THE RAKE'S CHALLENGE

Weary of society life, Giles Maltravers, the rakish Earl of Longwood, decides to flee it. Meanwhile, Anna Lawrence, nineteen and inspired by Lord Byron's poems, also determines to escape and seek a life of travel and adventure. Then, when Giles rescues Anna from her first escapade, despite her resolve to demonstrate her independence, he finds himself rescuing her from one potential disaster after another. He cannot live without her and Anna has come to love him with all her heart, but she hides a secret and can never be more than a friend to Giles . . . Can their love yet prevail?

Books by Beth Elliott
Published by The House of Ulverscroft:

APRIL AND MAY

BETH ELLIOTT

THE RAKE'S CHALLENGE

Complete and Unabridged

ULVERSCROFT
Leicester

First published in Great Britain in 2011 by
Robert Hale Limited
London

First Large Print Edition
published 2012
by arrangement with
Robert Hale Limited
London

British Library CIP Data

Elliott, Beth.
    The rake's challenge.
    1. Single women- -Fiction. 2. Nobility- -England- -
    Fiction. 3. Alienation (Social pyschology)- -Fiction.
    4. Love stories. 5. Large type books.
    I. Title
    823.9′2–dc23

    ISBN 978–1–4448–1174–2

Published by
F. A. Thorpe (Publishing)
Anstey, Leicestershire

Set by Words & Graphics Ltd.
    Anstey, Leicestershire
Printed and bound in Great Britain by
T. J. International Ltd., Padstow, Cornwall

This book is printed on acid-free paper

For Hélène

1

Sweet was the scene, yet soon he thought to flee,
More restless than the swallow in the skies:
Childe Harold's Pilgrimage,
Canto XXVII
Lord Byron

The first glimmer of light was sufficient for Giles to find his clothes. Shirt and breeches were swiftly donned and his cravat knotted. He slipped his waistcoat on and, as he buttoned it, he turned towards the large four-poster bed. Sophia was asleep, half covered by the silken sheets. But, even as he looked, she opened her eyes and stretched languorously.

'Are you leaving so early, darling? I'm surprised you have the energy. I'm sure I deserve a diamond pendant, at the least.' She was watching him closely.

With a tightening of his lips, Giles moved away. He pulled on his boots and straightened up, reaching for his jacket. Another glance towards the window warned him that the light was already stronger. It was time. He stalked out of the room without looking at

1

the beautiful, sulky woman in the bed.

In the entrance hall he paused to complete his dressing. He adjusted the ruffles of his shirt cuffs and buttoned up his jacket. His caped greatcoat was lying over the back of a chair. Shrugging it on, Giles surveyed himself in the pier glass. He frowned, dashed his thick black hair back from his forehead and made a tiny adjustment to his cravat. Giles Maltravers, Earl of Longwood, never appeared in public in anything less than impeccable style, and especially this morning, he must show all his usual elegance. He picked up his hat and cane, undid the bolts on the door and sauntered out into the grey dawn.

A carriage was drawn up at the edge of the pavement. Beside it stood a tall, willowy young man. On seeing Giles, a look of relief came into his face. Giles set his hat on at a rakish angle and leisurely descended the steps towards his friend.

'Everything is ready,' said Ned Caldecott, following Giles into the coach.

'So I see.' Giles picked up the slim wooden case and opened it to reveal a pair of Manton's duelling pistols. He lifted one and then paused, glancing sharply at the other man. 'Sometimes I only just remember in time that you are a poet,' he remarked.

Ned smiled slightly. 'I am also a crack shot, old fellow, as you well know. Of course, they are not loaded. I know my role.'

'And does that include composing an ode for this occasion?' drawled Giles. 'It would be something of a novelty. The newspapers would love it.'

Ned leaned forward, his expressive dark eyes very serious. 'Giles, are you certain this duel is necessary? Everyone saw what happened. Chilvers was so obviously in the wrong — '

Giles looked at him with hauteur. 'Ah, but he would not apologize, Ned. I had no choice.' He gazed out of the window at the trees alongside the road. 'Anyway, it relieves the tedium of existence. And if he annoys me by so much as a look when we meet now, I may decide to put a bullet through him.' He showed his white teeth in a fiendish smile.

Ned, who was checking the pistols once more, jerked his head up, an expression of horror on his long, sensitive face. 'But that would mean fleeing the country, old man.'

'No Maltravers *flees*! Ever!' said Giles coldly. 'But calm yourself, my poor, deluded poet. I only meant I might put a bullet through some part of his offensive body to remind him of his insolence for as long as possible. And to make him ridiculous, of course,' he added, with a sudden grin. 'That might afford me some amusement. And give the tabbies something else to whisper about me.'

Ned considered his friend. At length he shook his head. 'Trouble with you is, even raking and hell-raising bore you. You need something to keep you busy, old man.'

'How long have we known each other, Ned?' Giles asked softly.

Ned knew that tone. He folded his arms and gave a short laugh. 'Don't think you are going to frighten me. I have been saving you from the consequences of your own reckless-ness since we were both thirteen years old.'

'Hah! My recollection is that *I* saved *your* miserable skin more than a few times as well.'

'So we are even!' Ned slowly turned his head to look Giles in the eye. Giles had relaxed his haughty look. Something like a smile passed across his lean face. Then he stared out of the coach window again, his mouth a straight line. Eventually he sighed. 'Sophia wearies me,' he said softly. 'There is nothing behind that beautiful face.'

'Is that not how you like 'em?' asked Ned. 'Now I would be satisfied with all that beauty.'

'I grant she may be worth a sonnet or two, but after that you would be shocked by how her mind runs only on jewels. A veritable magpie.'

The coach slowed and stopped. Both men jumped down, Ned carrying the pistols in their box. Another coach was arriving from the far side of the common. Two men got out, followed by a third, older man.

'Ah, so they did bring a sawbones,' muttered Ned.

One of the men in the group began walking towards them. Ned went to meet him and they examined the pistols and loaded them. While they did this, Giles considered his opponent through narrowed eyes. To be obliged to defend his honour against such a coarse and clumsy dolt! True, the Regent's Victory Ball for Wellington had been an almighty squeeze, with nearly 2,000 guests, but not only had Chilvers knocked into him while he was waltzing with Belinda Beveridge, the idiot had pushed Belinda so hard she had ended up splayed all over Giles's chest. Then what must the fool do but bray with laughter and declare that they looked as good as any man and wife after a few months of wedlock. Of course, Belinda's mother had repeated that to anyone who would listen! A challenge was the only way to sort out the mess.

Chilvers was buttoning his dark coat right

up to the neck. Giles's lip curled. So the fellow was afraid now he was sober. Then they were back to back, pacing out the distance. Giles turned. He saw the handkerchief drop and waited, regarding his opponent scornfully. Chilvers jerked up his arm and shot. The bullet whistled past at a slight distance. Giles raised his brows. He considered. He saw Chilvers swallow. He was standing side on, so as to present the smallest possible target.

A wicked gleam came into Giles's eyes. At last he raised his arm and took aim, almost carelessly. He could see the sweat on the other man's face. Then came the crack of the pistol and at the same time a loud yelp from Chilvers. He jerked forward, still howling, a hand pressed to his backside. The doctor and his second raced towards him.

Ned retrieved the pistol and strode towards Giles. Both of them were grinning like schoolboys.

'That will remind him not to be clumsy on the dance-floor,' remarked Giles, giving the weapon into Ned's outstretched hand.

Ned chuckled. 'He will be eating his dinner off the mantelpiece for a week at least. Now, I'm for a large breakfast!'

★ ★ ★

Two hours later, Giles walked into the hall of the family mansion in Cavendish Square. He handed his hat and coat to Bilden, the stately butler.

'There is a letter from His Grace, my lord,' Bilden informed him.

Giles grunted and strode into the library. His father's letter was placed on top of a neat pile of correspondence on the large desk by the window. Giles set it aside and flicked through the rest. Nothing but invitations and bills, by the look of it. He recognized Sophia's handwriting on one little billet. He sniffed the scented paper and, with a disgusted frown, walked over to toss the letter into the fire.

His mouth tightened as he picked up the duke's letter at last and broke the seal. It was a short note, but even before he had finished reading it, his face was set in a surly expression, green eyes narrowed. He raised his head and glared at his reflection in the mirror over the mantelpiece. He rubbed a finger over the stubble on his chin and grimaced. Then his gaze dropped to the letter again. With another grimace he stuffed it in his pocket and went quickly out of the library.

'Tell Morgan to have my curricle at the door in an hour, with the blacks,' he informed Bilden. 'I am going out of Town.'

The lengthening shadows announced that the afternoon was drawing towards its end. The road was quiet and the driving needed no particular skill. The horses had kept up a good pace, but they were no longer fresh. Giles pondered his next move. His father's letter had decided him to leave Town. In truth, he was glad to escape the rest of the grandiose victory celebrations. Half the royalty of Europe was parading round London and the Prince Regent was enjoying his role as host at one extravagant event after another.

Giles was in no hurry to rejoin the fashionable world. He doubted his sanity would survive another insipid evening of dancing with debutantes, each one so like the next that he could not tell one from another. And always there were the eagle-eyed mothers, watching, hoping, trying to find a way of pushing their daughters at him. It was insufferable to be the target of their ambition, merely because his father was a duke.

The scowl descended on his face again. He resented having his carefree existence disturbed by all this scheming. He had long since shaken free of his father's authority and established himself as a hell-raiser, a way of life that was quite common among his fellow aristocrats. However, he always had to gamble deeper, fight harder, flirt more dangerously than the rest. Yet, however shocking his excesses, the ladies still pardoned him. The chaperons smiled on him and the mothers laid every possible trap to lure him into marriage with their daughters. Such was the burden of the immense dukedom of Hawkesborough that would one day be his.

They had left Richmond some way behind. The road was well maintained and busy with coaches and carts. Giles had kept his team in good form, making excellent time as far as Guildford, where he stopped for a drink of ale and to rest the horses. When they set off from the inn, he suddenly addressed his groom.

'Left or right at the next fork in the road, Morgan?'

'Left or . . . ' repeated the Welshman, in his singsong accent. 'Are we on a treasure hunt, my lord?'

Giles gave a bark of laughter. 'That's a novel way of putting it. Be quick, man, I can see a signpost ahead.'

'Right,' Morgan said, without hesitation. 'It's nearer to my home country, even if only by a few miles.' He looked at his master in sudden hope. 'Are we going to Wales, then?'

'Of course not. We are on our way to Longwood Hall, but I am in no hurry. This rural interlude pleases me. Let's see where we end up this evening.'

'So long as it's not in a ditch . . . just my joke,' said the groom hastily, catching a glance from dagger-sharp green eyes. 'Well, my lord, who knows how you will feel by morning, isn't it then?' Morgan shook his head, his expression saying plainly that he was used to Giles's sudden changes of mood.

The curricle swung to the right. It was a wide road with high hedges on either side. Occasionally Giles caught a glimpse of well timbered land but he was more interested in urging his horses to a cracking pace. Nothing loath, the fine beasts lengthened their stride and the curricle flew along the sunlit road. After a while, Giles laughed out loud.

2

'No coach?' Annabelle Lawrence stared at the landlord of The Swan in dismay. 'B-but I thought the Winchester coach departed from this inn?'

'And so it does, miss. It left at noon, as it does every day. There's no coach for Winchester now until tomorrow morning, at seven o' the clock,' said the landlord, already turning away in response to calls from the other side of the taproom. He had no time to waste on a young lady who had arrived too late. Anna bit her lip and sneaked a look around. This busy coaching inn by the town of Alton was too close to home for her to be certain that nobody would recognize her. Keeping her head down, she made her way outside.

Now what was she to do? She simply did not have enough money to take a room at The Swan. If only she could have arrived here earlier — but that would have raised suspicions at home. She walked out of the forecourt and a short way along the road towards the town. Already her portmanteau seemed to be terribly heavy. She set it down and inspected the hedgerow. It was thickly overgrown with dog roses at this point, so she pushed the bag under a mass of trailing sprays. A quick glance to each side assured her that the only witness was an old donkey in the field.

Anna squared her shoulders. She and her schoolfriends had long agreed that they would emulate Lord Byron's hero and never fear adventure. Here was her first trial — for the journey from home this morning could not count! Now she would walk as far as the cottages she could see in the distance and surely a kind old lady in one of them would give her a night's lodging. It was not cowardly, she assured herself, to leave the large coaching inn. If anyone recognized her there she would be hauled back to a home she could no longer endure. This was the only solution. If only she could have reached Alton before the Winchester coach departed.

She stepped out bravely along the road, a neat figure in her best straw bonnet with blue ribbons that matched her spencer. The July sunshine was hot, but it would not take many minutes to walk as far as the cottages. A curricle appeared, coming from the town towards her. The two men in it were talking and laughing loudly. As they came abreast of

Anna, they looked down and one of them whistled.

'There's sport, eh, Jerry?'

They both laughed, a drunken, coarse laugh that made Anna quicken her steps. She knew only too well what men in that condition were capable of. That was why she was here, after all. Surely, oh surely, they would continue to the inn? She kept on as fast as she could go without actually breaking into a run. Please, please, why could another coach not come by, or even some local person appear on the road?

Behind her she heard unmistakable sounds of horses being stopped and feet jumping to the ground.

'Hey, you!' a voice shouted.

Anna picked up her skirts and fled. The sound of running feet came closer. Both of them were following her, whooping and laughing hysterically as they tried to grab hold of her.

'Tally-ho! I have her!' cried one. Anna felt a hand touch her shoulder. She pulled free and raced on. Her heart seemed to be pounding in her throat. She absolutely must reach a cottage before they could catch her. But the hand clutched at her again, more firmly this time. She staggered and nearly fell. Somehow she pulled away and kept running. One of them was now overtaking her. His eyes were bright and his teeth were bared in a wild grin as he put out both arms and seized hold of her.

The force of their speed meant that they went down heavily in a tangle of arms and legs. Anna landed on top of him. She was sobbing for breath. He wheezed and choked, his breath stinking of spirits, but he was not drunk enough to relax his grip on her arms.

'Bravo, Jerry. Let's see the prize!' The second young man swayed over her. He tugged at her bonnet. 'What sport,' he panted. 'We have found ourselves a pretty wench to pass the time here.'

Anna saw with horror that both men were inspecting her legs. Her dress had pulled up when she slipped over. She reached out her hand to adjust her clothes but the first young man — Jerry — caught her wrist.

'Oh no,' he drawled, 'don't spoil sport.'

'Let me *go*,' she choked.

The two men convulsed with laughter at this. Anna scrambled to her feet and darted away. Fear gave her an extra burst of speed but the men overtook her in no time. Each one grabbed one of her arms.

'*Nooo*,' she screamed, jerking and twisting.

'I like a good chase,' said Jerry, 'but that's enough now, wench. Time to submit.' He pulled her arms behind her back, none too gently. 'Now then, Barty, let's get her into the field.'

Anna struggled and kicked out. Her jean half-boots made no impression on the man's hessians. She screamed again, a high, desperate wail. The two men swore at her and the one called Barty jerked at the ribbon of her bonnet.

In the struggle, none of them had heard the tall, elegant man approach. He did not waste time on words but slashed with his whip at the legs of both men. With a roar they swung round, fists clenched and ready to punch. But when they saw the dark, murderous face, they sobered in an instant, their faces appalled.

'M-Maltravers!' gasped Barty, taking a step backwards.

'You dogs!' snarled the dark-haired gentle-man. 'You should be taken up on a charge of rape.'

'She was just . . . ' Jerry faltered to a halt.

Anna retreated a little way and watched. She saw her two attackers cowering before the newcomer. She clutched at her throat, numb and not certain whether she was safe or not. This man was tall and very dark, of both hair and complexion. Whatever he was saying, it seemed to strike horror into the two young men. They bowed their heads, nodded and finally scuttled off as he made a sharp gesture towards their curricle.

Anna stood rooted to the spot. Her knees were shaking and her mind felt blank. A very long time seemed to go by before she realized the newcomer was still in the same place. He was inspecting her, but he had not come any closer. She eyed him warily. He was tall and strongly built. His face was harsh. She licked her lips nervously and glanced behind her towards the cottages. He would easily catch her if she ran. They were still too far away for her to reach them.

She realized that he was speaking and frowned at him, forcing herself to take in his words. His eyes were narrowed and he looked angry. Then he gave a lopsided smile and suddenly she knew he was not a villain.

'Perhaps you should retie your bonnet strings, ma'am.' His voice was deep, calm and disinterested.

Anna stared at him for a moment longer. At last she stopped clutching her throat and lifted her hands stiffly to her bonnet. It was almost slipping off the back of her head. She unknotted the bow and pulled the hat off. Mechanically she inspected it. The gentleman raised his eyebrows as her thick, flaxen hair tumbled down. Anna twisted her hair back into a knot as best she could and settled her bonnet on top, retying the bow with fingers that trembled. She shook out her skirts and jerked her spencer tidy.

'That's better,' he encouraged her. 'Now, may I present myself? Giles Maltravers, at your service. You will tell me how I may help you.'

Anna tried to speak. No sound would come out. She swallowed and tried again, but only managed a little sob. It seemed at that moment as if the bottom had fallen out of her world.

★ ★ ★

Giles remained quite motionless, looking at this pretty waif. He sighed. 'Yes, you are very young, aren't you? Have you run away from school?'

At that, the girl found her voice. 'Of course not.' It came out as an indignant squeak. 'But I-I missed the coach and needed to find lodging.'

'Are there no rooms available at The Swan?' His deep voice registered his disbelief.

She shook her head miserably. 'I did not ask, but in any case I cannot stay there — '

He held up a hand. 'You have not yet told me your name, Miss . . . ?'

The question seemed to alarm her.

17

Inwardly, he cursed. What the *hell* was he doing, getting involved with this chit? But how could he ignore the struggle going on just as he arrived at the inn? He was still furious at such a brutish attack on a young girl. She must have plenty of backbone, not to be drumming her heels in hysterics. However, she was as white as paper and looked ready to fold at the knees. He must not approach her, but coax her to come to him.

'Well?' he prompted her.

She turned her large blue eyes full on him. 'If I do tell you, will you promise not to tell anyone else?'

Giles gave an involuntary grin. 'I promise. Must I cross my heart and hope to die?'

She stared at him intently and seemed to relax a little. 'Oh, no, of course not. But it is important. I am Annabelle Lawrence.'

He offered his arm. 'Come then, Miss Lawrence. Let us get you somewhere where you can recover from your ordeal.'

After a minute's indecision, during which he waited, impassive, she took a step towards him. He did not move and she took another step, then she was by his side. She placed her hand on his outstretched arm and he turned back towards The Swan.

She stopped. 'Oh, no, I cannot — '

'There is no fear of seeing those two

rogues. I ordered them away.'

She stared at him in disbelief. 'And they will obey?'

He raised his brows. 'Of course.' He indicated that they should move on again. She did so but with obvious reluctance.

'Sir,' she began hesitantly, 'I cannot go into that inn.'

'I think you have no choice, Miss Lawrence. My groom will have obtained a private parlour and you can rest there. You need to recover from your ordeal.' He felt a tremor in the hand resting on his arm. He glanced down at her agitated face, and added, 'Have no fears, child. You are quite safe with me.' And the devil of it was, he meant it. Damn it! Giles thought, with a tightening of his jaw, he must be older than he realized.

3

A short time later, he was standing at the window of the private parlour, his hands clasped behind his back. He was torn between amusement at his new role as chaperon and annoyance at having his comfort disturbed. His protégée was seated in an armchair and he had ordered a maid to bring her a glass of wine.

'If you please,' he heard her tell the maid who had just set down the glass on a small table by her chair, 'I would much prefer a cup of hot milk.'

Giles's shoulders shook and he gave a sudden cough. He turned from the window to look at her keenly. 'Are you quite certain you are not still a schoolgirl?'

Anna sat up indignantly. 'No, sir. I am on my way to take up employment.'

His brows lifted. He said nothing more, however. He assumed a bored expression when the maid returned with the milk but watched as Anna accepted it gratefully. When she had drunk it all, she looked up with a smile. 'Now I feel better, sir. I think perhaps I can manage now.'

Her expression was so sweet and trusting that for an instant he was jolted out of his habitual cynicism. Perhaps, fortunately, at that moment there was a tap at the door and in came Morgan with her portmanteau. 'I found it where you said, miss,' he said, in his sing-song accent. Before she could thank him, he turned to Giles. 'Everything is settled as you ordered, my lord. If there's nothing else, I'll go and see the horses have been fed properly.'

Giles waved him out, then exclaimed and followed him. When he came back into the room the maid was setting the table for dinner. A serving boy appeared with a tray of covered dishes. At once a savoury aroma filled the room. Giles inspected the food through his quizzing glass.

'This looks perfectly tolerable,' he remarked, pulling out a chair for Anna. 'I must confess that I am more than ready for my dinner.'

Anna was standing by her chair as if frozen. He saw that her hands were clutching her throat again. Now what had frightened her?

'Miss Lawrence?' He smiled his best smile, the one he reserved for suspicious chaperons, and gestured towards the meal.

'Your groom called you 'my lord',' she said accusingly.

Giles nodded. 'Correct. I am Giles

Maltravers, Earl of Longwood. But lord or no lord, I am hungry. Come, Miss Lawrence, please join me.'

Reluctantly she came to the table and allowed him to push in her chair. Her head was bowed and she spoke with some difficulty. 'I should not be intruding on your meal, my lord . . . ' She clasped her hands together tightly. At the same moment, her stomach growled and she gave a little gasp of embarrassment.

Giles laughed. 'You are as hungry as I am.' He picked up the carving knife. 'Perhaps while I carve this capon, you will serve that dish of potatoes.' He hid a smile when she obeyed without further protest. This encounter with a very young lady was giving him more amusement than any number of London social events could do. When he handed her a plate with several slices of capon on it, she set to work with a good appetite, quite unlike the debutantes who would pretend never to be hungry when in society.

He needed to discover just what she was planning to do. As he poured wine into her glass he asked, as casually as possible, 'What time did you leave your home this morning?'

'Not early enough,' she said, eyeing him suspiciously. 'I missed the coach.'

'Yet the Hampshire roads are good,' he

remarked, lifting the cover of another dish as he spoke. He raised his quizzing glass to inspect it more closely. 'That looks like a beef pie. Could you serve me a portion, if you please?' As she did so, he continued, 'So you live some distance from Alton?'

She kept her gaze lowered and did not answer. There was a short silence then she looked up and said fiercely, 'If my stepfather had let me keep my pistol, I could have shot them.'

Stepfather! Oh! And he took her pistol away from her!

Giles raised his brows. 'Are you a good shot, Miss Lawrence?'

'Of course. My father taught me.' She sighed. 'But I am sadly out of practice since I went away to school.'

'And your stepfather does not approve of ladies who can shoot a pistol?'

She shook her head. He waited, hoping for a few more crumbs of information, but she suddenly seemed to notice the last slice of capon on her plate and busied herself with cutting it up.

'It is not the thing to go around shooting people,' he remarked eventually, 'even when they are as uncivilized as that pair today. Be assured, Miss Lawrence, I have punished them for you.'

'But you just sent them away.' The look she cast at him would have frozen a lesser man.

He emptied his wineglass and reached for the bottle. 'Even so, I have punished them,' he repeated, filling his glass again. 'They are now excluded from their London clubs until such time as I decide they are reformed.' He surveyed her over the rim of his glass. His smile faded as he realized she was watching him with some misgivings.

Was it the wine that was disturbing her? Could this be a clue as to why she was running away from her home? Giles racked his brains, but could not recall any family by the name of Lawrence. Yet she was obviously gently born and well brought up. She must be the daughter of a country squire.

'Which coach will you take in the morning?' he asked, as she set down her spoon at the end of the meal. Again he found himself being examined by those large eyes. He narrowed his own, unused to being weighed up by such a young lady. It was a novelty, and he decided he rather liked it.

'I am going to Winchester,' she admitted reluctantly. 'I will have to be ready before seven o'clock,' — she stood up — 'which means it is time for me to retire.' She took a deep breath. 'My lord, I cannot express how truly grateful I am for all the help you have given me . . . '

Giles raised a hand. 'Spare me,' he said drily. 'Pray sit down again — just for a moment,' he added, as she shook her head. Anna sat on the very edge of her chair, both hands resting flat on the table as if to jump up the next second.

Interesting! Giles had the impression that she was used to making sudden escapes. He took another sip of wine, noting again how she followed the movement. 'I have made arrangements for the maid to sleep on a truckle bed in your chamber,' he informed her.

She frowned. 'That is not necessary. I am sure I am safe here.'

'Maybe,' he allowed, 'but I wish to observe the proprieties. You are, after all, very young' — his eyes challenged her as she drew breath to argue — 'and on your way to take up employment. There must be no breath of scandal to sully your fair name, Miss Lawrence.' He took another sip of wine. Her large anxious eyes grew rounder.

He must be honest, damn it! He set down his glass sharply and sighed. 'I am — er . . . well known in Society for my rakish behaviour. My name will cause real scandal for you if it is ever known you met me.'

Her gaze kindled. 'What nonsense! When you rescued me from those horrible men and . . . and you have been everything that is kind and considerate. I will never forget how much I owe you.' She blinked and turned her head away.

Giles distinctly heard a sniff. His eyes widened. *Kindness?* That must be the first time he had ever been called kind! But he would not upset her further by laughing at her. He looked again. She was certainly a very pretty girl with a pure complexion and those expressive eyes, the colour of a clear winter sky. Her mop of flaxen curls framed her face delightfully. Her yellow dress was simple but well made and suitable for her age, which he judged to be about eighteen.

Very likely she was just out of the schoolroom and running away from a marriage arrangement she did not like. If he were really a true gentleman, Giles thought ruefully, he would insist on taking her back to her home. He had noticed how she kept her head down when going through the taproom. No doubt she must live fairly close by. It would surely be possible to find someone who could identify her.

But he sensed a certain desperation in her. She was brave enough to undertake a new life rather than submit to letting others arrange her future for her. And after all, he was doing the same thing. His father's letter, commanding his presence at a series of events, was tantamount to organizing his marriage to Belinda. Giles scowled. Even if the Beveridges were old family friends, he would not have his hand forced in that way.

'Are you angry with me, my lord?' asked a very small voice.

'Eh?' He whipped his head round. 'I was wool-gathering.' He summoned up a smile. 'You are tired. It is time to retire, Miss Annabelle Lawrence.' He rose on the words and moved to open the door for her.

'No one calls me Annabelle,' she protested, following him across the room. 'I am known as Anna.' She gave him a shy smile. 'Thank you for everything.'

And now what the devil was he going to do? Giles stared at the last remnants of the sunset as he swirled the brandy in his glass. He would not play the tyrant and force her back home, but neither could he allow her to wander off into more misadventures. She was far too pretty to be roaming the country alone. He took a sip of his brandy and nearly choked as a new and horrifying idea struck him. Did this anxiety on another person's behalf mean that he actually had a conscience?

He swore a few choice oaths as he hastily crossed the room to seize the decanter and refill his glass. Whatever was happening to him?

4

Anna went thankfully into her bedchamber. She sat down on the chair by the dressing table and shut her eyes for a few moments, letting the events of the day flow over her. She had escaped from home without raising any suspicions but then things had gone very wrong. If Lord Maltravers had not appeared in the nick of time, Anna knew she could not have defended herself against those two men. She was trembling at the memory. *So, learn a lesson from it,* she told herself, *if you want to live a life of adventure, plan ahead properly!*

Yet if she had not been molested, she would never have met Giles and that would have been a pity. She smiled as she recalled their conversation. There was that gleam in his eyes that said he was a kindred spirit. Somehow she knew he would not force her to return to her home. However, this was only a brief interlude. He had played his part. Tomorrow she would depart at a time when he would no doubt still be abed, or at the very most, involved in his elaborate toilet. It must take him hours to achieve such an elegant appearance.

She sighed and stood up rather stiffly to open her portmanteau. It only took a little rummaging to find a nightgown and her brush and comb. Turning back to lay them on the dressing table, she glanced in the mirror and gasped in horror. She looked a complete fright with her hair an untidy riot of tendrils and curls.

Quickly she undressed, hung up her clothes and sat before the mirror to brush her hair into smoothness. The light was beginning to fade so she got up to look for a candle. She struck a light and was setting the candlestick down by her bed when there was a tap at the door. In came the maid and bobbed a curtsy.

'If you please, miss, I'm Betsy. His lordship said as I'm to sleep here and wake you in time for your breakfast in the morning.' She peered at Anna's bare arms. 'Cor, miss, look at them bruises. You must be pretty sore.'

'I fell down,' said Anna, looking in dismay at the obvious mark of fingerprints on each arm.

Betsy raised her eyebrows but said no more. The two girls were soon in their beds and in no time at all, Anna could hear Betsy snoring. In spite of her own weariness, she was quite unable to sleep. By now she should have been in her new employer's home and safe from pursuit. Not that anyone would realize she had disappeared for a while. She had told the housekeeper at home that she was going to stay with her friend Elinor, as she often did.

Her mother and stepfather had gone to London to see something of the grand victory celebrations. It would be ten days before they returned home. It could well be even a day or two after that before they sent for her. Elinor, who knew all about Anna's problems, had come to fetch her in the gig that morning and so Anna was able to take her portmanteau without arousing any suspicions. It was fortunate that Elinor lived only eight miles away; near enough to visit but not so close that their parents could always keep track of the two girls.

Elinor knew all about the problems of life with Anna's stepfather and a mother who was too weak to stand up to him. He alternated between bullying and — when drunk, which was more and more often, being over-affectionate to his pretty stepdaughter. He was becoming a menace. Now that Anna had left school for good, her mother had summoned a distant cousin, planning to get rid of her daughter by a speedy marriage.

Cousin Frederick Swinton, a country pastor of five-and-thirty, was quite agreeable to the match. Why would he object, when

Anna was an heiress with a very handsome estate of her own? But Anna took one look at him and knew she could never live the kind of dull and confined life he would impose on her. So she had set about organizing her own destiny. She had answered an advertisement in the *Morning Chronicle* for a companion to a Lady Fording, who was in poor health.

The lady's home was far enough away to make Anna safe from discovery. If things went badly wrong, Elinor would help her find another position. It was obvious that she was not wanted at home and so Anna was determined that she would choose her own life. After all, she and her three friends, all entranced by the work of the poet Lord Byron, had agreed that they would seek adventure and travel to the utmost of their ability. She would be the first of them to carry out this plan!

Her thoughts turned to her rescuer. He was in every way suitable to be cast as the hero of a Byronic saga. He was tall, dark-haired and his stern features seemed to be carved in marble. But when he smiled and his green eyes sparkled, he looked as if he could be most entertaining. And he was quite the most elegant gentleman she had ever seen.

Those two brutes had absolutely cowered before him, yet he had not even raised his voice. Not like her stepfather, who began to shout the moment he was not getting his own way. Anna shuddered. How could her mother have been attracted to him, especially when she had been married to dearest Papa? Yet she knew the answer.

After Papa died suddenly of an inflammation of the lungs, Sir Benjamin Fox had been such a frequent visitor and so full of good advice that her mother, never confident about organizing her life, had gladly accepted his offer of marriage. Anna was just fifteen at that time. But what Sir Benjamin only discovered after the marriage was that he could not benefit from the large Lawrence estates. There had been a lot of shouting and door-slamming when he found out that everything was settled on Anna for when she reached the age of five-and-twenty.

By remarrying, her mother even forfeited the right to continue living there, so they had removed to Foxley Manor, Sir Benjamin's much smaller estate. That was when he started drinking excessively and seemingly confused over which lady was his wife and which his stepdaughter.

Not long after that, she had been sent away to school in Bath. She sighed and turned over once more, plumping up her pillow and trying to calm her racing mind. School had certainly been safer than living in Sir Benjamin's home.

The next thing she knew, Betsy was shaking her. Anna opened one eye and groaned.

'There's warm water in the ewer, miss, and I'll bring some breakfast up to your private parlour. Plenty o' time yet.'

When she did make her way into the parlour, she found Giles there already. He was so elegant that she at once felt slightly dowdy, even though she was wearing a new sprigged muslin gown, and had brushed her curls into submission and tied them back with a blue ribbon.

'There was no need for you to get up at this hour, sir,' she said, sitting down on the chair he held for her.

He said nothing, merely gesturing towards the coffee pot. She gritted her teeth and poured with a slightly unsteady hand. It felt as if she had escaped from school and from home only to fall under yet another person's authority. She refused the dish of ham he was indicating and took a slice of bread. She considered him under her lashes while she buttered her bread and dolloped a liberal spoonful of honey on top.

He continued to eat his eggs and ham placidly but made no effort at conversation. Why had he taken the trouble to get up so early? He must have risen before the dawn, she thought, noticing again how elegant he was and how smoothly shaven. His black hair was thick and lustrous and it curled attractively over his brow. Yes, he was an ideal model for Lord Byron's hero.

She held back a sigh. No doubt he wanted to be sure she had gone before setting off himself, then he could be free again. It was a melancholy thought. He was the first friend she had made in her new life. Probably he would be her only friend, as no doubt she would be living a very quiet life, fetching and carrying for the old lady. Better that, though, than marriage to Cousin Frederick or being pawed by her stepfather.

'Is there something amiss?'

Anna jumped and realized that she was staring out of the window while holding the slice of bread and butter halfway to her mouth. The honey was dripping gently down onto the table. 'Oh, dear,' she said, 'it seems I am the one wool-gathering this morning.'

There was a pained expression on Giles's face as he looked at the honey. 'More misadventures,' he murmured. 'I very much fear, Miss Lawrence, that you are what is known as a pickle!'

She giggled and gave him a look of pure mischief. 'I can do a lot better than that, sir.'

He sighed. 'That is what I am afraid of. In fact, it has been worrying me so much that I have decided to convey you to your destination myself.'

Anna gasped. 'Oh no, I could not possibly accept.' She set down the slice of bread, adding, 'Besides, you said . . . you said — ' She broke off in embarrassment.

'Ah, yes, my shocking reputation. I am aware of the irony. But I find I cannot be easy until I see you safely delivered to your new home. And we will hope that your employer lives retired and has not heard of me. In any case, we will have Morgan, my groom, as chaperon.'

It was too tempting. To ride in his curricle and talk with him for a while longer. She beamed at him and held out her hand. 'How kind you are. *Thank* you, sir.'

He recoiled. 'I am delighted to be of service, but pray excuse me — ah — when you have removed all the honey.' His face showed only a polite indifference but there was a gleam of amusement in his green eyes as she inspected her sticky fingers.

★ ★ ★

'This is splendid!' Anna turned a glowing face towards Giles. 'What beautiful horses. How smoothly they go.' She indicated the vehicle. 'And your curricle is so well sprung. I have not ridden in anything so sporting since Papa was alive.'

She had let some information slip at last! Giles allowed a short time to pass before asking, 'So your father was a keen sportsman?'

'Oh, yes.' It seemed as if the words were torn from her. 'We used to ride to the hunt together. And he taught me to drive and to shoot . . . I am a good shot,' she gave him a serious look. It was not boasting, he could see. *So she had been a cherished only child. And now . . . ?*

'Are both your parents dead, Miss Lawrence?'

He saw how she gripped her hands together in her lap. 'My mother remarried. I now have two young half-brothers.' She looked down at her clasped hands. 'Life is very different now.'

He nodded. 'Evidently. But that is not why you are running away, is it?' There was no answer to this. He drove on for a short while, then sighed. 'Miss Lawrence, my conscience is troubling me — and heaven help me, it is extremely distressing to find that I have one! You appear so youthful.'

She gave a peal of laughter. It made Giles

think of sunshine and roses. He caught himself up. This was strictly a charitable mission, soon to be over.

'Are you truly old enough to have left school?' he insisted.

Her smile faded. 'I stayed away at school until my mother could no longer refuse to allow me back home. I am past nineteen years of age.'

He cast a sideways glance at her lovely profile. 'An old maid indeed.'

'You are trying to provoke me,' she said. 'Why is it that men only see us in terms of wives and mothers? I have decided on my own path in life and it does not include marriage — not for a long while, anyway.'

'Ah!' The image of her struggling against those two overexcited young bucks the previous day was in his mind. He would not be unkind enough to remind her of it, however. But he wondered how soon it would be before she found herself in even worse danger. She was too pretty and too innocent to be let out alone. He cast her a swift glance. 'So where is this path leading you? I believe I said earlier that you are a pickle, Miss Lawrence.'

Anna cast her eyes heavenwards before replying. 'Well then, I am in good company. My three friends, my *best* friends, that is, and

38

I — have sworn to live our lives as fully as we can. We are inspired by Lord Byron's marvellous poem about the adventures of Childe Harold.' A thought seemed to strike her. Her cheeks became quite pink and she clasped her hands at her bosom. She leaned towards him and asked in a tone of reverence, 'Oh, sir, do you *know* Lord Byron?'

Giles kept a straight face, but it was a full minute before he could speak without a tremor in his voice. 'I — er — do occasionally see him at various functions. I cannot claim an acquaintance, however.'

She looked so downcast that he added, 'My own friend is a poet, so I am aware that writing verse is an incurable condition. Neither of them can help it!'

She merely gave a little nod. Clearly she felt no interest in Ned. He felt slightly offended for his friend, whose work was good and less flowery than the stuff written by that damned fellow Byron. And Ned did not trail mayhem everywhere he went, he was merely a trifle forgetful.

'Well, can you tell me if he is as good looking as they say?'

'Who, Ned?'

'*Lord Byron*, of course!'

He considered for a while, quite aware that she was holding her breath for the answer. 'I suppose he is well favoured,' he said at last, 'if you like a rather negligent appearance.'

'Yes . . . do go on.'

He glanced at her eager face. 'Er . . . ' He racked his brains. 'He has dark hair, very curly. The females all swoon over him.'

'And — have you not read *Childe Harold's Pilgrimage*?'

Giles gave a bark of laughter. 'Of course not. But I have not been able to avoid the dam — er . . . the poem. All the females were sighing over it, quoting from it, using it as a theme for masquerade balls. Enough to turn your stomach.'

She bristled with rage. 'If you do not know the work, how can you presume to judge?' Her nose poked several degrees higher in the air.

'Allow me my own tastes in literature,' he drawled.

'Oh, so you do read,' she flashed.

Giles felt a strong urge to put her over his knee and wallop her. He merely nodded stiffly and confined his attention to his horses. He allowed the pace to lengthen. The road was straight and the day a fine one. The blacks needed little urging. They raced along the road. Soon Anna was holding onto her bonnet and laughing with joy. Then a scatter of houses warned that they were approaching

40

a town. Giles became aware of Morgan coughing to attract attention.

'I know, I know,' he called over his shoulder, 'they need a rest.' He glanced at his wind-swept companion. 'This is Alresford. If you do not object we shall stop at an inn here.'

She had forgotten her sulks and smiled at him sunnily. 'That will be delightful, thank you. A glass of milk will be most welcome.'

Once again he had to choke back a laugh. There was not a single young lady in the ton who would admit to drinking milk. He swept under the archway and through to the yard of The Swan. Ostlers came running to attend to the horses. Giles jumped down, and helped her descend. He noted how gracefully she managed this.

'Do you always stop at hostelries called The Swan?' she asked as they approached the open door where the landlord stood waiting.

'What?' Giles had been busy thinking how tall and willowy she was and how her athletic stride matched his own. 'I always stop at the *best* hostelry, whatever its name.' He was aware that several heads turned towards them as she laughed merrily. He nodded towards the land-lord. 'Private parlour, at once.' He must protect her from any unnecessary attention. Then it occurred to him that he was too busy looking after her to feel his usual boredom.

5

Anna was impressed by the ease and speed with which Giles whisked her into a private parlour. She was even more impressed when a meal started to appear almost immediately. The drive had made her hungry. She removed her bonnet and came to survey the food on the table. The serving boy was hurrying in with a large dish of vegetables. Anna sniffed appreciatively. 'That smells delicious.'

The young man looked up, gaped at her and set the dish down too close to the edge of the table. There was a mighty crash, which brought him back to his senses. 'Sorry, sorry, miss . . . sir . . . ' He fled.

Giles shook his head, his mouth thin with annoyance. Anna smiled uncertainly. 'That was a silly thing to do,' she began, but stopped as the landlady bustled in and quickly cleared up the mess. She gave the floor a last wipe and straightened up. She glared at Anna then turned her fearsome gaze on Giles before sweeping out. The serving boy came back in, eyes lowered and bashfully set another dish of vegetables down carefully before scuttling out and closing the door behind him.

Giles sighed as he carved the sirloin. 'I must remember not to come here again for some considerable time.'

'Why ever is that?' Anna inspected all the dishes eagerly and helped herself to a generous portion of vegetables. 'Mmm, carrots, my favourite.' When there was no answer to her question, she looked up. Giles was leaning back in his chair, watching her.

'Are you not hungry?' she asked, eager to begin her meal but making herself wait until he had served himself.

He shook his head slowly. There was a strange little smile on his face. 'Miss Lawrence, you are an education. I begin to perceive that I have taken on a new role in life. Perhaps it is doing me good.' He poured some lemonade into her glass. 'Behold me in the position of chaperon!'

Anna frowned over this. 'Surely we are only two travellers, whose paths go together for a short while?'

He laughed. 'You just do not understand, do you? You have been too sheltered from the real world. You bewitched that poor mooncalf of a serving boy. And you are not aware of why, are you?' He set his glass down abruptly. 'And the landlady evidently thinks I am running away with you. It's time to accept that you are far too pretty to escape attention, my infant.'

Her face became uneasy. 'Oh no, no. Mama is the beauty in the family. I am nothing to her, I assure you.'

He said no more and set about eating his meal. But now Anna's appetite had deserted her. She did not want to be singled out for her looks. It had already caused her enough trouble yesterday, and of course, her stepfather . . . She shook her head and tried to swallow another morsel of meat.

A quick glance under her lashes showed her that Giles was not looking at her but staring out of the window. She laid down her knife and fork and admired the clean cut lines of his face while he was looking elsewhere. He was not as dark as he had appeared at first. It was only when he scowled that he seemed to have a dark complexion. His nose was delightfully straight and his hair was so thick, she wanted to take hold of a handful and feel the silky curls — or at least to smooth back that lock that fell so persistently over his forehead.

'Where exactly are you going?' he asked abruptly, turning a keen gaze on her before she could look away. His eyes glinted very green as if he knew she had been inspecting him, but his expression was quite bland.

Anna jumped. 'If you take me to the coaching inn at Winchester, I will hire a gig to get to my destination . . . ' Even as she said the words she saw the anger flash into being. Those green eyes were darting fire at her. His face became extraordinarily haughty.

'I believe I told you that I will convey you to your destination.'

'Yes but . . . but . . . what about your own journey? I must be taking you miles out of your way.'

'It doesn't signify. In any case, I am in no hurry.' He was still glaring at her down his nose. 'And that was not my meaning, as you very well know,' he added frostily.

She gave him a look of pure mischief that changed abruptly to alarm as he leaned forward menacingly. After a moment while she decided he was merely teasing her, she shrugged. 'It is the first step of my life of adventure,' she began.

'Life of *what*?' he echoed, his brows rising almost to his hairline. 'Why do you require a life of adventure?'

'I told you, sir. But of course, you do not value Lord Byron's ideas. My three friends and I have sworn to travel and experience other, fascinating cultures.'

Giles wrestled for words. Eventually he

asked, 'But how can going into service be considered an adventure?'

'Oh,' she waved her hand airily, 'that is merely until I come into my inheritance. When I reach the age of twenty-one, I will have an annual income.' She tossed her head. 'And *then* I shall travel overseas, with my friends, probably. But for now,' — she bit her lip and fidgeted with her knife — 'this is a start. I told you, I could no longer stay at home.'

Giles began to laugh. 'The dreams of youth!'

Anna set down her knife and fork with a clatter and placed her hands on her hips. 'You have no right to mock me. I assure you, I am serious. Just because you have old-fashioned notions, it does not mean you can scorn my point of view.'

She saw the immediate transformation from a laughing young man and fellow traveller into a haughty aristocrat. 'My apologies, ma'am.' His eyes were chips of ice and his tone sent a chill down as far as her toes. 'And pray be good enough to tell me where exactly I shall have the pleasure of taking you today?'

She considered, eyeing him doubtfully. 'Rosevale Court, in the village of Hurford,' she muttered at last. 'It is about forty minutes' drive beyond Winchester.'

He gave a curt nod and turned his attention back to his meal. Anna sat motionless. She had spoiled it all now. But he should not have laughed at her. Why would men not allow women to depart from their traditional role? She forced herself to cut up another tiny square of beef and chewed determinedly. At last he put his knife and fork down and drew out a gold watch.

'If we are to arrive at a respectable hour, we need to set off within the next thirty minutes,' he announced, getting to his feet. 'I shall inform Morgan.' He left the parlour.

Anna pushed her plate away in relief. She wandered to the window, looking out at the busy main street. It was getting harder not to feel apprehensive. Her new employer might be difficult to please. She tapped her fingers on the window ledge, beating out a little rhythm that grew faster and faster. Then she heard the door open again and hastily jerked her hands behind her back.

'I have been thinking,' she announced, 'that it would be a good idea to have a pistol. Do you think we could procure one in a shop here?'

'No!' said Giles without hesitation. 'You cannot go about ready to fire at people. Why are you so bloodthirsty?'

'Because I wish to defend myself,' she retorted. 'Who knows whether I shall meet more creatures like those two vile rogues.'

Giles studied her with his head on one side. 'There are other weapons, Miss Lawrence, but I think you have yet to discover them.'

'Swords?' she asked doubtfully.

Giles laughed out loud at that. 'You are very refreshing.' He suddenly assumed an air of great hauteur. He maintained it until Anna looked slightly alarmed. 'Like this. With a haughty manner, you can intimidate people. They at once imagine you have status and influence. Then they are afraid to touch you because they fear the consequences.'

Anna sighed. 'That would not work for me. I prefer a proper weapon. I will find something.' Unconsciously, she rubbed at her bruised arm. Giles followed the movement and he grimaced. He made no comment, however, merely picking up his hat and gloves and holding the door for her to leave.

★   ★   ★

The afternoon was warm, the roads were dry and a fine layer of dust drifted onto the curricle and its occupants. They made their way through Winchester without stopping, although Anna wondered aloud if there were any bookshops where a copy of *The Corsair* could be found. 'My friends and I searched for a copy all over Bath but in vain,' she said, shaking her head sadly.

'Believe me, Miss Lawrence,' said Giles, 'all existing copies of that poem are in the hands of the ton. It is so fashionable that everyone wishes to be seen to possess a copy.'

'It is very unfair on we true admirers,' she sighed. Suddenly she brightened. 'My new employer is a member of the *ton*, so perhaps she has a copy.'

'It is something to speculate about,' he agreed, negotiating a narrow alley where several carts were drawn up and various merchants haggling over the wares in them.

'Do you know anything about the subject of the poem?' she asked impulsively. But she had not chosen a good moment. Just ahead of them in the narrow street leading to the Westgate, there was a commotion. A man was being chased out of an inn. His dog, a large and savage looking mongrel, objected to this, launching himself at the innkeeper while barking furiously. Several urchins came running to see the show. Amongst so many hazards, Giles had to give his full attention to keeping his blacks moving smoothly.

Anna watched in admiration as they passed

the noisy fight 'Now that is real skill!' she declared, looking at Giles with a gleam in her eyes. 'You handle the ribbons even better than my father.'

Giles did not seem overwhelmed by this praise. They proceeded in silence for some time. It seemed to Anna that her heart had sunk down to her boots. She did not regret leaving home but it was impossible not to feel some apprehension about what lay ahead.

Almost as if he had read her thoughts, Giles commented, 'It is only about another six miles to Rosevale Court. There is still time to change your mind.'

She gripped her hands firmly in her lap. 'No, my lord. I *cannot* return to my home.'

He leaned forward and looked directly into her eyes. 'That was said in a very serious tone. What are you fleeing from, my child?'

Suddenly, there was a lump in her throat. She wanted him to put a strong arm round her, so she could lean against his shoulder and sob away all the hurt and frustration of being an unwanted stranger in her own home. She swallowed hard several times and at last managed to say, 'My mother kept me away at school until I was nineteen. And almost as soon as I came home, she had a suitor arranged for me.'

'Was that so terrible?' he asked, 'It is the

usual way of our world.'

'Yes, but he is so *old*,' she exclaimed, 'at least thirty-five!'

'Ah!' he said faintly. 'My infant, I myself am thirty years of age. I shall need a cane any day now.'

She gave a shaky laugh. 'I cannot believe that, sir. Why, there is no comparison between you and Cousin Frederick. He is bald and stooping and . . . and he is a parson and very conscious of his moral superiority.'

'Oh, I have no moral superiority,' he murmured, 'no moral anything, in fact.'

'Well, I am sure you would not come running only because it was suggested you could marry an heiress, sir.'

The horses broke into a gallop. Giles muttered something under his breath and gripped the reins, slowing them to a canter. He gave a heavy sigh. 'Miss Lawrence, just what am I doing, helping you to disappear in such a way?'

Anna gave a gasp of horror. Her cheeks went white with apprehension. One shaking hand flew up to her throat. But before she could speak he went on, 'If I were a man of honour, I should undoubtedly insist on returning you to your family forthwith. But . . . ' — he shook his head — 'I do sympathize with your point of view. You see, I

51

am fleeing from my family also.'

She frowned over that. 'But you are a man. You can do as you like.'

He gave a short laugh. 'Alas, not always. However, I do my best. Which is why my reputation is so bad. You do realize you must not admit to knowing me.'

'I will not be so base,' said Anna hotly. 'You are most truly a gentleman.'

He shook his head. There was a strange, twisted smile on his lips.

A short while later they were driving past high walls and soon came to a set of imposing entrance gates. The woman at the lodge confirmed that it was indeed Rosevale Court and Giles turned into the avenue. Anna surveyed the large building in silence, her hands pressed against her throat.

'I do trust you will be well treated here.' Giles swept the curricle round the circular drive and pulled up in front of the main door. Morgan leapt down to take her portmanteau. Giles helped her down without leaving his seat. Anna clung to his hand, the last bit of solid comfort in her uncertain new world.

'Thank you . . . for everything . . . ' she whispered. She had to blink hard to see his face clearly.

His gloved hand briefly touched her cheek. His green eyes were glinting at her. 'Courage, little Anna. This is your first big adventure.'

The butler was standing in front of the open door. Morgan climbed back into the curricle. Giles touched his whip to his hat, gathered up the reins and then the curricle swung away. Anna took a deep breath and turned to walk through the door into her new life.

6

Anna vaguely registered an impression of old-fashioned elegance as she followed the stately butler across the wide entrance hall. Now that the moment had come, her heart was beating loudly enough to deafen her. He ushered her into an airy parlour. The side doors were open onto a colourful garden. There was a lady in the room, arranging flowers in a large bowl. She turned and gazed silently as Anna approached.

Anna came to a halt about halfway across the room. She curtsied. 'Good day, your ladyship. I am Annabelle Lawrence.' She looked at her new employer and suddenly she knew there had been a terrible mistake. This woman was certainly not an old lady in need of a companion. True, she looked thin and drawn, but she bore herself regally. She was possibly in her late thirties, olive-skinned and dark-eyed. Her dark hair was elaborately styled under a wisp of a lace cap and her emerald green dress was made of silk and lace.

Wild ideas of having come to the wrong house chased through Anna's mind. And by now Lord Longwood must be too far away to come to her rescue. The woman laid down her flowers and inspected her very thoroughly. Anna clasped her hands in front of her and waited. Her teachers at school had trained the girls in many social skills, including the art of standing for long periods without fidgeting. She kept her expression politely interested, but inside she was wondering how she could get away and where she would go.

Then the lady nodded slowly. 'Miss Lawrence,' she said in a husky voice, 'we have been waiting for you.'

Anna blinked. So she *had* come to the right address. She forced her lips into a stiff smile. The lady turned away and picked up her flowers again. Deliberately, she placed them in the bowl. She considered the effect, and at length turned back to Anna.

'Let us sit down.' She led the way to two chairs facing each other in an alcove. A gesture invited Anna to sit, while she went to pull on the bell rope by the fireplace.

'Now, Cronton will bring us tea and we can talk about your duties.'

'Yes, ma'am.' Anna tried to keep the bewilderment out of her voice.

The lady clapped her hands together. 'Oh, but I have not yet told you my name. I am the

Contessa di Callamontese. It is an Italian title. Ah, I see that you are surprised. You came expecting to meet Lady Fording, yes? She is my mother.'

A wave of relief swept over Anna. 'That was the name in the letter I received.'

'This is my mother's home. She is a widow and she does not enjoy good health. Recently she had a heart seizure.' The *contessa* pressed a lace-edged handkerchief to her lips. Her eyes were fixed intently upon Anna. 'I require a young lady to keep her company and see that she does not overtire herself. My mother is . . . impulsive and she forgets that she must take life slowly. So you must be a calming influence on her, you understand!'

Anna nodded. 'Yes, I will do my best, your ladyship.' She accepted the cup of tea the *contessa* offered her and gladly took a sip.

'I selected you because you told me in your letter that you are well educated,' she went on, sipping her own tea. 'Mama will only respect a person of intelligence. She is fond of reading and music. Do you sing?'

'Yes, I can both play and sing — only tolerably though,' said Anna, biting her lower lip.

The *contessa* waved her hand. 'It will be enough to keep my mother entertained quietly. I will not have her being over-excited.

Now, if you have finished your tea, we will go and meet her.'

Lady Paulina Fording was a vivacious little lady dressed in a pretty lavender muslin gown with much lace trimming and ribbons. She still showed traces of having been a great beauty. They found her reclining on a sofa by the window in her private drawing room on the first floor. On a low table close by was an untidy heap of fashion magazines, Minerva Press novels and boxes of sweetmeats. A small pug dog sat beside her, but on seeing Anna, it leapt down and started yapping.

'Be silent, Beppi!' commanded his mistress. Beppi sniffed at Anna's outstretched fingers, rolled his eyes and consented to let her stroke his head.

'*Benissimo*,' said Lady Fording, 'I see you like animals.' She smiled at Anna. 'I hope you also like horrid romances, Miss Lawrence? You do? Then we shall go along famously.'

'Mama, dearest, I have explained to Miss Lawrence that you are to avoid all excitement.' The *contessa*'s tone was very firm.

Her mother fluttered both hands. 'But, of course, Beatrice. You tell me every day.' She lifted her shoulders in a little shrug, her dark eyes twinkling wickedly at Anna. 'This young lady will spare me every fatigue and even write my correspondence for me, yes?'

Anna nodded and smiled back at her. It was plain that Lady Fording was far more Italian than her daughter, and probably much easier to like. The *contessa's* manner conveyed a chill. She also seemed nervous but maybe, if her mother's health improved, she would relax.

Anna's spirits rose. Life here promised to be easier than at home, where she had many duties to perform, including spending a lot of time looking after her two small half-brothers. Lady Fording seemed very good-natured. And even if her daughter was a little cold, she was not haughty and full of orders — so far at any rate!

At last Anna was shown to the room she would occupy. It was on the second floor, and faced the garden. She quickly unpacked and poured water into the basin for a much needed wash. Then, having dressed in a fresh muslin gown in soft pink and arranged her hair in a simple knot, she went back downstairs to tap on Lady Fording's door.

They went down to dinner together, Lady Fording leaning heavily on Anna's arm. The old lady sighed as they reached the bottom of the staircase.

'I used to run up and down these stairs fifty times a day,' she said. 'But I was young and happy in those times.'

There was much to ponder in this statement. The old lady was so chatty, Anna was sure she would hear all about it very soon. They walked slowly to the parlour, where a footman was waiting to open the door for them. To Anna's surprise, there was a gentleman seated there. He rose swiftly from his chair and bowed to both ladies. Anna curtsied, wondering who he could be. The *contessa* had not mentioned a husband. He came forward and kissed Lady Fording's cheek.

'You are in good looks this evening, Zia Paulina.'

Zia! That meant aunt. Anna was thankful she had worked hard in her Italian lessons at school. She had not realized that she was coming to a houseful of Italian people, and who spoke their native language. Were any of the servants Italian, she wondered? But now the *contessa* entered the room. She was dressed in a low-cut amber silk robe. It was so beautifully styled that Anna's mouth almost watered with envy. How she would love to possess such a gown.

'I see you have met my cousin, Miss Lawrence. Enrico, this young lady is to keep Mama quiet and help her recover. Miss Lawrence, this is Signor Enrico di Cassagna.'

He inclined his head slightly but said

nothing. Anna thought he glanced at her simple dress with disdain. He was very fine himself, in a velvet jacket that was moulded to his form and with high, stiff shirt points. His jet-black hair was smoothed sleekly back from his face, emphasizing his prominent cheek-bones and narrow dark eyes. His expression was irritable and he made little attempt to take part in the conversation throughout dinner.

The meal was delicious, but after drinking her soup, Anna felt so tired she could have set her head on the table and slept. It was an effort to reply to the frequent comments of Lady Fording. Not even the floating island pudding could rouse her to any enthusiasm, although she usually considered it a big treat. She was simply relieved when the contessa rose to take the ladies to the drawing room. They went up the wide staircase together and, at the top, Lady Fording announced she would retire.

'And you should also retire now,' she told Anna. 'My maid will come to fetch you when I need you tomorrow.'

'Thank you, ma'am. You may be sure I shall be ready.' Anna stifled a yawn and made her way up the second flight of stairs to her room. She could hardly wait to set her head on the pillow. She scrambled out of her clothes and shook out her hair. She picked up her brush, but after a few half-hearted strokes gave it up. She was just too tired to bother. Sinking thankfully onto the bed, she pulled the sheet up to her chin. She wondered drowsily where her dear, kind Lord Long-wood was tonight and if he was glad to have got rid of her. How much more personable he was than the *contessa*'s surly cousin! How she wished she could see him again. She yawned and burrowed her head into the pillow. In a very few minutes, she was asleep.

Over the following week, Anna settled into a comfortable routine. In the mornings, she sat with Lady Fording and dealt with her correspondence, then they took lunch together. After a nap, Lady Fording liked to go downstairs and walk a little in the garden. Beppi, the pug, enjoyed a sedate stroll around the rose arbour or even as far as the lake and summerhouse. Then he would collapse and pant, eyeing Anna soulfully. She could never get him to run or chase a stick, however hard she tried.

Meanwhile, Lady Fording would sit on a bench under the shade of a great old oak on the lawn, from where she had a view both of the house and the lake. A footman would bring out lemonade and small cakes. The weather was settled and warm, so these days had a pleasant, dreamlike quality for Anna.

Occasionally, she remembered her ordeal with the two young men at Alton and she would shudder and clasp her throat. But that memory led inevitably to the happier memory of the dark-haired, green-eyed Earl of Longwood. How she had enjoyed that curricle ride when he kept those beautiful and spirited horses at such a smooth but fast pace.

While he was very masterful, and she had had to fight his ideas, she knew she had not felt so well cared for since her father's death. It had been a great comfort to feel that she was important to someone, even when it was just for a day. And it had been so hard to say goodbye.

'You are sighing again,' Lady Fording would remark. 'Do you not like it here, Anna?'

'I am very happy here, ma'am,' Anna would reply. 'It was just a-a certain event that sometimes comes to mind.'

'Well then, we must cure that. Come, have another of Cook's gooseberry tarts. Nothing is more certain to cure *la melancholia*.'

Lady Fording's remedy was always to have another biscuit or another drink of cool lemonade. Anna marvelled at how she had managed to stay so small and birdlike. Poor pug, who was always ready to gobble up a good half of Anna's cake, was certainly much too plump. During these peaceful afternoons, they would sit and sew and chat companionably. One particularly sultry day, on seeing Anna wafting a fan, Lady Fording's eye brightened.

'I always loved to send messages by using my fan. How skilled are you in this art?'

Anna stared at her. 'Messages? Do you mean writing on it?'

The old lady fluttered her hands. 'No, no, no. Like this.' She raised her fan and drew it across her eyes. 'There. Do you know what I just said?'

Anna shook her head, eyes wide with surprise.

'It means: 'I am sorry'. And this?' She flicked the fan open and laid it against her left ear. 'That is: 'Do not betray our secret'.' She beamed. 'Now I shall teach you.'

'But I shall not need this skill, ma'am,' protested Anna, laughing.

'A lady always needs this skill,' insisted Lady Fording. 'Besides, it will amuse me.'

So Anna learnt to place her fan against the right or left cheek, or at her bosom, to furl and unfurl it, even drop it at her feet, depending on the message these gestures conveyed. It was all accompanied by much laughter and added to the interest of the days. The *contessa*, when she came to sit for a while with her mother, joined in the lessons. At dinnertime, the two ladies made Anna demonstrate the movements she had learned.

Even Signor di Cassagna roused from his usual indifference to watch attentively. When he actually addressed her, Anna realized just how important they all considered this art. They all three tested her, occasionally arguing about the exact meaning of a gesture. Anna felt proud of her new skill. Was the Earl of Longwood as knowledgeable as Signor di Cassagna? She was sure he would be. One thing alarmed her, however. She became aware that Signor di Cassagna had started to look her up and down out of those narrow dark eyes of his. But, as he only ever appeared at the dinner table, and the whole family was there at that time, she told herself not to worry.

One afternoon, when Anna brought pug back from his walk, Lady Fording set down her plate and glass and gave her characteristic little shrug of the shoulders. 'Anna, my dear, let us leave our sewing for today. I simply cannot wait any longer to discover if Melidora will resist the advances of Count Grigorevitch. And you read it so well. I must hear the rest.'

But a search through the workbasket amongst the silks and materials failed to turn up *The Bandit's Quest.*

'I fear I have left it in your parlour, ma'am.' Anna jumped up. 'It will not take many minutes to fetch it.'

'Hurry, my dear! I so long to listen to the next episode.' Lady Fording fed a biscuit to Beppi, who snuffled happily and wagged his little tail. Anna hurried back into the house and soon found the book, lying on the table where she had left it the previous evening. As she sped down the stairs she heard Signor di Cassagna's voice coming from the ground-floor parlour. The door was open.

'Things go from bad to worse. He becomes intolerable. I shall have to go to Town and send an express through the embassy. He must accept that I — *I* am the rightful leader!' He then lapsed into a torrent of Italian.

Anna hastened past on tiptoe and scampered out of the front door. She had never heard those Italian words before but they sounded very rude. Whatever could have roused Signor di Cassagna from his habitual languor? Anna suspected that most of his attention went on his clothes and appearance. He was forever adjusting his hair or his cravat in front of any looking glass. She giggled as she decided that probably he was furious with his tailor for not sending his new jacket home in time for some event.

Well, whatever it was, it would make no difference to her new life. She smiled as she approached the tree where Lady Fording and pug sat waiting for her. Now they would enjoy an hour reading their story. What nicer way to spend a hot afternoon? She was delighted with her job as a lady's companion.

7

Signor di Cassagna left the following morning, accompanied by his Italian valet, in a coach laden with luggage. Anna found they got on better without him. He had never contributed very much to their evening's entertainment anyway. Now Lady Fording spent an hour with her daughter in the main drawing room after dinner and they asked Anna to play and sing for their entertainment.

From little bits of information let fall by Lady Fording, Anna was learning something about the *contessa*. When Napoleon's forces had conquered northern Italy, the commanding French general had confiscated the family's main residence, the Palazzo di Callamontese. The family had been living in a smaller property they owned, in a remote village in the mountains. But now that Napoleon had been vanquished, they were hopeful that she would soon be able to return to her former home.

'It is such a beautiful region,' Lady Fording told Anna, 'so picturesque and nature so bountiful. *Che meraviglia!* The land of my childhood — I would never have left it but for Sir Alfred Fording. However, when he came to stay with my elder brother, I lost my heart to him.' She gestured to the portrait over the mantelpiece. A bluff, fair-haired man smiled out from it. Lady Fording smiled and shook her head. 'You understand, child, that one does not give up one's country unless it is for love.'

This was very much in agreement with Anna's own ideas. 'It is as good as a novel, dear ma'am,' she said eagerly. 'What an adventure to leave your home and come to England. But if you were living here, how is it that your daughter married an Italian?'

'Ah, we used to return to my family for visits. Beatrice had many suitors here in England. But once she met Paolo — the Count di Callamontese, she made up her mind he was the man for her. Yet she has come to help me in my time of need, just when she has so much to do to restore her own home.' She shrugged and sighed. 'And Enrico is obviously impatient to return to his life in Florence.' She gave Anna an almost apologetic look. 'He is my brother's youngest son and very active in politics.' She said this in a whisper.

Anna's eyes grew round. 'Is politics a dangerous activity in Italy, then?'

Lady Fording nodded her head vigorously. 'We will not mention it again,' she stated.

Another week went past, the only difference being that the weather turned wet and they had to stay indoors during the afternoons. Anna walked pug so that she herself could get exercise and fresh air. They finished *The Bandit's Quest* and began *Prince Kaspar's Secret Bride*. Anna was looking forward to reading another chapter of this as she brought pug back from a walk. But when they reached Lady Fording's parlour, Anna found the Contessa sitting with her mother.

The *contessa* indicated a dish of sweetmeats. They were conical in shape, made of chocolate and tipped with a cherry. 'We are waiting for you, Miss Lawrence. It is a hobby of mine to make these traditional sweetmeats from our region of Italy. I suppose it is a kind of nostalgia.' She sighed as she picked up the dish and offered it to her mother. 'You will tell me, Mama, if I have succeeded.' She turned towards Anna. 'They are called volcanoes.'

'Yes, I see.' Anna bit into the creamy chestnut paste and chocolate confection and exclaimed in delight. 'This is delicious, ma'am.'

The *contessa* seemed pleased. 'So I have

not lost my skill.' She gave Anna an almost embarrassed look. 'It may seem a strange pastime, but it is something the ladies of my husband's family all enjoyed doing.'

'Yes, I remember that from when I was a girl,' nodded Lady Fording. 'I was often a visitor at the Palazzo di Callamontese. I was very friendly with the girls of the family.' She sighed and shook her head. 'Ah, my dear daughter, your lost home.'

'And God knows what state it is in.' The *contessa* rose and walked swiftly over to the window, gripping her hands together. 'Doubtless those French villains have stripped out most of the treasures. But we will set it all to rights.' She broke off and put one hand over her mouth, remaining at the window with her back to them.

Lady Fording looked at Anna and placed a finger to her lips. She shook her head slowly. Anna nodded slightly and bent her head over a book that was on the table by her side.

'Are you already considering your return, Beatrice?' her mother asked at last.

'I must do so, Mama.' She returned to sit next to her mother as she spoke. Anna kept her eyes on the book but she was all ears. This was exciting.

She heard a deep sigh from the *contessa*. 'Mama, I cannot bear to leave you alone here.

I will wait until you are well enough to travel back with me.'

Anna thrilled with excitement. Did that mean she would go as well? Just like her hero, Childe Harold, she would embark on a ship and travel in foreign lands. She waited hopefully, her head still bent over the book, but the ladies said no more.

At dinner that evening, the *contessa* disclosed that she had received a letter from her cousin. 'Enrico says the victory celebrations are drawing to a close,' she informed her mother. 'Most of the foreign dignitaries will be leaving within the next week. Enrico says everyone is talking of rest and sea air. He wants us all to go to Brighton. Mama, it would be good for you to spend a few weeks at the seaside. Now we have Miss Lawrence and she has proved so good at caring for you, I think we can make the journey.' She waved away the dish that was being presented by a footman. 'I am not hungry tonight.'

She glanced at Anna, who was helping herself from a bowl of green peas. A slight smile touched her mouth. 'It is good to see the appetite of youth.' Her eyes narrowed as she considered Anna's hair. As usual, Anna had brushed it smooth and pulled it into a knot at the back of her neck. It was the style favoured by the teachers at her school in Bath and she considered it suitable for her current role.

'Miss Lawrence, do you know how to dance?'

Anna looked up from her green peas and stewed veal. 'We had a good dancing master at school. I know all the steps . . . but I have never danced at a ball.' Where was this leading? The *contessa* was definitely planning some new scheme. Could it be because she felt free without Signor di Cassagna and his rather stifling presence? Anna's eyes grew wide with anticipation. 'Will there be a dancing party here, ma'am?'

She was disappointed when the *contessa* raised her hand in a negative reply. But when the ladies were in the drawing room, the mystery deepened.

'So you can dance,' said the *contessa*, 'and now, will you please ring the bell? I require my dresser to take your measurements. We must see about some new clothes for you.'

Anna stared in bewilderment. She felt as if she was inside one of Lady Fording's more lurid stories. The feeling grew as the evening progressed. The *contessa's* dresser was an Italian and she spoke little English, so they all discussed Anna and her new clothes as if she were a dummy. She followed the conversation reasonably well and when it was a matter of the colour, she was able to make her own suggestions. It sounded as if she was to have some beautiful new dresses. But why?

'It seems to be a lot of very smart clothes just to go to the seaside,' she ventured to remark, when the dresser had finally left the room.

The *contessa* sighed and opened her hands in a gesture of resignation. 'In his letter, Enrico reminds me that Brighton is a very smart town. Even as my mother's companion, you must be seen to be smart. And surely, no young lady ever minds having new clothes.'

Anna coloured. 'It — it is very kind b-but it will be very costly, I fear.'

'That is nothing,' announced the *contessa*. 'It will please me to see you looking stylish. It is time for you to become a young lady of fashion.'

When she was alone in her room, Anna went over the evening's events again. She had a niggling suspicion that there was more to this than appeared. She was not being given this new wardrobe just to satisfy the *contessa's* idea of her own importance. And why was she expected to dance? Whatever did grand people do at the seaside?

She also wondered about her mother and stepfather. If the victory celebrations were over, they were probably back at home. How long would they leave it before sending to order her to return from Elinor's house? And then, how would Elinor handle the matter? Well, perhaps going further away from home for a while was a good idea. And it would be really exciting to visit a spa town. She would see the sea for the first time in her life. What good fortune! Brighton was such a smart place — and she might even see the Prince Regent, who had his own magnificent summer residence there.

Even better than the Prince, it was quite possible that Lord Byron would be there. Anna had to clap both hands over her mouth not to shout out with excitement at this idea. She jumped up and twirled around. Suddenly, new gowns became very important.

8

Giles took a turn along the seafront before going into the Castle Tavern. The smooth surface of the water reflected the evening light, turning gold now. There was quite a crowd of people strolling about, in no hurry to join the throng inside the assembly hall. Giles raised his hat to several acquaintances but did not stop. Ned was waiting for him and he wanted a full account of the latest events in Town.

At the open door of the Castle Tavern Giles paused. He raised his eyebrows at the sight of the constantly moving mass of people. They were of all ages, all dressed in the latest London fashions and all gossiping as usual. He was aware of a ripple of extra sound and heads turning towards him and just as quickly glancing away. A few fans fluttered while the ladies' eyes continued to hold his. The bold ones, of course.

Should he feel gratified at this display of interest? He had only been away from society for a month. It had been an agreeable change to live on his country estate just like any ordinary gentleman, discussing crops and harvests with his steward, helping some of his labourers dig a new drainage ditch and tackling various jobs that required hard physical effort. If his father could have seen him, the duke would have been apoplectic with rage. But Giles did not share his father's views on keeping a wide distance between himself and his tenants.

However, a month alone had been enough. That leaden feeling of boredom was creeping over him again. His life was basically lonely and lacking in challenge. He had only to express a wish and someone — his valet, the butler or some other servant, hastened to complete the task. It was stifling, but that was the order of things in his father's household and the servants were trained to their duties. Giles longed for a life where he must struggle to achieve his goals. He envied Charles, his younger brother, who had become an officer in Wellington's army. Ah, now there was real value in a life like that!

But as the heir to the dukedom, Giles knew he was destined for a different kind of duty. And yet his father kept him away from managing the vast estates, so that his life was a desert of insipid entertainments and social events. And all the time the ambitious mamas were trying to catch him for their particular daughter. They were so alike, these empty-headed, dutiful chits; they would bore him to distraction within a day of marriage. Yet his father was growing insistent about the need for an heir. And someone had informed the duke that Belinda Beveridge was a willing candidate.

Giles grimaced. That ball, where he had ended up with Belinda plastered all over him because that clumsy fool, Chilvers, had cannoned into them, had given Belinda's mother an excuse to claim her daughter was half compromised. She had even prodded her usually inert husband into paying Giles a visit. It had taken a lot of skill and a great deal of brandy to avoid discussing the topic of the viscount's daughter and expectations. That had been a close call!

That was the trouble with families with whom one had a long standing acquaintance. It was impossible to shake them off altogether. As youngsters, he and Belinda had been on friendly enough terms. But Giles was damned if he would be leg-shackled to her or anyone until — at some time in the distant future — he found a girl he knew he could live with.

He raised his hat to yet another friend and strolled on. Had a month been long enough to cool their fevered hopes? If he came across

Belinda and her family here he was going to have to be freezingly correct and distant. It was only Ned's plea that had brought him to Brighton. They could attend the races and take part in some sporting activities. There would be card parties and the theatre. And no doubt he would endure a dinner at the Pavilion before the suffocating emptiness of it all overcame him.

'There you are at last! I have been waiting here this age.' Ned appeared in the doorway. He grinned. 'You lucky dog, Giles. It seems the entire female population considers you to be manna from heaven. Why do they never give me those looks?'

Giles was considering a particularly bold pair of brown eyes above a fluttering fan, but at his friend's plaintive tone, he turned his head. 'Oh, but they do, Ned! They do! Only you are always busy composing a poem at such moments. You attract the artistic souls, whereas I get the harlots. If you really tried, even Lady Caroline Lamb would allow herself to be diverted from her current amour.'

'Byron? Ah, but you are behind with the latest gossip. He is to be married.'

'Spare me the details. Now, who was it who mentioned Byron to me . . . ? Ah, yes — ' He broke off, a smile lighting up his face as he remembered fiery little Anna. Poor girl, what a waste of so much spirit. No doubt she was already wishing she had not left a comfortable home — even with a bullying stepfather — just to fetch and carry for some cantankerous old lady.

'Come on, then,' Ned led the way inside, where the orchestra had just stopped playing a country dance. The couples were moving off the floor and the noise of conversation soared. Waiters began weaving their way round the room with trays of drinks. Giles assessed the girls as they made their way back to their chaperons. His lips tightened.

He put a hand on Ned's sleeve. 'I think we shall find more entertainment in the card room,' he murmured. And then, he saw her! His brows drew down as he watched through narrowed eyes. He saw the energy in her as she took a drink from a waiter and turned to make her way to a table in an alcove, where an older lady sat. He saw them smile and exchange a remark as the flaxen-haired girl placed the glass on the table. She was wearing a white dress that enhanced her tall, slender figure. Giles drew in a deep breath. So Anna Lawrence had gone from pickle to grown up young lady in a remarkably short space of time.

Her shining hair was brushed free of curls

and swept up into a classical style, bound with a silver ribbon. His practised eye noted how the dress cleverly defined her figure. The tiny puffed sleeves showed off her white arms. He was surprised to discover his thoughts whirling, he who was so jaded by the endless procession of debutantes. He never lost control of his emotions. But now he could not tell what he felt. Was it relief that she had apparently found a kind employer? Or was it simply pleasure at seeing her again?

'Well, come on then.' Ned's voice was impatient. Giles turned slowly away. After all, he had warned her not to admit to knowing him. He reached the doorway and took a final glance back. And received another shock.

'It would have to be him!' he muttered.

'What now?' Ned followed the direction of Giles's gaze. 'Well, by Jove! Is that Charles hanging round that yaller-headed female?'

'Need you ask!' growled Giles, frowning at the sight of his younger brother hovering close to Anna and her companion. Lord Charles Maltravers, resplendent in his hussar's uniform, made a striking figure. It was clear that Anna was impressed. Swallowing a most unbrotherly feeling, Giles strode over to the alcove, followed by a puzzled Ned.

Nobody could be surprised that he would greet his brother. What a perfect way to gain an introduction to his former travelling companion. He saw how her eyes widened as she saw him approach. But she kept the polite smile on her face as she listened to Captain Lord Charles. No doubt he was using all his usual wiles, the dog! For once, Giles was not prepared to leave his brother to his seduction routine. This was *Miss Lawrence* and she was *his* protégée.

By now Charles had seen his brother. He straightened up, very tall, blond and broad-shouldered, the silver facings on his blue uniform shining. In this period of festivities to mark the downfall of Napoleon and the end of the wars, all soldiers were heroes. Charles certainly looked the part and he was enjoying the many glances of admiration cast at him. With a whole roomful of girls ready to swoon, why did he have to pick this one to flirt with?

'Giles!' Charles gripped both his brother's hands, a warm smile on his face. 'Where have you been hiding, you dog?'

'Thought you were still parading round London,' Giles responded.

'All finished now, old fellow. Prinny took it into his head to take a bolt to his summer farm.' This was said with a sneer. The Prince's Marine Pavilion, might have once been a farm but now it was a growing sprawl of exotic appearance.

'Ah,' said Ned, shaking Charles's hand, 'it's true you have been abroad and so this is the first time you have seen the — er — improvements.' He grinned as Charles rolled his blue eyes heavenwards.

There was a tiny pause. Giles cast a glance towards the ladies seated behind his brother. Charles gave a start. 'Oh, I forget my manners.' He bowed to the old lady. 'May I present my brother, ma'am? My older brother, Giles Maltravers, Earl of Longwood. And Mr Caldecott. Giles, Ned, this is Lady Fording and Miss Lawrence.'

Giles bowed with exquisite grace. He addressed himself to the elderly lady, who was watching him with a twinkle in her sharp eyes. 'I trust you are enjoying your stay in Brighton, ma'am.'

She gave an expressive little shrug of her shoulders. 'Thank you. It is a town I like. And this young lady is taking great care of me.'

Giles gave Anna a quick glance and turned back to Lady Fording. He raised his brows. 'Indeed? You have had the misfortune to suffer an indisposition? I trust you are regaining your health.'

She unfurled her fan. She was watching something behind Giles but he was too polite to turn round. The next moment another lady came into view and went to stand behind

Lady Fording. Giles saw the physical resemblance, but there could not be a greater difference in character. She was elegant but as cold as ice. Lady Fording waved her fan generally. 'My daughter, la Contessa di Callamontese. Is this not amusing, Beatrice? We now have three so handsome young men gathered round.' She beamed at them all.

The master of ceremonies announced the next dance. Giles looked at Lady Fording. 'With your permission, ma'am, I will dance this with Miss Lawrence. That is' — he looked directly at her at last — 'if you care to dance?'

Behind him, his brother cleared his throat pointedly. Giles took no notice. Anna looked to the *contessa*, who nodded an assent.

'Thank you, Lord Longwood.' She placed a hand correctly on his outstretched forearm and they moved away to take their places in the set.

'At last,' he breathed. 'I am anxious to know if all is well.'

She gave him a demure smile. 'I am very fortunate.'

He saw Charles leading the *contessa* into the same set. Damn! No further conversation would be possible. But he could maybe learn a few things while they danced. For a start, the transformation was remarkable. She knew it as well, the little minx. She was pleased with her softly flowing gown and her cleverly styled hair, decorated with its silver ribbons. He quickly found that she was light on her feet. For the first time in a long time he had a partner with whom it was a pleasure to dance.

It was not many minutes before she whispered, as they joined hands to complete a figure, 'Why is everyone staring at us?'

'Curiosity.' But he was at fault. He had been so pleased to see her again he had been indiscreet. Now he had drawn attention to her. But he wanted to discover if she was in good hands. The change in her appearance troubled him a little. The old lady seemed kind and open, but that daughter of hers was up to something. A lady's companion was normally treated very little better than a servant, not displayed in charming gowns and taken to dancing parties. Dressed and groomed in this way, Anna was now stunningly attractive. She was being used as bait. But who was the intended victim?

Giles stifled a sigh. Once again, he was going to have to rescue her.

★ ★ ★

Anna heard the sigh and wondered if he was bored dancing with her. She bit her lip, her happiness punctured at this idea. She had been so delighted to see him again. She had recognized his tall figure and broad shoulders as soon as he entered the room but, mindful of his warning, she had pretended not to know him. But then he had invited her to dance — actually dance — with him. Her first dance at her first ball and she was dancing it with him. But then he sighed and all her joy shattered.

Of course, he moved in the topmost circles of society. Was that why everyone was taking discreet looks at them? At least she was presentable. Her dress was stylish and Maria, the maid, had dressed her hair into this Grecian knot. And she did know the dance steps. In fact it was a delicious sensation to move in this way, especially when her partner was the most splendid man in the room and her own special friend.

She stole another quick look at Giles as they linked hands with the other dancers in their set to move in a circle. His face with its sculpted cheekbones gave no clue to his feelings. His dark curls, as always, fell over his brow. But those green eyes, under his thick, straight brows, glinted at her.

'Is this your first visit to Brighton, Miss Lawrence?'

'Yes, sir,' she replied. It was some form of

conversation, after all.

'And have you seen much of the town so far?'

'We arrived yesterday, sir. There was only time for some shopping.'

The dance separated them again. When next they came together he was still grinning. 'Is shopping your main interest? There are other things to do in the town.'

'So I understand, sir,' she replied, with a gleam of mischief, 'but everything depends on Lady Fording's health. She must not overtax her strength.'

He merely raised his brows at this. The final chord sounded and they bowed and curtsied and Giles led her back to where Ned was sitting with Lady Fording. Anna felt she was walking on air.

'I have discovered something very wonderful,' exclaimed the old lady to her daughter, who reached her side at the same time as Giles and Anna, 'this gentleman is a poet.'

'What, Ned, are you still scribbling your verses?' Lord Charles clapped him on the shoulder with a hearty laugh.

'I greatly admire poetry,' said Anna, examining Ned keenly. 'But not everyone does so. I have heard it described as an incurable condition.' She saw Giles's eyes crinkle at the corners as he took in her remark. He gave a slight shake of his head at her, just as she was drawing breath to ask Ned if he knew Lord Byron. She stuck out her lower lip and fanned herself instead.

Lord Charles requested the next dance. Anna accepted but it was an effort to appear pleased. Before Giles appeared, she would have been delighted to dance with Lord Charles. But now any other partner would be an anticlimax. However, she was cheered to discover, when they returned after the quadrille, that Giles and the *contessa* had agreed to make up a party to go to the races the next day.

9

The three open carriages made a fine convoy the next morning on their way to Race Hill to the east of the town. The sky was blue with just a few small clouds and the day promised to be warm and settled. Lord Charles Maltravers led the way in a yellow curricle. Giles and Ned brought up the rear in the racing curricle. The black horses gleamed like satin and were full of spirits. The ladies were in their open barouche between these two very dashing carriages.

Anna sat with her back to the horses. Lady Fording and the *contessa* were opposite her, both looking very elegant. Anna was dressed in another of her new gowns, a delicate blue muslin with much pleating at neckline and sleeves, and trimmed with ribbon at the hem. She had a long yellow scarf draped over her elbows, just as the *contessa* arranged hers. She wore a sweet little straw bonnet trimmed with a spray of yellow flowers and carried a tiny parasol. Both these items had been purchased on their first day in Brighton. Anna was glowing with pleasure at her new elegant possessions.

Very occasionally, during school outings in Bath, Anna and her friends had examined the smart clothes and bonnets in the expensive shops in Milsom Street but she had never been able to purchase any. Her mother had made no attempt to dress her daughter in fashionable clothes. Everything was made by the local dressmaker, who came once a week to the house to sew.

She put up a hand to touch the blue ribbons of her bonnet, tied under her left ear by the *contessa* herself. Just for a second, Anna's pleasure was eclipsed by a worry that all this finery was part of some scheme and she was a pawn in a game she did not understand. Then she looked up at the carriage following theirs. She caught a glint of jewel green eyes. He was observing her. Hastily she looked down, smoothing away an imaginary crease in her glove.

'Are you sure, Mama, that you are well enough for such a long excursion?' The *contessa* was examining her mother closely.

Lady Fording made a sweeping gesture, taking in the view and the sky above. She smiled warmly at her daughter. 'This is medicine for me. You know how I enjoy animation and company. And we could not ask for three more handsome and energetic young men to care for us.' She raised her eyebrows and grinned wickedly at Anna, who felt a blush rise in her cheeks. At this Lady Fording chuckled and leaned forward to pat Anna's knee. 'Ah, yes, child, you should be more pleased than anyone! These are young men of the first style of elegance and good family.'

The *contessa*'s face was its usual cool mask. She merely said, 'Well, Miss Lawrence, I rely on you to watch carefully. If Mama appears in the least fatigued, we will return at once.'

'Of course, ma'am.' Anna gave her a wide, innocent look. Lady Fording, already used to Anna's facial expressions, had a satisfied look. She and her young companion would contrive to do much as they pleased. Lady Fording nodded towards the first curricle, driven by Lord Charles. 'Now he is a fine young man, full of dash and he is extremely handsome with his blond hair,' she commented. Her eyes held a question.

Anna merely smiled back. The old lady chuckled softly. 'But he does not please you, huh?'

'It is not my place to be pleased or . . . or — '

'Mama, do look over this way,' said the *contessa*, her tone arctic. 'See how delightful the sea is along this bay.'

'Nearly there,' called out Charles over his shoulder. 'Quite a crowd ahead though. Where shall we make for, Giles?'

They had to proceed slowly in the line of carriages. The three young men began to see people they knew and frequently exchanged greetings. One or two men on horseback seemed inclined to join the group, but Giles gave them no encouragement. It was he who manoeuvred them into a good place to watch the races, near the finishing line and on the upper side of the track so they had a good view down the valley to the sea.

Anna sat entranced by the whole spectacle of the crowds and the jolly atmosphere. There were so many well-dressed people, all apparently in good spirits. It was not long before Charles appeared at the side of their barouche. He addressed the *contessa*. 'My lady, you would have a better view from my curricle. And then Miss Lawrence will be able to watch the races without twisting her neck.'

'Well.' The *contessa* hesitated. 'I shall only be in the next carriage if there is any problem, Mama.'

'Yes, go on, my dear, the young man is right. As we are now, Anna will block our view just at the most exciting moment.'

So Charles helped the *contessa* to climb

into his curricle and they appeared to enjoy a conversation about horses. When Anna saw the first race she was completely enthralled. She had always loved horses and she and her father used to ride a great deal. It had been so long, however, that she had forgotten how much she enjoyed watching the superb grace of a proud horse galloping.

'Yes, yes, go on!' she shouted, then recollected herself and sat down, embarrassed. Her choice won the race but she did not dare open her mouth. Lady Fording merely chuckled.

'Royal Hawk is a splendid animal, is he not? He seems almost to fly.'

'I was sure of it! It is you,' said a woman's voice by the barouche. Anna tensed, but, turning her head, she found two completely unknown people there. A rather portly middle-aged gentleman and an elderly lady were smiling at Lady Fording. At the same moment, Lady Fording exclaimed, 'But my dear Henrietta! How wonderful to see you. And John. How are you? And the children?'

The gentleman laughed. 'The children are quite grown up. But you will see them soon enough.'

The old lady was beaming. 'Dear Paulina. It has been such a long time.'

'Oh, do get into the carriage and we can

have a comfortable coze,' urged Lady Fording. Pug began to bark shrilly, so Anna picked him up.

'I think I will take him for a little walk, ma'am.'

'And I,' said the other lady's son, 'will go and find some refreshments.' He winked at Anna. 'I think the coze will last for quite some time.'

She set Beppi on his feet and looked for a way through the groups of spectators who were gathered at this point, close to the finishing line. At once she became aware of someone at her side. Giles gave her an inscrutable look, his eyes narrowed beneath his dark brows.

'My dear young lady,' he said, in a pleasant tone, 'you cannot possibly wander off alone. Allow me to escort you.'

'This is not a lonely road,' she objected, 'and I have pug to protect me.' She hid a saucy smile when she heard him give a derisive snort.

'Protection? I think a large cat would be more use.'

'But . . . your horses?'

'Mr Caldecott can handle them.'

They walked on in silence. Anna could hardly believe her good fortune. Here she was, strolling at a society event with her own special friend. And she thought he was quite the most good-looking gentleman there, as well as the best dressed, in his bottle green jacket and snowy linen. Even his boots shone like mirrors, she noticed, darting a glance at his long, well-shaped legs.

She was glad of her own smart new dress and bonnet. She hoped she looked fashionable enough to please him. He steered her towards a fairly open space where they could talk without being overheard. 'Tell me, Miss Lawrence, are there any menfolk in your new establishment?'

She stared at him. 'Why do you ask?' Then she gave a little skip. 'Are you going to give me a pistol if I say yes?'

'Of course I am not going to give you a pistol. Maybe a glass of hot milk.'

'Now you are laughing at me.' She sighed. 'It was always our supper at school. And it is not very long since I was still there.'

'You have not answered my question.'

'Oh, well, yes and no. Lady Fording's nephew came to escort her daughter on the journey to England. His father, Lady Fording's brother, is too elderly to make the journey. But Signor di Cassagna went to London soon after I arrived and we have not seen him since.'

He walked beside her in frowning silence.

Anna glanced at him. 'Is it of any importance?'

He pursed his lips. 'I merely wondered. As I took you to that family, I feel a certain — ah — responsibility to be sure you are not in any further scrapes.'

She laughed, bringing a gleam to his eyes. 'Oh, you are remembering how nervous I was when we arrived at Rosevale Court. Indeed, I could not have a kinder employer. We read horrid novels and do embroidery and my chief duty is walking this poor little creature.' She glanced down. 'And I see he has reached his limit now.'

Giles looked down with disfavour. 'What? Already? But we have scarcely been walking for a minute.'

Anna chuckled. 'It is certainly longer than that. See what a distance we have come from the carriage. But Beppi never goes very far. His mistress is elderly and he is spoiled — and lazy.' She smiled sunnily up at Giles. 'Now he has to rest before I can walk him back.' Beppi sprawled on the grass, panting, his bulging eyes staring sadly at Giles.

'Good lord! And you told me you liked your new life. Can it be that you have changed your ideas on what constitutes an adventure?'

She was about to retort but caught the

fleeting gleam of humour on his face. That made her laugh out loud and his smile grew broader. They stood in perfect amity for a long moment. Then Beppi wheezed and Anna caught her breath and looked away. She became aware of other people strolling close by. A gentleman was passing close to them. He gave her a keen look and raised his hat to Giles. When Giles touched his hat in return Anna sniffed discreetly, inhaling the spicy fragrance that clung to him, mixed with the smell of fine leather and soap.

They turned to face the track as the growing thunder of hoofs and clamour of raised voices told them another race was approaching the finish. Anna could just see the horses with their brightly dressed riders whipping their mounts towards the line. There were shouts and cheers as the winner was declared.

'I think Charles put his money on that one,' Giles remarked, vaguely interested.

Anna nodded. She wondered how one set about making a bet. Her father had not taught her anything about that. Could she ask? She decided there was no point, she did not have any money for such things. She bent gracefully over the little dog. 'I think pug is ready . . . ' she was saying, when from behind her a woman's voice barked out, 'Longwood!'

Startled by the brusque tone, Anna whipped her head round to give Giles an enquiring look. She saw his brows draw together. His nostrils pinched. She distinctly heard an exasperated sigh before he assumed a bland expression and turned towards the voice.

'Lady Beveridge, Miss Beveridge.' His voice was so cold that Anna decided these people must have offended him. She stood quietly, and looked at the newcomers. Here were a pair of very well-born ladies, judging by their air of consequence.

'Well, so here you are, Longwood,' said the older lady, a gaunt woman with a prominent chin and with a loud, rather deep voice, 'it is an age since we saw you in Town. I was expecting you at our dinner party. And dear Belinda was most cast down that you were not there.'

The young woman by her side was a dark-haired beauty. She had good features but her expression was proud. She was wearing a very elaborately stitched spencer over a silk gown. Anna was somewhat astonished to find that both ladies were examining her from head to foot. She struggled to contain her indignation at this impertinence. However, she would not disgrace herself before her dear Lord

Longwood, so she clasped her hands, and in her turn, coolly inspected the girl's dress.

It was pug who caused a diversion. Restored by his lie-down, he scrambled to his feet and yapped angrily at the newcomers, straining on his leash to jump up at the younger woman. She took a hasty step backwards with an exclamation of annoyance.

'Quite so,' murmured Giles. 'As you see, ladies, we are exercising Lady Fording's dog. Ah, permit me to introduce Miss Annabelle Lawrence to you.'

Anna smiled into two pairs of hostile eyes. Neither lady so much as gave her a nod.

'Shall we see you at the theatre this evening, Longwood?' Lady Beveridge demanded.

'It is by no means certain, ma'am.' He bowed and took a step back. 'Come, Miss Lawrence.' He drew her arm through his and swept her round. In an undertone he added, 'If that animal cannot walk, pray carry him.'

Pug, however, seemed as keen as Giles to get away from these ladies. With a final wheezy yap, he scuttled off as Anna gave a tug on his leash.

'Who are they?' whispered Anna.

Her only answer was a growl.

'I see,' she exclaimed. '*She* is the fate you were running away from when I met you.'

He drew in a sharp breath. 'No Maltravers

ever runs away — from anything! But I prefer to avoid them, yes.'

'And you just used me to help you. Perhaps I could have become friends with her, she looks very elegant and sophisticated . . . and I expect,' she added wistfully, 'she has a copy of *The Corsair*.'

'I doubt if she would lend it to you anyway,' he snapped. 'But I suspect her mama would never allow her to read anything written by Byron, in any event. Ah, here is Lady Fording's carriage. Get rid of that damned dog!'

'Oh, but I cannot get back in yet. Can you not see she is still talking to her friend.'

'I did not say you should get back in. Just get rid of the dog and I'll take you for an ice.'

'Oh! Thank you, yes,' she twinkled up at him. 'Well, if I cannot have a pistol, I shall at least have my very first ice at my very first race meeting.' She could tell he was laughing although his face remained quite bland.

★   ★   ★

Giles had the impression that he was wandering into new territory with this girl. She appeared so innocent and unworldly, yet she was capable of such flashes of dry humour. She was a pleasure to talk to, unlike so many young ladies who seemed not to have two ideas in their heads. And as for her appearance, he, who was accustomed to society beauties, was quite amazed at how very striking she was with the benefit of more stylish clothes. If a top London modiste took her in hand, she would be absolutely dazzling . . . but then he checked himself sternly. He was honour-bound to maintain his role as her secret guardian.

Even so, if truth were told, he was piqued that she did not look at him in the admiring way she had been looking at Charles in the ballroom last night. The chit smiled at him in that open way she had, that made him think of summer sunshine. She treated him almost like a favourite uncle. Giles discovered that that was a very lowering idea.

True, they had made each other's acquaintance in a most unusual manner. And he had set himself up to keep her safe. It had not been easy. When he thought back to all their arguments, he felt exhausted. But he put these thoughts aside as they reached the refreshment stall. He watched with amusement how long she took to choose her ice and then how she savoured every mouthful, even licking her pink lips several times not to lose any of the treat.

'I think you are very fond of ices, Miss Lawrence?'

'I shall be from now on, Lord Longwood.'

He wondered again what her home life had been, if such a simple pleasure was a novelty for her.

'Found you at last, Brother.' Charles was beaming at him. By his side, Belinda Beveridge stood, coldly composed. Giles cursed under his breath. So Lady Beveridge was going to fight to the last ditch to shackle him to her daughter.

'Have you abandoned your companion?' He frowned at his brother.

'The *contessa*? Boot's on the other foot, Brother. She's busy talking to that gentleman, Mr . . . Mr Barton — old family friend.' Charles shrugged. 'And Ned has that faraway look on his face. Bet you any money he'll have a sheet of poetry finished by now.'

Belinda cleared her throat. At once Charles broke into speech again. 'Miss Lawrence, allow me to escort you back, while Giles and Belinda get ices.'

'I fear not,' purred Giles, giving his brother an arctic glare, 'we have had our ices and now it will be my pleasure to take Miss Lawrence back.'

'Let us all go together,' said Belinda. Her voice was low and emphatic and as cool as her appearance. 'Miss Lawrence, have you been here long?' She finally looked at Anna properly, 'Do tell me what are your favourite pastimes in Brighton.' She contrived to draw Anna to her side and they walked on ahead, chatting.

'Sorry, old man,' muttered Charles, 'just obeying orders.'

Giles speared him with a look. 'Whose?'

Charles shrugged his broad shoulders. Then he nodded towards Belinda. 'Her mother.'

'Understand this,' Giles's voice was low but deadly, 'I will deal with my affairs my way. *Never* do that again if you value your handsome face. I will surely rearrange it for you.'

10

Anna left the villa on Marine Parade by the side door. It was not yet eight o'clock and the air was still chilly. She soon came to the spot Belinda had described, where a path led down from the edge of the road to the beach. The sea looked vast and beautiful, sparkling in the early sunshine. From the edge of the beach came the constant shush-shush of waves pushing up and then retreating. They seemed to be calling her.

Anna looked at the bathing machines, drawn up in a row. The horses were standing in their harness, munching in their nosebags. The women who took ladies into the water to bathe were sitting in a group chatting and smoking their pipes. There was no sign of Belinda. Anna sighed. The road was still deserted, but she must make haste if she was going to take a dip. Soon people would start coming out to take the air and then the opportunity would be lost. And it was such a lovely morning.

Maybe Belinda would arrive soon. Meanwhile, since she was here, at least she could take a closer look at the machines. She picked her way down the steep track. Walking on the shifting surface of the beach was not as easy as she had thought. It struck her that a girl as elegant as Belinda would not enjoy this sensation. But she had been so very eager to try the benefits of sea bathing.

By the time Anna reached the first machine, her light summer shoes were full of small stones, which made walking uncomfortable. She needed a quiet spot to sit down and remove them. But one of the women rose and came to meet her.

'Be you Miss Lawrence?'

Anna looked at her. She was a burly creature, her face leathery from so much time spent outside in all weathers. Her huge, floppy hat was tied firmly under her chin by a wide red scarf. The pipe she held in her hand gave her a piratical air. This really was an adventure!

'Because, if you be 'er, I've a message for 'ee.'

Anna nodded, 'Yes, I am Miss Lawrence.'

'Arr, then, yer friend is already out there.' She jerked a thumb towards a cabin out in the water. 'She says to 'urry up 'n join 'er.' She nodded towards the door. 'In yer goes, missy. Yer can take yer clothes off while old Jimmy pulls the machine into the sea.'

Anna looked at the swimmer splashing in

the deep water. She longed to do the same, so, without another word, she climbed the three steps into the machine. It was a struggle in the tiny space to remove her outer clothes and hang them on the peg. The horse pulled steadily but progress down the beach and into the water was very jerky.

She could hear the woman calling, 'Get up, there, do!' and a few rather colourful swearwords that she had not heard since her father was alive. She grinned and bit her lip. They seemed to work on old Jimmy, who tugged even harder. Soon Anna could hear the waves lapping around the wheels and even slurping up under the floor of her moving new home as it lurched into a sweeping turn. The horse must now be facing the shore.

'Be 'ee ready, missy?' called the dipper. 'Open the door.'

Anna drew in a deep breath. She opened the door and gasped. The sea was lapping at the step. This really was something quite new. The woman grinned at her, her own feet under water. Anna laughed with pleasure at the sensation of being on the same level as the waves. She could see the woman swimming near the other machine. It was not Belinda, however.

'Where is my friend?' she asked.

'Never mind 'er, jump in, now. Best to get in fast. Do 'ee want to wear yer shift? Shame to get it wet.'

Anna goggled at her. 'Of course I must wear it.'

The dipper shrugged. 'Arr. Nobody to see. Old Jimmy don't mind if you swims naked.'

'Not me,' retorted Anna, 'I always swim in my shift.' She plunged in and screamed at the sudden shock of the cold water. But at once she found it pleasant. She kicked her legs and stretched out her arms, splashing and enjoying the freedom of movement and the sensation of being buoyed up. The salt stung her eyes and tongue. She spluttered and laughed. Then she swam strongly out towards that great horizon. Tired at last, she turned on her back and floated, looking up at the expanse of the sky. This was heavenly. She heard a whistle and saw the dipper making beckoning signs at her. Reluctantly, Anna swam back.

'That's fair long enough, missy,' called the woman. 'Old Jimmy's gettin' cold. An' you get yerself dressed now, smartish!'

This time it was really hard to pull her clothes onto her wet skin. She twisted her dripping hair into a rope and pinned it at the back of her neck. By the time the woman shouted 'whoa' and the machine lurched to a halt, Anna was ready. But she was angry.

'Why did you tell me my friend was in the water?' she asked, descending from the cabin. 'It was no such thing!'

'That was the message I got told to say, missy. No 'arm done, eh? You enjoyed that dip.' The woman crossed her brawny arms.

Anna looked at her suspiciously. But maybe Belinda had decided the water was too cold for her. She was not a very good friend after all. Well, never mind, the swim had been an enjoyable new experience. And now it was time to make herself presentable before Lady Fording needed her.

That afternoon, Lady Fording was going to take tea with her newly rediscovered friend of the day before. Mrs Barton was staying in a villa close to the Old Steine. When the coachman stopped to let them out of the barouche, Lady Fording said to Anna, 'Well, my dear, I shall stay for an hour. You may have that time for yourself.'

'Thank you, ma'am. I shall go to the subscription library. But I will be here in one hour, you may be sure. Your daughter is most anxious that you must not get tired.'

'She worries about everything! Can she not see that I am very well now?'

Anna smiled and saw the old lady safely up the steps and into the care of the butler. She sped off down to the Steine and then across into the streets where there were such interesting shops. But today she did not spare them a single glance in her hurry to reach the lending library. It was too much to hope that they would have copies of Lord Byron's books but she would certainly find a gorgeously grisly adventure story or two.

Having made her choice, Anna discovered she still had almost half an hour of her free time left. She found her way to the parade ground on the Steine. It was near the Marine Pavilion, the residence of the Prince Regent. This side of the park was a quiet open space with benches here and there. Down the road she could glimpse the sea. From here it was about five minutes' walk to Mrs Barton's house. There was enough time for her to see how the story began. She sat down and smiled as she opened the book.

She was already lost in the adventures of the fair Porphyria when she became aware of loud voices very close by.

'Got her clothes on now . . . '

'No matter, we know what she looks like without 'em, hey. Swimming all alone, it ain't decent.'

'By Jove, Barty, see that yaller hair, it's the same wench we tumbled that day in Alton.'

Anna felt her cheeks burning. What

misfortune to encounter these brutes again! And how dare they discuss her as if she was simply an object. She kept her head bent over the page, wondering if they would dare to grab at her here, where there were other people about. Worse still, how could they have seen her swimming? Were they following her? The bathing area was on a secluded part of the beach. In any case, it was an accepted activity for ladies. Belinda had assured her of that. But Belinda had tricked her.

She did her best to pretend she was engrossed in her book. She turned a page, trying to stop her fingers from trembling and still they stood there, sniggering and watching her. She gritted her teeth. Eventually she heard their voices fade as they gave it up and walked off towards the town. From somewhere close by, a clock struck the hour. Anna gasped. Lady Fording would be waiting. She gathered up her books with hands that shook and set off. She dashed across the road, taking no notice of the numerous vehicles and narrowly escaping being run down by one of them. Something cold slid down her cheek. Angrily, she shook her head to shake the tears away. It felt so humiliating to be sneered at like that.

A hand grasped her upper arm and obliged her to stop. She gave a shuddering breath and looked up unwillingly into a pair of furious green eyes in a dark face.

'What in thunder are you about?' snarled Giles. 'You nearly ended up under that tradesman's cart.' He looked more closely and muttered under his breath. Still keeping a firm hold on her arm with one hand, he pulled out a large white handkerchief and gave it to her.

It smelled of him and his spicy cologne. Anna received it thankfully and wiped her eyes. Now he was here, somehow the tears just kept coming. She blinked them back valiantly.

'We cannot stand here,' he said, 'we are attracting attention. Where are you going?'

She realized that there were a lot of passers-by. Giving her eyes one last wipe, she held out the handkerchief. 'Thank you.'

'Er — pray keep it. Which way, Miss Lawrence? Quickly!'

She gestured towards the seafront. 'To the corner of Marine P-Parade. Mrs Barton's house. I'm late.' She sniffed and raised the handkerchief again.

He said no more but pulled her arm through his and walked her along the road. It seemed that everyone they passed knew Giles. He responded to all greetings with a curt 'Good day', and kept walking steadily.

Anna kept her head lowered. It must be obvious she had been crying and her bonnet had only a small brim, so her face was fully visible.

Thanks to Giles and his comforting presence she found herself turning left into Marine Parade in a very few moments. Anna saw the coach drawn up outside Mrs Barton's house. 'That is where I am going,' she said. 'Thank you for your assistance. I seem to be forever causing you trouble, sir.'

'It is no trouble,' he retorted, 'but I would like to learn what it was that upset the redoubtable Miss Lawrence so much. As I know, she can usually handle a crisis with the utmost calm.'

Anna gave him a watery smile. 'You are very good to me. I must hurry now, sir. Please excuse me.'

'No,' he said, 'I will not. But I will wait until tomorrow for the explanation. I take it your party will attend the assembly?'

'I believe so. Oh, there is Lady Fording. She will be cross if I am not there. Goodbye, sir.'

★   ★   ★

Giles watched her hurry along the pavement. She reached the carriage at the same time as the old lady. She was safe now and could compose herself. Whatever had happened to cause such distress? He rolled his eyes. Yet again he was involved with this schoolgirl — for she was a schoolgirl in her innocence. And when had he ever bothered with innocent schoolgirls?

Yet she had no one else to turn to and he found that he cared about her safety. Yes, he consoled himself, he was doing what any gentleman with a shred of decency would do. And now it was time to put her out of his mind. He was already late for his meeting. Ned and his other friends would be getting impatient. It was time to set off for the boxing match they planned to see in a nearby hamlet. But, as he strode along the seafront, his frown deepened. It was not just decency. It seemed to him that he also cared about Anna's happiness. And that was a frightening thought.

11

'I will go to the card room,' stated Lady Fording, when they were on their way to the Castle Tavern for the Thursday assembly. 'Henrietta and I can find partners for a hand of whist.'

'I shall sit and watch you, ma'am,' offered Anna, concealing her disappointment at the thought of missing the dancing, 'in case you need anything.'

But when they arrived, Mrs Barton had her granddaughter with her. She at once suggested that Anna and Emily could stay in the ballroom with the *contessa*.

'That way,' she said, 'Paulina and I can play cards in peace and the girls can get some practice on the dance-floor.'

Emily smiled happily at Anna. She was a buxom girl of seventeen. Her father was a widower and her grandmother lived with them and chaperoned her, she told Anna. 'But she is not too strict,' she added. 'I think so long as she can have a peaceful life, she does not enquire too much into my activities.'

'So you have a great deal of freedom?'

'Unfortunately, not at all. There is also

Miss Thorne, my governess. She supervises my study of French and music and we have a reading programme.' She pulled her mouth down. 'It is rather serious . . . '

They both laughed. 'I don't suppose,' said Anna hopefully, 'that you have read — '

'*The Corsair*?' Emily shook her head. 'Miss Thorne would have apoplexy. But for the moment I am on holiday. Dear Papa insisted I should come to Brighton, so I may be more confident when we go to London this winter.' She broke off to inspect a group of young officers entering the room.

Anna was glad to have another young person for company. She had lain awake worrying about how the two young bucks knew she had been bathing and why it should be so scandalous when it was considered beneficial for health. But she would prefer not to draw attention to herself. A glance towards the *contessa* showed her to be deep in a serious conversation with Mr John Barton, Emily's father. Of course, they were all old family friends.

'Oh, look.' Emily unfurled her fan and cooled her round, pink cheeks. 'There is Lord Longwood and his brother, Lord Charles Maltravers. How handsome he is in his hussar's uniform. What a pity they are both such desperate rakes.' She sighed wistfully.

'Grandmama says I must not accept if Lord Longwood offers to dance with me.'

'I am a little acquainted with them,' said Anna, bristling at this criticism of her special friend, 'and I have found them both to be perfectly gentlemanlike.' She feasted her eyes on Giles's profile and lustrous black hair. 'In fact, I have already danced with both of them — in this very room!'

'Oh dear me! But you can probably get away with it because you did not know.'

'Know *what?*' Anna's eyes flashed.

'Well, Jack says — Jack is my brother, you understand — that there is no one with a worse reputation than Lord Longwood. If he were not the son of a duke, he would not be received.'

'Yet I could not help but notice that Lady Beveridge and her daughter were on very good terms with him.'

Emily nodded. 'That is because Lady Beveridge wants her daughter to be Duchess of Hawkesborough. She would be fabulously wealthy, you know. It is certainly worth a try. And with such a title, Miss Beveridge would be willing to overlook her husband's rakish life.'

'But how shocking,' exclaimed Anna. 'I would never settle for that.'

Emily gazed at her in amazement. 'How

could you prevent a man from behaving as he wishes? But I daresay Miss Beveridge will not succeed in catching him. They say he has the most exquisite mistress.'

Anna digested this unwelcome news. She looked across the room again, but Giles had disappeared. He must have gone into the card room. Now Anna wished she had stayed with Lady Fording in there. One of the young officers came and invited Emily to dance. Anna fanned herself and looked at the *contessa* again. She was struck, as always, by how tense and pale the woman looked. Surely she had lost weight since Anna had first seen her? She was a woman who lived on her nerves.

When the dance ended, Emily reappeared and sat down again. 'He trod on my toes twice,' she whispered. A few minutes later she frowned and looked closely at Anna. 'Why are those men looking our way? They seem to be discussing us.'

Anna followed her gaze and swallowed as a sick feeling made her stomach clench and her heart pound. A group of several young men were looking at her and sniggering. She turned to Emily in bewilderment.

'I think they are talking about me. But why? Surely not because I danced with Lord Longwood!'

'Well,' said Emily slowly, 'maybe they are just admiring you.'

Anna shook her head. 'They would not be laughing, would they?'

The next dance was announced. A rather older man detached himself from the group and made his way over to the *contessa*. He bowed and spoke to her in a low voice. She shrugged and nodded an assent. The man approached Anna and bowed with a great flourish. 'I would be honoured to dance this set with you, ma'am. Your chaperon has given permission.'

She did not particularly like the look of him. He seemed to be near to her stepfather's age and that in itself made her wary. He was lean and tall and his clothes were highly fashionable. His hair was so black, Anna was sure it was dyed. But it would be impolite to refuse so she stood up and gave him a small tight smile.

'Charming,' he purred, his glance sweeping her from head to toe. 'I am Sir Bilton Kelly, Miss Lawrence.'

'Oh, you know my name,' she said foolishly.

He smiled. 'Of course.'

The music began to play and so she could remain silent. He moved with expert grace and was in every way polished and charming. Too charming for Anna. She could not overcome her initial suspicion that he wanted something. He seemed to be inspecting her in minute detail. It gave her the feeling that her dress was too thin and clinging. She knew her cheeks were red and it was not from the dancing. At last the music stopped and he offered to take her for a glass of champagne.

'No thank you,' replied Anna, 'I must return to my party, sir.'

He protested, but she was adamant. At last he gave it up and offered his arm. Reluctantly, she set her fingertips on it and let him escort her back across the wide room to the *contessa*. She was surprised to see Giles standing watching her. His eyes were like chips of ice, but his face was a polite mask.

'Kelly!'

'Ah, Longwood. Not your usual haunt.'

'I could say the same,' retorted Giles. The two of them bristled, then Sir Bilton Kelly gave a bark of laughter and, after bowing punctiliously to Anna, walked away, stroking his impressive side whiskers.

This evening was full of mysteries and each one seemed to be more unpleasant than the last. Anna suppressed a sigh and wondered how long it would be before Lady Fording decided to go home. She cast a look under her lashes at Giles. He was tight-lipped, his face dark with anger again. Anna suddenly felt exhausted by it all. She rubbed a hand across her forehead, wishing desperately that she could be back at Rosevale Park, sitting under the oak tree and reading another chapter of the latest story to Lady Fording.

'What is it?'

His voice was so gentle that she looked up, startled. The anger had gone. There was a warm look in those green eyes, that made her long to blurt out all her worries. She made an attempt at a smile, not aware that she was twisting her hands together.

Couples were taking their place in two lines for the next country dance.

Giles bowed. 'Miss Lawrence, please do me the honour.'

It was a bittersweet pleasure, but she could not resist the chance to spend the next fifteen minutes close to him. They had not been dancing long when Giles again looked as black as thunder.

'I fear I have done you a great disservice,' he murmured.

Anna took her four steps away and then turned to take his hand for the figure. 'How is that, sir?'

He shook his head as if puzzled. 'I sense that people are watching us. Not good!' His beautiful lips tightened.

Anna swallowed. 'Perhaps it is because I

have done something I should not . . . ' She shot a glance at him. 'And who is that man who was dancing with me?'

She felt the warning pressure of his hand on hers as they moved three places down the line. 'Later, perhaps,' he murmured. 'But I am still waiting to learn what was the problem yesterday. Has it had any consequences?'

At that she lowered her eyes. So he *had* noticed the young men talking about her. It took a great effort to maintain a composed expression. And when she thought that perhaps this was the last time she would dance with him, she felt a huge ache in her chest that made it painful to breathe. But Anna had her pride and somehow she kept her face serene until the end of the dance.

Then it was over and she had managed! Giles was escorting her back across the long room, while her face positively ached from smiling.

It was over, she was thinking, when Belinda suddenly appeared in front of them. She was clad in a discreetly expensive robe of green silk with diamonds flashing in her ears and in the combs holding her elaborate coiffure in place.

'Miss Lawrence,' she said, with a pretty smile, her eyes darting to Giles's face and then back to Anna, 'I have been meaning to call on you to apologize for yesterday. Mama found out what I intended to do and she forbade it. I could not even send you a message. I do trust you simply went back home?'

'Well, no.' Anna bit back the reproach she wanted to make. 'The dipper told me you were already in the water and had left a message that I should join you.'

'Oh good heavens! You actually went into the sea — alone?'

'So it turned out — but only because I thought I would find you out there.'

'Interesting!' Giles's deep voice made both girls turn abruptly towards him.

'What can you mean, Lord Longwood?' tittered Belinda, flicking her fan open in her left hand. Anna recognized what the gesture was saying — *come and talk to me*. Belinda was looking at Giles. Anna saw that he had assumed a bored expression. Someone cleared their throat. Lady Beveridge had sailed up to them, looking even more gaunt in puce crêpe and with several ostrich plumes in her turban. Once again she seemed not to see Anna.

'You may join our party, Longwood. Your brother is already there.' She gestured towards a sofa under the long window.

'Charles? In that case, ma'am, pray hold me excused.'

Anna felt the anger of these two ladies as if it were a physical blow. They were hunting Giles and they considered her to be an obstacle. But Giles was not going to let them catch him. She saw how his nostrils pinched and his mouth set in a firm line. Well, she owed him a favour and besides, she had a score to settle with Belinda.

'The *contessa* is looking this way, my lord,' she remarked, fluttering her own fan and giving Belinda a cool smile. 'I really must see what she requires of me. Miss Beveridge, perhaps we may meet tomorrow. Donaldson's Bookshop is such a wonderful place, is it not? I could spend all day there.'

Giles cleared his throat abruptly and, placing her hand on his arm again, led her away.

'Did you see her expression?' Anna gurgled, still wafting her fan. 'I think she will stay away from Donaldson's — and that will annoy her.'

'Minx!' said Giles with feeling, 'I believe you will soon get the better of them all.'

The *contessa* was indeed looking for them. 'Miss Lawrence, please go and see how my mother is getting on,' she ordered.

When Anna returned to report that Lady Fording was enjoying herself hugely, Giles had gone.

12

The noise of the ballroom faded and then was cut off entirely as he stepped out of the main door of the Castle Tavern. Giles took a deep breath and stood for a minute in the fresh evening air. He strolled down towards the sea. In the gathering twilight he could just make out the constantly moving lines of white as the breakers tossed and fell. He crossed the road and watched for a little while, listening to the scrape of the shingle as the waves pushed and tugged at the shoreline.

At last he gave a shrug as if to cast off a burden. He turned back to walk across the Steine. As he passed Donaldson's, with its wide veranda, he smiled and shook his head. So little Anna had already discovered this bookshop. Of course she had, she would have been hoping to find Byron's latest book there.

Thinking of Anna brought back his frown. Perhaps he should not have danced with her, but he had done it to warn that rogue Sir Bilton Kelly that she was not a friendless little waif. When one of the Prince Regent's aides showed interest in a girl, everyone knew what was coming next! She would receive an invitation to the Pavilion for the Prince to look her over. And in her cleverly cut gown and with her hair styled, Giles had to admit she was indeed a striking little beauty.

And now he had danced with her, the curst libertines hanging around the town probably thought he was planning to add her to his conquests. Damn it all to hell! His reputation really could damage her. So now it was his duty to protect her from any harm. He stopped in his tracks. *Duty!* He was developing a conscience and that made him very uneasy. Life was so much sweeter when one only had to choose which activity promised most pleasure.

He set off again, lengthening his stride as he turned up the hill in the direction of The Nag's Head. He needed relief from these new responsibilities — as well as from the irritation of Lady Beveridge's blatant attempts to trap him into marrying Belinda. Tomorrow he would deal with all these intertwined problems. But for tonight he was going to forget it all. His friends were slumming it amongst the fishermen and labourers. They would all be discussing the previous night's boxing match and he was keen to join them. A skinful of gin and maybe a pretty girl would help to chase away this unwanted mood. He reached The Nag's Head and pushed open the door into the crowded and smoky taproom.

* * *

The sound of his valet opening and shutting drawers in the dressing room eventually pulled Giles back to consciousness. He cast an arm over his eyes to block out the daylight. Blue sky was not what he needed in his current state. He lay on his back and waited for the pounding in his head to stop. But already he was remembering a certain number of tasks he wished to carry out. With a groan, he swung his long legs over the edge of the bed and sat up.

Slowly, slowly, he raised his head and squinted up at his valet's impassive countenance.

'Yes, Daynton,' he said ruefully, 'I expect I look rough. Well, come on, man. Let's set to work.'

An hour later, freshly shaved, hair expertly brushed, clothes faultless and carrying with him the faint aroma of his usual spicy cologne, Giles made his way downstairs to the dining room. He was mildly surprised to find Ned sitting at the table, his head clutched in both hands.

'Did you spend the night here?' he enquired, reaching for the coffee pot.

Ned raised a paper-white face. His large eyes were startlingly dark, with huge shadows under them. 'How can you look so neat and fresh?' he groaned, putting his head down again.

'I take it we helped each other home?' Giles sipped the coffee.

The only answer was a grunt. Then Ned hauled himself up and went to the sideboard. He came back with a glass of porter. 'Daynton says it cures a hangover,' he commented, and set about swallowing it. It did not produce any noticeable effects. The two friends soon abandoned any attempt to eat breakfast. They left the table and went silently into the small drawing room.

Giles sat at the writing table and scratched out a letter. He rubbed his forehead as he read it through, thought a bit and added a couple of amendments. With a sigh of relief he sanded it and sealed it with his signet. 'I should have done that much sooner,' he muttered, ringing the bell. 'See that this is taken by special messenger,' he ordered the footman, who appeared at once.

He glanced at the wing chair in which Ned sat like a statue. 'What we need is a swim. Are you ready, Ned?'

It was hours later when they returned to Giles's villa on the Steine. Both looked much better by this time. Ned had lost his deathly pallor and Giles was tousled and had regained the spring in his step. Ned accompanied him into the house to retrieve his gloves and various items he had discarded in his drunken state the previous night. He popped his head round the drawing room door to say goodbye and Giles called him in.

'Here's an unwelcome surprise. An invitation to a musical evening at the Marine Pavilion.'

'When?'

'Tonight! The Prince usually does send out at the last minute.' He sighed, thinking how Sir Bilton Kelly had looked at Anna. He was scouting for pretty girls to entertain the Prince Regent and thought he had found one. By dancing with her, Giles knew he had given the wrong message to the Prince's aide. 'I was afraid this would happen.'

'Why 'afraid'?' Ned raised his brows. 'Are you thinking you will have no peace from Lady Beveridge?'

Giles glared at him. 'I know they are laying bets on whether or not she succeeds in foisting her daughter on to me.' He drummed his fingers on the table, frowning in thought. At length he sighed. 'I have to go,' he said.

Ned's jaw fell open. 'You can't be thinking straight, old man. Terrible dragon, Lady Beveridge.'

'Well then, I shall rely on you to protect me,' said Giles with a flash of humour. 'And I expect all our friends have also been invited, so there is no hope of spending the evening playing cards at the tavern. No, seriously, Ned, we have to be at the Pavilion. If it is as I fear, I may need your help.'

Bemused, his friend nodded at him, then beat a retreat to go back to his own lodgings. Giles smiled faintly. Ned was always loyal but not very practical. However, once he knew what was wanted, he never refused to help. Giles rose and paced the room as he decided his strategy for the coming event.

13

Anna had passed a quiet morning, running a few errands around the house for Lady Fording and taking Beppi for his walk. She did not meet anyone she knew, which was a relief to her jangled nerves. For reasons she did not understand, she seemed to have become the object of spiteful gossip. But still she wondered who had given the dipper the message that Belinda was in the sea and, even more, how the young men had seen her bathing. The men's bathing machines were at the far end of the beach, and surely nobody could swim such a distance.

In the afternoon, the *contessa* decided they would all go out to look at the shops. Anna, thinking of the unpleasant looks she had received at the assembly the previous evening, felt at first that she would prefer to stay at home. Then she tossed her head. Why should she hide? They were only silly young men and she did not know any of them.

If she were Emily, looking to make a splendid marriage, then it would be a matter for some concern if people gossiped about her. But Anna had other plans for her future, schemes she had made a long time ago in agreement with her friends, Elinor, Sally and Tess. They were all determined to enjoy a number of adventures involving travel, and living an independent life. So she absolutely must harden herself to criticism, especially from people who could have no real impact on her future.

Anna thought she had made a good start to her own adventures. It was certainly a big change from life in her mother and stepfather's home. On her mother's remarriage, they had gone to live at Foxley Manor, Sir Benjamin Fox's small estate at Warnborough near Alton. It was very shortly after that that her mother had sent Anna away to school in Bath. And from that time on, school had been Anna's home. Life as she had known it when she and her father had enjoyed so many sports and discussions over books together, was over.

She made a determined effort to banish all these sad memories. Peeping in the mirror, she pulled on her little straw hat and tied the ribbons under her left ear. Today they were pink, matching her sprigged muslin dress. She chose a long white shawl and draped it elegantly over her elbows. Now she would devote herself to Lady Fording.

The three of them spent an agreeable hour

strolling along St James Street with many pauses for discussion of the fashions displayed in the windows of the various boutiques. They made some small purchases, which Anna carried for them. Finally they reached the Steine and turned towards Donaldson's library and shop with its veranda packed, as always, by ladies enjoying a chat.

Anna took another look along the shelves of books but there was no sign of anything by Lord Byron. She sighed her disappointment and rejoined Lady Fording to examine the marvellous range of fans, ribbons and other little trinkets. The parade was crowded with people out for their promenade. Already Anna recognized some of them. She kept a careful lookout but she did not really expect that any acquaintance of her mother and stepfather would be in Brighton.

There were two surprises when the ladies eventually returned to their villa at the far end of Marine Parade. The first was the arrival of Signor di Cassagna from London. He seemed to Anna to be in an even worse mood than when he had left. His expression was peevish and he made no attempt to be polite, even to Lady Fording. He had a long and private conversation with the *contessa*, during which time Anna served the tea for

Lady Fording and found her a warm shawl to spread over her legs while the old lady took a little nap.

This was disturbed when the *contessa* came into the room with a hurried step. 'Mama,' she began in an excited tone, then, 'oh, I am sorry, I should not have disturbed you . . . '

'Whatever is it, Beatrice?' her mother exclaimed, sitting up and putting up a hand to straighten her lace cap. Her voice sharpened. 'Has Enrico brought bad news?'

'No, he is — as always — preoccupied with his political ideas,' sighed the *contessa*. 'But here is a big surprise.' She held up a large, gilt-edged card. 'It is an invitation to a musical evening at the Marine Pavilion — and for this very evening. Oh, Mama, are you well enough to go?'

'I would not miss it for anything,' Lady Fording beamed. 'I have not been there since your father was alive. The Prince's receptions are always splendid, you know. It is an opportunity to dress in our best.'

The *contessa* nodded. 'Yes, Enrico says we must all do so.' She glanced at Anna. 'Let me see, yes, I think you should wear the ivory silk.'

When they arrived at the Pavilion in the midst of a large crowd of other guests, Anna was almost speechless with excitement. When her family had gone up to London to see the victory celebrations and all the famous people taking part in them, she had been left at home as a punishment for refusing to marry Cousin Frederick. Yet here she was, six weeks later, actually the guest of the Prince Regent. And she knew she was looking very elegant although her dress was cut low on the bosom. The *contessa* and her maid had insisted that this was modest by fashionable standards.

'Yes, but I am here as your mama's companion, my lady,' persisted Anna, wondering why she must be as fashionably dressed as her employers.

'Silly girl,' scolded the *contessa*, 'would you rather be dressed in grey flannel? You will soon discover that the Regent expects everyone to be very fine. Just look at my gown.'

Anna had to admit that it was even lower-cut than hers. It was fortunate that the *contessa* was so thin, she thought privately, but she stopped protesting. After all, she had a gauzy scarf to cover herself up a little bit.

And so she was actually walking into the Prince Regent's Marine Pavilion amongst a crowd of high-born and well-dressed people. A discreet survey reassured her that her dress was indeed no lower-cut than most of the others. Seeing how much jewellery the ladies were wearing, Anna was grateful that the *contessa* had insisted on lending her a set of emerald clips for her hair. Anna clutched her fan in one hand and held Lady Fording's elbow lightly with the other. She had quite forgotten the malicious gossips in her eagerness to see this summer palace. She gazed wide-eyed at the exotic splendour of the reception room where the Prince's staff were greeting the guests.

Two of the rooms were set out for cards and other games of chance. Lady Fording soon found a partner to set about playing whist. From the third brightly lit room came the sound of a small orchestra, playing a light and cheerful piece.

Lady Fording turned round. 'Anna, my dear, do go and listen. You may find the Prince himself is playing.'

'Oh, I should like to see that,' said Anna. 'Thank you, ma'am. I will not stay long and then I can bring you some refreshment.'

She hastened through the main salon towards the music room. Everyone said the Regent's orchestra was excellent and for Anna, any concert was a rare treat. But she was only halfway through the main saloon when she found her way blocked by Sir Bilton Kelly.

'Ah, Miss Lawrence,' he drawled, raising his quizzing glass. She was obliged to stop. He made her a fine bow and she curtsied in return, inwardly using one of the swear words she had learnt from her father. Please let him be quick so she could get to the concert.

'You are the very person I was looking for,' he went on, surveying her bosom with an approving eye.

'Oh?' she enquired, resisting the urge to tug her dress up to her throat. Now what?

'I understand you are a great reader, Miss Lawrence. Allow me to show you the Prince's fine collection of books. I am sure you will be fascinated.'

He indicated that she should precede him through the doorway into yet another room. It was not very well lit. Anna glanced around, looking for help, but nobody came forward. She saw that people were watching discreetly. If she did go apart with this detestable man, that would be the end of her good name. Not far away Belinda stood, a look of cold disdain on her face. Anna held her eyes for a moment but Belinda merely glanced down.

Anna looked up at the waiting man, leering at her and oozing self-assurance. The rather sickly sweet smell of his cologne and the pomade on his hair repelled her. She narrowed her eyes as she looked into his smirking face. He was so sure he could make her do as he wished but she *would not* be trapped in his schemes.

'Pray excuse me one moment, sir,' she said, 'I was carrying out a commission for Lady Fording. You know she is an invalid and it will not do to keep her waiting. I will return when I am able.' She curtsied and took a step backwards.

His face took on a dull flush and his eyes sparked. 'I will do myself the honour of accompanying you,' he growled.

Her heart sank. But at least she had thwarted his first plan. She turned back towards the card room, deliberately walking up to Belinda and giving her a burning look.

Still with the cold look on her face, Belinda took a step back and half turned away. Giles was there and he was looking daggers at Belinda. Anna moved on, but not before she heard a gasp and saw Belinda turn back, looking dismayed now.

At least I am not the only one in the middle of a drama, she thought. But how was she going to escape this pest?

14

According to his plan, Giles was among the first arrivals at the Pavilion that evening. He had Ned and Charles as his lieutenants, not without a vigorous argument beforehand. Charles was still tight-lipped and mutinous but at least he had promised to carry out his brother's instructions. Ned would be fine just so long as he did not get distracted by a sudden inspiration. Giles heaved a deep sigh. How could one slip of a girl make his life so complicated?

'There they are,' he murmured to Charles, as Lady Beveridge and Belinda appeared in the entrance to the saloon. 'Just see you keep them well away from me.'

Charles gave him a fulminating look. 'Don't think I shall forget what you promised me for this,' he hissed. He straightened his impressive shoulders so that the silver braid on his uniform jacket sparkled in the candlelight. His blond hair shone and he looked magnificent. Several young ladies followed him with their eyes as he moved through the reception room and greeted Lady Beveridge, bowing with exquisite grace and leading her and Belinda into the next room.

Across the salon Giles met Ned's eyes and he gave a tiny nod. So far so good. Now it was a matter of waiting and watching. He saw Sir Bilton Kelly appear, take a quick survey of the guests and return to the inner room. And then Giles saw the *contessa*, entering on the arm of a very polished dandy. This must be the Italian cousin. A man to be wary of, decided Giles, disliking him on sight.

Behind them came Anna, close to the old lady. She was staring wide-eyed at the decoration of this salon, obviously impressed. A smile quirked the corner of Giles's mouth but it was quickly replaced by a frown. Her gown was too sophisticated for her age and far too low-cut! All that snowy bosom on display! His frown deepened. Her hair was dressed high, with jewelled clips sparkling in it. Little tendrils curled by her ears and at the back of her neck. The effect was breathtaking. Giles breathed hard. In normal circumstances, he would snap up such a little beauty for his own pleasure and entertainment. But she was the waif he had rescued and sworn to protect.

Then anger flashed through him. They were up to something! Anna was going to attract a lot of male attention. And this was the place where attracting male attention was certain to lead to trouble and seduction! Did she realize what message her appearance gave out? Somehow, he found it impossible to believe she would willingly join in any underhand plot. She was too open and direct for that. But . . . his eyes shot to the *contessa* and her escort. He could well imagine they were scheming something very underhand.

So, his task was even more delicate than he had foreseen. Anna was in need of protection from all sides. He kept in the background, observing how the Italian gentleman looked carefully round the room. From his sulky pout it seemed the person he sought was not there. Giles followed at a discreet distance until he saw Anna assist Lady Fording into a chair at the card tables. After a brief conversation Anna walked away in the direction of the music room.

When Sir Bilton Kelly appeared and gestured towards the darkened bookroom, Giles excused himself from the group with whom he was chatting. He edged forwards through the clusters of guests. Anna would certainly need rescuing from whatever that toad had in mind. As he wove through the crowd, he could see her look round, seeking help that nobody offered. Yet they knew what was going on! Curse them, all eager for a bit of scandal.

Then to his astonishment and joy, he saw her take a step back and Sir Bilton Kelly's face at once flushed with anger. Bravo to her for her spirit! Then, close by Anna, he spotted a profile he recognized. It was Belinda. Why did she not step forward to offer help. Only a day or two before, she had seemed to be Anna's friend. Instead she turned away from Anna, and so in his direction. Her face held an expression of scorn. If she had been a man, he would have driven his fist into that smirking face in front of everyone.

Charles was not far away, trying to make conversation with Lady Beveridge. She spotted Giles and began to gobble something, beckoning to him imperiously. He ignored her, following Anna back towards the card room. He could see Kelly keeping close behind her, his face still red. Anna would never get rid of him without help. Giles came up to Ned and whispered to him urgently. Ned cast up his eyes but slipped away to the library.

One more element in place to foil his plans, thought Giles, reaching the card room where Sir Bilton Kelly was attempting to charm Lady Fording. Giles strolled up to the group, every inch the languid, bored aristocrat.

'Miss Lawrence,' he drawled, 'you wished to hear the music, I believe. Make haste! The

Prince himself is about to play. You must see this. I am sure Lady Fording can spare you for a while.'

His reward was the light that shone in those blue eyes, at once a message of relief and thanks. She took his arm without a word and he winked at Lady Fording and whisked Anna away.

'Thank you,' she breathed, giving his arm a slight squeeze.

He nodded in reply and kept walking, past groups that parted so readily now to make way for them. The music was playing, so they slipped silently into the music room and found seats on a long bench by the wall. Giles was aware that Anna was sitting bolt upright. He heard her rapid breathing and saw the rise and fall of her bosom above the low-cut line of her bodice. He heard a stifled sigh and felt the draught as she fanned herself. The fragrance of roses came to his nostrils. It suited her absolutely.

The audience was appreciative and their attention was on the Mozart concerto, not on gossip. Gradually, Anna was swept into the spell of the music, especially the soaring notes of the violinist. Soon she had a slight smile on her lips and was totally absorbed. From time to time, Giles took a covert glance at her, examining her finery. Her gown was silk and net, an elegant ivory column that clung to her slender form. The jewels in her hair were of excellent quality. Whose were they? How appealing she looked, her youthful freshness emphasized by these fine things. But, considering her position as merely an old lady's companion, he very much feared she had been set up to attract the Prince himself.

In order to understand their plans, Giles knew he needed to discover a little more about the cousin. What motive could he have? Was he one of these European exiles who had lost his estates to Napoleon and so hoped for help from the British Royal Family? It looked as if Anna was the bait . . . but just what did they plan to do with her?

The concerto ended. Anna clapped enthusiastically. She turned towards Giles, her cheeks delicately flushed. 'How much I enjoyed that. Thank you for . . . for . . . '

He stood up and drew her to the side of the room. 'I believe it is my duty — as your friend — to warn you never to go aside with any . . . ah — er — gentleman in this Pavilion.'

The colour burned in her face now. 'I could see that,' she retorted, 'and I managed to escape. But he followed me.'

'Well, Miss Lawrence,' drawled Giles, allowing himself to inspect her from head to foot and back up again, 'you *are* dressed in a very eye-catching manner.' He was totally disarmed by her frank embarrassment at this rebuke.

'I did protest,' she blurted, 'b-but the *contessa* insisted I must be as fine as the rest of her party. Signor di Cassagna is such a dandy.' She took a step closer and whispered, 'Pray believe I do not wish to be remarked upon.' Her eyes pleaded.

For an extraordinary moment, Giles almost drowned in those blue eyes. The lovely line of her throat was so fresh and pure that he was conscious of an urge to stroke his fingers down it and on down to that slender waist. He pressed his hand to his side and forced his mind to consider what was going on here. She was still watching him anxiously so he smiled at her teasingly.

'It is no great matter,' he said, 'except that it draws creatures like Sir Bilton Kelly, like a moth to a candle.'

She looked anguished. 'I cannot forget what happened in Alton. And I fear that by going sea bathing, I have been guilty of an indiscretion. But I still do not understand how those horrid young men knew of it.'

Giles gave her a sardonic look. 'You were not aware that the young men come to Brighton armed with telescopes? Half their pleasure is spying on bathers so they can enjoy the sight of a female ankle — and maybe a lot more than that.'

'Oh no!' she gasped, horrified. 'How terrible!' She hung her head, giving him the chance to admire her silky flaxen curls. Then she looked up, her jaw set angrily. 'So why did Miss Beveridge suggest we should go sea bathing in the first place? She must have — '

Giles reached out a hand to give hers a warning squeeze. 'Your Highness!' He bowed. Beside him he heard Anna gasp and saw her sink gracefully into a deep curtsy. So she had been well educated in social manners.

The Prince was affable. The music had put him in a good mood. But to Giles's experienced eye, he was deciding that this new blonde beauty would suit him very well. With an inward groan, Giles knew that only by removing Anna from Brighton could he keep her safe from the Prince's staff, who would be instructed to bring about an opportunity for her to be alone with the Prince.

'Oh, my dear, there you are.' It was the contessa, making an artistic appearance at precisely the right moment for the Prince to greet her. She also sank into a curtsy and then lingered as Anna told the Regent how much she had enjoyed the music.

'Splendid, splendid,' he exclaimed, in his rather high pitched voice, obviously pleased. 'Next time we have a little playing, we shall make sure you are invited. You, too, Longwood, what? See to it, eh, Kelly.' He nodded and walked on with no more than a nod to the others.

Signor di Cassagna glared at the Prince's retreating back. Anger radiated from him. The *contessa* was paler than ever. 'Enrico — ' she began, but he made an impatient gesture and turned away. The *contessa*'s bosom rose and fell in a sigh. Automatically she opened her fan and half shielded her face as she moved towards some other visitors and began to make conversation with them.

Giles observed all this in silence. Signor di Cassagna, he noticed, was sulking in a corner of the magnificent room. The Regent had not wanted to talk to him, that was clear. But he and the *contessa* — were desperate to talk to him. Was that why they had dressed Anna so enticingly? Thoughtfully he turned towards her. In spite of his unease, he had to hide a smile. She was so excited at being noticed by the Prince. But she did not realize what that meant. Now, how was he going to tell her?

'Oh, dear me!' Anna put a hand to her mouth. 'I really must see how Lady Fording goes on.'

Giles laid a restraining hand on her arm. 'Allow me to escort you. This is no place for a young girl to be alone.'

She gulped. In all the excitement, she had forgotten why he had brought her to the music room in the first place.

'And while I have the opportunity,' he went on, 'there are a couple of things I must say to you.' He drew her along a side corridor and into a small lamp-lit room. Giles closed the door behind them both.

'This is where they store the chairs,' he said, 'They will start bringing them back shortly. But I need to speak to you.'

She was puzzled. 'This is like an episode from a horrid novel. What is the mystery, sir?'

'Don't be pert!' but his lips twitched and she gave a gurgle of laughter. Giles fought the urge to pull her close and kiss those tempting lips. He shook his head. 'Miss Lawrence, you have no chaperon and so, ironically, it falls to me to warn you that you must take great care. As a rake myself, believe me when I tell you that you are attracting attention from some dangerous people.'

She swallowed. 'I . . . ' Her hands stole up to clasp her throat. 'I d-do not wish to do that.'

'So why do you flaunt yourself in such an immodest dress?' he flashed angrily.

Her eyes slid away from his. 'The *contessa* said I must have fashionable dresses to come to Brighton. Her maid created them for me. And she also dressed my hair for this evening.' She came up to him and laid a hand on his arm. 'Oh, sir, what do you think it all means?'

She was staring up at him, looking so young and so vulnerable that Giles reacted without thinking. He opened his arms and she cast herself against his chest and heaved several mighty sobs. Giles did not care for weeping women, but this child's distress moved him. He patted her cheek and slid his hand under her chin, raising her face to his.

'Anna, Anna, stop crying. Nothing will hurt you, I promise . . . ' But the huge blue eyes, drowned in tears, made him forget what he had been going to say. He took her face in both hands and kissed her. He felt her tremble, heard her gasp of shock. Then slowly, her lips parted under his and he deepened the kiss. She pressed herself against him and her hands slipped around his shoulders.

Then as suddenly as he had begun, he wrenched his head away. 'Oh, God! I should not have done that.' He took a step back from her.

She was staring at him, her lower lip caught between her teeth. 'Did you not want to do it?' she asked, her voice trembling. She was rubbing a finger over her swollen lips.

He stared back. 'That has nothing to do with the matter. I am a scoundrel.'

She smiled. 'You are a rake. You said so yourself.'

He gave an unwilling laugh. 'Upon my word, you are mighty cool over it.'

She considered him, her head on one side. 'Well, that is what rakes do. I could never be afraid of you. And now I know what a kiss is like.'

He could not help grinning at her innocent remark. It had been a very chaste kiss. But he was having to exercise considerable restraint not to pull her back into his arms. The combination of sweetness, beauty and mischief was very tempting. He would have to leave his little lecture for another time. He must get her away from him before he burned up completely.

She was twisting her hands together. Then she said, 'You are right about men noticing me. And I have made some mistakes . . . the sea bathing.' She made a helpless little gesture.

'That was not your fault.'

'But it meant that I attracted notice. The

young men were making rude remarks about me later that day.'

'Was that why you were crying when I saw you on the Steine?'

She nodded. 'I will do my best to be discreet from now on, sir.' She opened the door. 'I really must return to Lady Fording.'

He heaved a sigh and followed her out into the corridor, still thankfully deserted. 'Stay close to her,' he advised. 'I think you are safe when you are with her. And, in spite of what I just did, I will always help if you need me.'

She looked at him over her shoulder and smiled.

15

It seemed an interminable length of time before the entertainment was over. Giles kept a discreet watch on Anna until he saw her leave with her party. She looked subdued and that made him angry with himself. He should not have kissed her! Worse still, he should not have kissed her in a store-cupboard, like a schoolboy, for God's sake. But she had been so sweet and scared and helpless, he just wanted to offer comfort. What the hell was he doing? It made no sense trying to protect her from the *roués* of the Prince's household, only to seduce her himself.

Giles noticed how Signor di Cassagna was so busy fussing over arranging his own evening cloak that he gave no help to his female relatives. In fact, he appeared to consider himself above being pleased. His sole aim had been to approach the Regent — who had not taken any notice of him. Now that was strange, as the Prince was always a kind and considerate host. His aides would certainly have briefed him on all his guests. Possibly there was a political reason behind this mystery. But as it involved Anna he was determined to discover just what was afoot.

Behind him he heard a footman yawn. A glance at one of the ornate clocks informed him that it was indeed late. That damned Signor di Cassagna had lingered to the bitter end. There were very few people left now, but Ned had still not appeared. Giles went to fetch him from the library where he was deep in a book he had taken from the shelves.

'Nothing happened,' he assured Giles, when the latter had succeeded in rousing him from his story. 'Is it time to leave already? Pity! This is a damned interesting tale.'

'So I see,' replied Giles caustically. 'Devil take it, Ned, there could have been an orgy in here and you would not have noticed!'

'Assure you, no one came in. I did as you asked and kept guard all evening.'

Giles gave it up and ushered his friend out.

'Did you manage to avoid the dragons?' asked Ned, a little too loudly. A few heads turned in their direction.

Charles loomed up, all his smiles gone now. 'He certainly did! Left it to me to keep 'em away from him. What are you up to, Brother? Belinda was most upset, saying you frightened her with your dark looks. And then you were chasing after that — ' He saw the menace in his brother's eyes and checked. 'Oh well, have it your own way. You've promised me your blacks for a week, after all.'

They crossed the open area towards Giles's house. Ned was deep in thought but Charles, still full of energy, was suggesting they go on to the tavern, where he hoped to find some friends for a decent drink and a hand of cards.

'And a wench or two,' he added, grinning. 'All that civility has sunk my spirits. I need a cheerful lass to coax me back into good humour.'

Neither Giles nor Ned answered him so he kept on talking. 'I tell you what, Brother. Good job if you do keep your distance from Belinda. She's got a damned sharp tongue when she's crossed. And her mother is full of self-consequence!'

By this time they had reached the bottom of Edward Street. Charles set off along it, then realized he was alone. He looked back.

'What, surely you are coming with me? The night is young.'

'I need to write something,' murmured Ned. 'Excuse me, must do it while the idea is fresh . . . ' He wandered off towards his own lodging.

'I have had enough of being civil this evening,' drawled Giles.

'*You've* had enough! Well, that does it! I'll see you in the morning.' Charles swung round and marched off towards The Nag's Head.

Giles clasped his hands behind his back and walked down as far as the sea. He stood for some time gazing out towards the unseen horizon, just listening to the murmur of the waves as they swelled and sank. He was uneasy for his protégée. The Prince Regent had shown unmistakable interest in her. She was now in real danger of being caught in a trap.

For a second he even considered giving her a pistol. But, if she shot at the Prince, she would be in much worse trouble! Yet he could not allow her to be seduced and cast aside. She was a young lady of good family, if he guessed aright. She had mentioned a large inheritance. She had unquestionably been well educated and perhaps was expected to fill an important role one day.

Whatever it was that had caused her to flee her home, he felt sure that in a while she would go back to her family. She would soon learn to place more value on her true position in life. The unwanted suitor would have disappeared and she would perhaps have more choice over her future. For the present, he acknowledged with a twisted grin, she was doing exactly the same as himself, and running away from her duties.

Oh, how he understood that urge. Yet again, he cursed his fate for being the older son and the heir to the mighty dukedom of Hawkesborough. Yet with awful clarity, he knew that he could not hide from his destiny forever. How he had envied Charles his career as an officer. But it was no good to hanker after that now. He paused for a moment and drew in a deep breath.

He seemed to be on the verge of reforming his way of life. Somehow, he had come to realize that he took no pleasure in doing everything to excess. He had been a rakehell for a long time but his view of life was shifting. And it was no pleasure to see that his shocking reputation was damaging his little friend. What on earth had made him kiss her? At the time he simply could not help himself. After all the years of raking, one slip of a girl in tears had overturned his cold-hearted indifference to female wiles.

He must behave like a proper guardian. With a foul curse he kicked a stone down onto the beach. It made a satisfying clatter as it bounced down and thumped against other stones. He kicked a larger stone and heard the correspondingly louder clatter.

'Tut-tut!' said a soft voice from behind him. 'Anyone would think you were still a schoolboy.'

Giles clamped his teeth together. He turned slowly, his expression unreadable. 'Sophia.'

'Hello, darling!' She smiled at him, her oval face beautiful, her figure alluring in the shimmering gown that clung to every curve. 'I think I have arrived just in time to save you from a night of boredom. Have you missed me?' She came close and put her hand on his chest, rubbing gently against the silk brocade of his waistcoat. Her blonde hair shone in the light from the lamp across the street. Her perfume filled his nostrils. She was still smiling up at him, but her eyes were watchful.

Giles stood motionless, his arms by his sides. Slowly, slowly, she slid her hand down his chest to his narrow waist, down over his flat stomach towards his inner thigh. At the last moment, he caught her fingers in his own and moved her hand away, pushing it back to her side.

Sophia raised her brows. 'I have found you at an inopportune time, then. But if you wish to see me later, I am staying in the new villa on the corner of St James Street.'

He tightened his lips. 'Not the most discreet place.'

'Oh, darling, don't be stuffy. This is Brighton! And shopping is such fun.'

He bit back a sharp retort. Already her

mind was calculating what treasures she could acquire. He looked past her towards the Steine.

'Are you out here quite alone?'

She shrugged. 'Mrs White is there somewhere. She knows how to make herself scarce if need be.' She raised her face towards him, her lips inviting.

Giles took a step backwards.

She threw up her hands. 'You are very disagreeable tonight. I will leave you, then.'

He said nothing, merely nodded. She waited a moment longer, then pulled her hood up, and slipped back across the road towards the tall shape of the Castle Tavern. Giles saw another female figure appear and they both continued walking away until they vanished into the darkness.

The heavy scowl descended on his face again. Damn Sophia! He had enough problems without her tiresome attempts to charm him. No doubt she would discover where he lived and start sending her endless messages. It was time to make it clear that the relationship was over. And it was definitely over. She had sensed it as well. He had not felt the faintest flicker of desire in spite of her intimate caresses.

But that did not mean she would give up trying. He was well aware she hoped to persuade him into marrying her. She was well born and had a large circle of acquaintances. Even if there were whispers about her reputation, she was discreet enough to be accepted in polite society. That meant she would have plenty of opportunity to meet him at all kinds of events. Moreover, her elderly father was a highly respected gentleman. Indeed, her one virtue was her great affection for this scholarly recluse.

He paced on along the road, hands clasped behind his back. What must he do to keep Anna out of danger? Just what was that Italian gentleman plotting? The one moment when the man actually looked pleased was when the Prince Regent noticed Anna and made it plain he found her attractive. So now what was the next stage in the villain's plans?

None of it made sense — yet. But he would discover what was going on. As he turned for home he tipped back his head and looked up at the stars. A low laugh escaped him. Whenever Anna was involved, he lost that crushing sense of boredom. She wanted a life of adventure but Giles was certain she would end up out of her depth. He would have to see she came to no harm. It was a challenge he found he welcomed.

16

'I have not seen you anywhere in town during the past two days,' Giles remarked in a low voice to Anna. It was the interval in the play and he had come to pay a visit in their box. He gave her a keen look. 'However, I have not heard of any earth-shattering events so I assume all is well?'

Anna considered his impassive face then she gave her usual sunny smile. 'You are teasing me, sir.'

He raised his brows, 'What, no adventures? Alas, poor Miss Lawrence, life is dull, indeed. But perhaps you have been indisposed?'

'Not I.' She shook her head, setting her curls dancing. They were tied back with a spangled blue ribbon, but in a looser style than usual. Giles's eyes lingered on them as she confided, 'Lady Fording was not very well. Her daughter made her stay at home so I have been keeping her company.'

'I am glad to see she is in good spirits now.' He glanced across at the old lady, who was talking to the cousin. Giles narrowed his eyes as he inspected the man. He was dressed with great elegance from his crisp shirt points and

158

artfully tied cravat to his flawless pantaloons and evening shoes. And yet . . . perhaps it was the crimson silk lining in the evening cloak draped so carefully over the back of a chair that stirred Giles's animosity, or maybe those pomaded black locks. Or perhaps it was the fellow's complete lack of interest in anyone but himself. Whatever it was, he felt an intense dislike of Signor di Cassagna. He sensed an unpleasant mystery.

He turned his attention back to Anna. This evening she was dressed in a pale-yellow gown. It was made of fine muslin, with cleverly gathered puff sleeves, trimmed with ribbon. The high waist was bound by matching yellow ribbons. It was a much simpler style than the evening gowns she had been wearing recently. He thought she looked charming. Then he saw that she was considering him with her head on one side.

'What is it?'

'How did you guess? I need to ask you something . . . but not here.'

'A secret?' he teased her and watched with wicked amusement as the flush spread over her cheeks. He was about to ask her if she had remarked a pistol in a shop window when the door to the box opened abruptly. He paused as the *contessa* appeared. She was far more animated than usual, with some colour in her thin cheeks and her eyes sparkling. She was ushering in a visitor, none other than Sophia.

Giles's features hardened. *Trouble!* Sophia paused in the doorway. There was satisfaction in her eyes as they met his and he knew she had come hunting him. She was wearing that damned triumphant smile of hers, the one that meant she had everything under control. She continued to look at him while he stood there, languidly raising his quizzing glass. Then she noticed Anna. Her eyes narrowed and she darted a quick glance at Giles. *Trouble indeed, especially for Anna, unless he was very careful.*

'Mama', said the *contessa*, 'This is Mrs Chetwynd. I have brought her to make your acquaintance.'

'Ah, you must be the lady with the so elegant bonnet,' said Lady Fording. 'Beatrice was telling me how you met yesterday in that milliner's boutique in St James Street.'

Sophia was at her most charming. Giles watched, impassive, as she exchanged polite small talk with the old lady. Then Signor di Cassagna bowed over her hand. Giles could see the calculating glance she cast over him. She would try to bewitch him anyway, in case he turned out to be useful to her. Finally she turned her attention to himself.

'Oh, how remiss of me,' said the *contessa*, 'but perhaps you have already met Lord Longwood . . . '

She was interrupted by a silvery laugh that set Giles's teeth on edge. He knew it well.

'But of course,' trilled Sophia, stepping across to place a hand on Giles's arm. Still clutching him, she smiled around. 'We move in the same circles . . . don't we, darling?' Then she appeared to notice Anna for the first time. She looked up at Giles. 'A young friend of yours, darling?' She smiled at Anna. 'I cannot keep up with all the young ladies he seems to know — and, of course, they change so often.' She fluttered her fan. 'It has been delightful to meet you all, but I believe both Lord Longwood and I should leave you now. The next act is about to begin.' She placed her hand on Giles's arm again, smiled a general smile and drew him out of the box.

Giles submitted to this. If he stayed, Sophia would avenge herself by spreading gossip about Anna being his latest love interest. Then Sir Bilton Kelly would be in hot pursuit of the poor innocent. In the doorway, he reached out his free arm to pull the door shut. He glanced at Anna. She was watching him with her lower lip sticking out.

Sophia kept her hold on his arm. 'This way,' she said, with a triumphant sideways glance. She swayed her hips and smiled graciously as they passed other spectators, all returning to their seats. It seemed her box was at the very end of this interminable corridor. Her long suffering companion, Mrs White, was standing by the door.

At last Sophia released her grip on Giles's arm. 'Will you join us?'

Frowning, he smoothed away a wrinkle from the sleeve she had been clutching. It took several minutes, during which nobody spoke. Finally he raised his head. 'Did you ask me something?'

Her smile was still firmly there but she was less confident now. She gestured towards the interior of her box. 'Do join us.'

He raised a hand. 'The first act was more than sufficient. Good evening.' He bowed and walked away along the now empty passage. He was too angry to sit through the rest of the play. Damn it, between Belinda and Sophia, he could scarcely get a moment's peace! Whichever way he turned, one of them was sure to appear. Add to that his responsibility towards his little protégée and life was becoming unbearably complicated. Since when was he, the worst rake in London, to be hounded by a pack of females?

He strode along the streets until he came to the open space of the Steine. By this time his first rage had cooled. He debated on how to organize a meeting with Anna without attracting unwanted attention that could damage her reputation still further. It did not seem that the problem was too urgent, but they would need time to discuss it. Besides, he must impress on her the need to keep herself safe.

He slackened his pace crossing the gravel path of the Steine towards Edward Street. People were still out, most of them on their way to card parties, no doubt. But Giles was in no mood for another social gathering. He would pay a call on his oldest friend. The women could not get at him there.

He reached Ned's lodgings and went up the stairs. There was no answer when he tapped on the parlour door so he simply walked in. He knew that if Ned was reading or in the throes of composition, he would need a lot of rousing.

And, sure enough, Ned was seated at the table, frowning over a closely written page, with many crossings out. Several crumpled balls of paper were lying near the hearth and a pile of sheets lay untidily on the table. Ned's hair was disordered, his necktie discarded and his shirt collar open. There was an inkstain on his cheek where he had rested smudged fingers.

Giles shook his head at this spectacle and crossed to the sideboard. He poured brandy into two glasses and carried them over to the table.

Ned blinked at him, and appeared to come back from a far distance. 'Oh, it's you, Longwood. Have you been here long?' He looked round vaguely.

'I need your help.' Giles thrust one of the glasses into Ned's hand. 'Leave your poem for now, Ned. I am in the devil of a coil.'

Ned frowned. 'What? Another duel?'

Giles gave a mirthless laugh. 'I wish it were that simple.' He took a gulp of his drink and grimaced at his puzzled friend. 'Women!'

'Women,' repeated Ned incredulously. 'You never complained about 'em before.'

Giles took another gulp of brandy. 'Perhaps that was because I never really cared before.' He sighed and leaned his head on one hand.

Ned drank some of his own brandy. He gazed thoughtfully at Giles and waited. At length, Giles looked up and shrugged. 'They are hovering like harpies, ready to pounce.'

'Well, you are a big prize, old man.' Ned narrowed his eyes as he considered Giles's words. 'You could just leave Brighton . . . '

Giles shook his head vigorously.

'So — the problem is that you care for one of them.'

Giles heaved a sigh. 'I care enough to protect her from harm.'

Ned's mouth fell open. 'This is a new start for you!' Shaking his head, he went to fetch the decanter. 'Well then,' he said, refilling both glasses, 'what do you have in mind to do?'

17

The ladies were sitting together in the drawing room, watching the coaches that passed up and down the road, as people began to go down towards Donaldson's and the Steine for the afternoon promenade.

'Do you feel strong enough for an outing, Mama?' enquired the *contessa*. 'I was a little anxious — you were tired after the theatre last night.'

Lady Fording chuckled. 'Oh, Beatrice, just because I fell asleep at the end of the play, it does not mean I am unwell.' She leaned forward and patted her daughter's arm. 'How many times must I tell you, animation and company is medicine for me?'

There was a tap on the door and the housekeeper came in with a card on a silver tray. The *contessa's* face brightened as she read it. 'Show her up,' she instructed the woman. Shortly afterwards, Sophia came into the room, a vision in almond green silk and a charming little hat with a turned back brim. Anna privately thought that her ensemble was more suited to a royal reception than an afternoon visit. The ladies curtsied to each

166

other, then settled down for a chat.

Anna took a seat a little to one side. Sophia ignored her. Her smiles and conversation were all for her new friend, with occasional remarks to Lady Fording. The tea tray was brought in and Anna set aside her embroidery to serve everyone.

'I did not quite catch this young lady's name last night,' remarked Sophia, deigning to notice Anna at last, as the latter placed a cup of tea on the table by her chair. The *contessa* explained Anna's role in the family.

'Oh!' Sophia opened her grey eyes very wide. 'Merely a companion. Well, then, she is very fortunate that you include her in visits to the theatre. And perhaps not so fortunate if Lord Longwood is condescending to notice her. I assume you know his dreadful reputation?'

Anna was handing round a plate of lemon cakes and was hard put to it not to throw them at the guest for this remark. How dare this woman criticize her special friend!

'Dreadful?' chorused Lady Fording and her daughter. Their eyes lit up in the expectation of delicious scandals.

Sophia gave her silvery laugh. 'Quite the worst rake in Town. No mama will allow her daughter even to dance with him.'

'Yet last night at the theatre, you claimed to

be a close friend of his,' stated Lady Fording, with a sideways glance towards Anna, sitting very straight backed on her chair with her plate clenched in one hand.

'Oh, the case is quite different,' Sophia tossed her head. 'We belong to the same circle of friends. And I am not a debutante, thank heavens.' She picked up her cup and sipped delicately, prolonging the suspense. Both the *contessa* and Lady Fording were hanging on her every word.

Anna got up to see if anyone wanted more tea. She was simmering with rage. This woman was a nasty tattle-monger. She set the teapot down again and resumed her seat.

'Do you mean he has ruined some girl's reputation?' the *contessa* prompted her.

'Oh, he does not bother with debutantes, he prefers ladies of experience.' She nibbled at her cake and cast a sour glance towards Anna. 'However, he has such charm, foolish girls can never resist him. But he gets bored so quickly. And then he lives such a wild lifestyle. His friends are all like him. He plays very deep, but I suppose one cannot expect it to be otherwise,' Sophia continued, 'when his family is so very wealthy. And as for the money he spends on his horses . . . ' She broke off as Anna choked over her tea.

'Well, it may be as you say,' said Lady

Fording, 'but we have found him to be a perfect gentleman. Anna, my dear, I think Beppi needs a drink of water.'

When Anna returned to the room, Sophia was discussing the various entertainments and bemoaning the lack of company.

'This year it seems a lot of people decided not to come here,' she sighed, 'as the peace festivities took so long, I suppose they all simply went home to their estates for a rest before the Season begins.' She placed her teacup on a side table and smoothed her skirts down. 'Of course, all these military celebrations mean that everyone is in love with a uniform. I saw Lord Longwood's brother — Lord Charles Maltravers — last night. I must say he looks very dashing in blue and silver. He has the height for it.'

'I agree with you,' said Lady Fording. 'A very pleasant young man but not, I suspect, a great thinker.'

Again Sophia gave her tinkling laugh. Anna repressed a grimace. It was such a mirthless sound. 'Ah, yes. He is nearly as bad a rake as his brother. I shall have to keep an eye on both of them, for the sake of the innocent girls in Brighton. If any girl is seen with either of them, she will damage her reputation.' She rose and pulled on her gloves. 'Do you go to the card assembly this evening?'

'You cannot keep me away from such an event.' Lady Fording looked round with a smile for her young helper. 'Now I have Anna to watch over me, I can enjoy these outings again.'

It seemed to Anna that Sophia was haunting them. They had scarcely arrived at the Castle Tavern and entered the rooms where the card games were starting up, than she came gliding over to them again. She was dressed in another low-cut but exquisite gown that drew many admiring glances. She engaged the *contessa* in conversation and when Signor di Cassagna noticed her, he actually came back from the card table where he had been waiting for a vacant place.

For a while Anna was occupied in finding seats for Lady Fording and Mrs Barton so they could join in a game of whist. At last she had them settled together with two of their acquaintances. They were preparing to deal their cards.

'Just one more thing,' said Lady Fording, as Anna settled a shawl carefully around the old lady's thin shoulders, 'a glass of wine, Anna, then I can enjoy my evening.' She glanced towards her daughter, who, together with Signor di Cassagna, was still chatting to Sophia. '*Che meraviglia!*' muttered the old lady, more to herself than to Anna. 'Enrico appears to find that lady sufficiently stylish for his taste.'

Anna thought her tone was ironic. Did she not care for her nephew, then? Or maybe she wanted Anna to understand her opinion of him. She debated this idea while working her way through the crowd and into the next room. The refreshments were set out at the far end. At length she reached the front of the crowd and it was her turn to ask a waiter for the wine.

'Miss Lawrence,' a man's voice exclaimed enthusiastically, 'by Jove, yes, yes, I thought it was you.'

With a sinking heart, she looked round. Sir Bilton Kelly was beaming at her. He nodded and moved alongside. 'Charming,' His eyes, she saw indignantly, were fixed on her bosom. The waiter had still not returned with her glass of wine so she must wait.

He cleared his throat and went on, 'The Prince particularly required me to see that you are invited to his next musical entertainment. In fact, you know, if you are willing, he would be delighted to entertain you as soon as tomorrow afternoon?' He raised his brows expectantly.

Sheer disbelief held Anna silent for the space of a minute. He was waiting with a half-smile on his thick lips. She drew herself up to her full height, her hands clenched into fists by her sides. 'I think you mistake me for a very different kind of female,' she spat at him. 'I may be young but I am not a fool.' Her eyes sparked blue fire and her jaw tightened. She glared at him again, then turned on her heel and pushed her way through the press of people.

Anger held her rigidly upright as she struggled through the crowd. She felt acutely aware of everyone. Their glances seemed to burn her. Was she really considered to be freely available? Her lips compressed tightly and two spots of colour burned in her cheeks. At that moment she spotted Giles. He was in a group of men, all talking and laughing. He looked dangerous and superbly arrogant.

For the first time she was seeing him in his true setting. And in a flash she saw just how rakish he was. So it was true that being friends with him meant that creatures like Sir Bilton Kelly assumed she was ready to be pawed by his master. She nearly screamed with rage. The horrid man had examined her as if she were a piece of meat!

It seemed an age before she reached the group of elderly ladies again. They were all intent on their game and took no notice of her. Then she realized she had forgotten Lady Fording's glass of wine. If she had been holding it, Anna thought, she would have thrown it in that detestable man's face. But now she must go back and get another one. With a sigh, she began to weave her way back through the crowd.

'Miss Lawrence.' A male voice spoke close by.

Anna hunched a shoulder and carried on. She knew who it was but now was not the time for a quarrel.

'Miss Lawrence, pray spare me one moment.' Giles was directly in front of her.

She looked up. To her annoyance, she found him as attractive as ever, his green eyes glowing this evening and that lock of dark hair falling over his brow. His eyebrows rose as she stared at him angrily.

'Yes, I know I abandoned you last night,' he said, 'but it was the wisest course, I think.' He gave her a dazzling smile. 'Surely you are not so angry you cannot open that pretty mouth of yours?'

This was intolerable! Now he was treating her to his rakish manners. She shook her head and pressed on. She reached the table, took a glass of wine and turned to go back. Giles was waiting in the doorway, watching her, his eyes narrowed.

'You are not just angry,' he murmured, following her into the card room. 'What is it?'

'Go away, please!' she hissed, not looking in his direction. At last she was back at the table. She set the glass down by Lady Fording and then turned round. But where could she go? The *contessa* had disappeared. Anna did not know anyone else in the room. Most of them were engrossed in their card games anyway. She shot a despairing glance towards Giles and quickly turned her head away again.

'Longwood,' someone called, 'are you going to keep us waiting much longer?'

'In a minute, Danby,' Giles called back. He moved very close to Anna. His eyes were on her hands. She knew they were still trembling and hurriedly clasped them behind her back.

'Tomorrow afternoon,' he whispered, 'by Donaldson's.'

She bit her lower lip and gave him an angry look. 'No!' She moved away. A minute after that, he had vanished. Anna looked cautiously around the room. Eventually she saw his dark head at the faro table. He seemed to have a large pile of guineas in front of him and he was drinking brandy. The group of men with him were all intent on the throw of the dice.

Anna checked to see that Lady Fording was still absorbed in her game. Then she looked up, across the heads of the card players and into the next room. She could see

Sophia chatting to Sir Bilton Kelly. Anna saw her put a hand on his arm and then they both laughed heartily.

★ ★ ★

Dawn was showing its first light when Giles eventually reached his own front door. He was far from sober, but even so he had not drunk enough brandy to dispel the bitter anger he felt. What had made Anna turn so decidedly against him? Now how was he going to warn her to keep away from rakes and rascals? Damn all these women, making his life so uncomfortable.

He shook his head to clear it enough for him to make his way up the stairs. That job at last accomplished, he steadied himself and pushed his bedroom door open. His coat and hat had disappeared somewhere on the way upstairs. Never mind. Daynton would sort that out.

Giles just wanted to lie down but he must undress! He made a huge effort and pulled off his first hessian. And as he did so, an idea came into his mind. Hopping over to a chair to grapple with the second boot, the idea took shape. Yes, that would be a way to impress Anna! Make her smile at him again . . . He would sort out the details later when his head was clearer. He dropped jacket, waistcoat and cravat on the floor in a heap that would cause Daynton anguish. He smiled. Yes, it was a *brilliant* idea. He shed the rest of his clothes and fell onto the bed with a sigh of relief.

18

'Really, Beatrice,' said Lady Fording, smiling up at her daughter from her position reclining against a heap of cushions on the sofa, 'you must not look so anxious. Of course I am tired after the excitement of winning such a lot of money last night.'

'I should not have taken you to the card party,' lamented the *contessa*, wringing her hands, 'now you are ill again.' She gave Anna a look of burning reproach. 'Miss Lawrence, you were there to watch over my mother. Why did you not tell me she was over-exerting herself?'

'Beatrice,' said Lady Fording in a long-suffering tone, 'I am tired because I am an old woman, not because I am a sick woman. But this argument is tiring me. All I need is to rest today. And, thanks to this abominable weather, we have to stay at home anyway.'

They all looked towards the window. Outside the rain hissed down. Further out, the sea tossed in grey and angry waves. It was enough to make anyone feel dismal. Anna stifled a sigh. She glanced at the *contessa*, still watching her mother, her hands twisting as she bit her lip in nervous worry. In Anna's opinion, she was the last person in the world to care for an invalid. She was restless and fretful, her butterfly mind flitting from one silly idea to the next.

'Miss Lawrence?' she said now, 'have you given my mother her medicine this morning?'

'Yes, of course,' began Anna, but Lady Fording interrupted.

'Beatrice, please, calm yourself. Anna is most efficient about my medicines.' She waved a hand towards the magazines. 'Come, let us look at the latest modes and then, when the weather improves, we can go shopping.'

At this the *contessa*'s face brightened. Typical! thought Anna. It was poor Lady Fording who had to look after her daughter. By now Anna had realized that the *contessa* was about as feather-headed as it was possible to be. She panicked for the slightest problem and had no interests to occupy her mind other than gossip and fashion. At least she had a marvellous eye for cut and colour and always looked stylish.

'Anna . . . ' Lady Fording's voice made her jump. 'Look, my dear, the rain has stopped. It is time to take Beppi for a little walk.'

Peeping from under a large umbrella, Anna grimaced at the state of the road. Poor Beppi protested but she dragged on his lead and he gave in and trotted along, giving her a reproachful look.

'Yes, it is horrid,' she told him, 'but a bit of fresh air and peace is better than sitting inside all day.' There was no doubting the *contessa*'s affection for her mother but the woman's constant fussing and tension made her very tiring company.

As they walked, Anna listened to the scrape of the shingle as the waves battered relentlessly upon it. To her surprise, there were some boats out on the water. They rose and sank with an alarming rhythm, making her feel queasy. Then she remembered Lord Byron's tale of Childe Harold and his voyage from England to Portugal. She took another look at the boats. Of course one could not expect the sea to be always calm. So she should try to go out in one for a sail and decide if she could manage a journey by sea.

The agreeable dreams of travel diverted her mind for a few minutes, but, as she turned back towards the house, she began to worry again over the fact that she was being pursued by Sir Bilton Kelly. She had not needed Giles to reproach her over her low-cut evening gowns, she knew they were too eye-catching, in the style of Mrs Chetwynd. Why did the *contessa* want her to dress in this manner?

Even more depressing was the fact that she had allowed her temper to get the better of her and now Giles was no longer her friend. Anna had seen the cold look in those green eyes when he turned away from her. She blinked furiously. It was wet enough without any tears!

There was a carriage outside the house when she returned. Who would pay a morning visit on such a wet day? Just for a second, hope flared, but Giles would not come in a closed carriage. He would not care about the rain.

Still, visitors meant that the atmosphere would be more cheerful. Anna hurried up to the drawing room, where she was very pleased to see Mrs Barton and Emily comfortably settled. The ladies were already drinking tea and eating some of the *contessa*'s Italian sweetmeats.

'Grandmama has spoken of these,' said Emily. 'I never had anything half so delicious. What do you call them?'

Lady Fording gave her little shrug. 'We just say *dolci*.'

'Sweet things,' translated Anna.

'So you speak Italian,' remarked Mrs Barton, giving her a sharp look. 'Did you study it at school?'

That was a mistake, thought Anna. She

should not give away anything about herself but keep in the background. Recently she had made so many mistakes, it was hard not to feel cast down. How could she be so thoughtless? But, fortunately, the *contessa* had other matters on her mind and created a diversion. 'So you saw Mrs Chetwynd at Celeste's boutique,' she said, 'and she chose a bonnet? What was it like?'

Emily did her best to describe the expensive bonnet.

The *contessa* sighed. 'She has exquisite taste,' she said enthusiastically. 'Oh, how I wish I had been there.'

'I expect you will see her wearing it as soon as the rain stops falling,' said Mrs Barton. 'It had three ostrich plumes, dyed green, so it is not a hat for a damp day. It cost too much to risk spoiling it.'

'It is very dashing,' said Emily. 'I saw several gentlemen looking in through the shop windows admiringly while she was trying it on.'

Mrs Barton frowned at her. 'Yes, well, Mrs Chetwynd is famed for being dashing. You must remember that she is a wealthy widow, my love, not a debutante like yourself.' She waited until Emily nodded submissively, then asked, 'Now then, have you spoken to Miss Lawrence about your plan?'

Emily shook her head. 'I was just about to do so.' She clasped her hands tightly. 'Miss Lawrence, do you ride?'

Anna hesitated a moment. This was giving away yet more information. But in the end she smiled and nodded. 'I do. I love riding.'

'Oh, splendid,' breathed Emily. 'I wonder if you would join me tomorrow morning? Miss Thorne does not ride and I do not care to go out with just a groom.'

'I would be happy to join you,' said Anna, 'but only if Lady Fording can spare me?' She looked enquiringly towards the old lady.

Lady Fording smiled at her old friend. 'I am happy to oblige you in this, Henrietta,' she said, 'I agree that riding is good exercise for Emily and of course she needs a companion. Anna is also young and energetic.' She smiled as she turned towards her, 'You know I do not rise very early. You will be back before I am settled in the drawing room here.'

The following morning it was still overcast but no rain was actually falling when Emily and her groom called for Anna. She had dressed in a moss-green walking dress and a plain hat with a matching ribbon. The horse they brought for her was a neat grey mare and very definitely sturdy rather than spirited. However, she was so pleased to have the chance to get out into the fresh air that she felt very happy to ride even this docile creature.

The groom indicated the way up onto the Downs near the race course. Anna soon found that Emily was only a reasonably competent horsewoman and not willing to take risks. Anna suppressed a sigh at having to stick to the paths. She would have preferred to take a more adventurous route across the hillsides. However, she wondered if her mount would cope with anything more difficult than a sedate trot along a well-marked road. And so they rode in a plodding fashion for about half an hour, at last making their way up to the crest of the hill.

'Ah, this is splendid,' said Anna when they stopped for a minute to let the horses blow. She waved her crop around. 'There are pretty views in all directions, green fields and trees and the sea is so much more impressive from up here. Why, I feel I can see almost all the way to France.'

Emily agreed. They admired the different prospects.

'There is plenty to explore,' said Anna. She looked longingly at the smooth sloping turf where a spirited horse could gallop for miles. The groom caught her look and grinned sympathetically.

'This is evidently a popular place,' Emily remarked. 'Just look how many other riders are out as well. Dear me, I did not expect so many people to be up here.'

'No doubt they want more exercise than they can get just by walking along the promenades.' Anna was gathering up her bridle, ready to move off again when she saw a lone horseman close by. He raised his hat to her. She looked warily, then recognized the long, pale face and huge dark eyes. It was Mr Caldecott, Giles's poet friend. He was simply a friendly face. She felt a wave of relief and nodded in return. He was mounted on a gleaming bay horse and had a very good seat, she noticed, as he cantered away across the open land.

'Somehow I did not expect a poet to be such a good horseman,' she whispered to Emily.

'A poet?' Emily stared after him eagerly.

'Yes,' Anna sighed, 'but not Lord Byron, I'm afraid.'

'Oh.' Emily lost interest. 'Have you managed to find a copy of *The Corsair* yet?'

Anna shook her head. 'It seems an impossible task.' But for once Lord Byron's work held no interest for her. Why was her heart thumping in this silly way each time another rider came close? And why did it sink when the rider was not the tall, devil-may-care Lord Longwood? She had told him to keep away from her. It was all her own doing. She forced herself to smile and nod at Emily's chatter.

They trotted on and kept going until a few spots of rain came down.

'We had better turn back,' called Emily. 'I do not want to get my habit all muddy.'

'I do not want to ruin my hat,' Anna urged her mount to a canter but had to stop when Emily called out that she was going too fast.

'You are an excellent horsewoman, I can see,' said Emily, as they trotted along side by side. 'I expect Jack would enjoy riding with you. He refuses to go out with me, he says it is too tame.'

'Surely your brother would want to see you came to no harm?' Anna was a little shocked.

'Not he,' said Emily cheerfully. 'And I would not want him. He fumes and frets and criticizes all the time. I much prefer your company. You are too polite to say how slowly I ride. I must say, though,' she added after a short pause, 'that if Jack hears you ride with me, he may join us after all.'

It was on the tip of Anna's tongue to warn Emily to say nothing to her brother but she held her peace. She must remember she was just a paid companion. But young Mr Barton sounded like a coxcomb and she wanted nothing to do with any more of them.

The day turned wet again and so the *contessa* insisted they must stay at home that afternoon. Anna was secretly glad of a respite from mixing with society and worrying about such people as Sir Bilton Kelly approaching her again. On the other hand, she longed for a chance to see Giles. She must find some way of apologizing for her behaviour. She could not bear it if they were no longer friends. And then there was the matter of that kiss and the feel of his long, hard body against hers. That was going to be her most precious memory through the years of her life.

She wandered to the window yet again but the rain was still falling from a leaden sky.

'Anna!' Lady Fording sounded amused, 'I think tomorrow we must venture into town even if we have to swim through a flood. You are obviously desperate to meet someone.' Her twinkling eyes watched as the colour crept into Anna's cheeks. 'Come, sit just there — with your fan — and show me those gestures I taught you the other day.'

19

'Go and talk to her, damn it!'

'Why me? Surely Charles could do the job better.'

'I have no intention of allowing Charles within arm's length of her,' said Giles through his teeth. 'He's a worse rake than I am. And he was sniffing round her when we first arrived in Brighton. I had the devil's own job to warn him off. I can trust you.'

Ned looked discreetly at Anna as he and Giles paused in their stroll. 'She's certainly the prettiest girl here this summer. Causing quite a stir, ain't she, one way and the other?' He turned his attention back to Giles. 'Know something? Never seen you like this and I've known you for a long time. You're nervous.'

Giles gave his old schoolfriend his haughtiest glare. 'No I'm not. I just have to be careful. She's young and unprotected. You know as well as I do that any attention from me can only harm her.' He brushed some imaginary fluff from his lapel as Ned continued to examine his face.

'It's a bit late for all this nobility, ain't it?

After squiring her all evening at the Pavilion — '

'Don't remind me,' said Giles with feeling. 'That was a nightmare.'

There was a faint smile on Ned's lips. 'Well!' was all he said.

'What do you mean, 'Well'?' Giles took a few steps away. Ned caught up with him, still smiling. 'You never considered any lady's reputation before,' he pointed out ruthlessly.

'You have completely misread the situation.' Giles knew he sounded defensive. He directed another discreet glance towards Anna. She was sitting at a small table outside Donaldson's, next to Lady Fording. The two of them were examining rolls of ribbon. Anna seemed her usual composed self. Giles cast a critical eye over her clothes and was relieved to see that she was well covered up. Her bonnet was the same saucy little straw one she had worn to the races, but with green ribbons today to match the spencer she wore over her pink muslin gown.

The Steine was crowded. Everyone was out, glad to resume their usual occupations after two days of such foul weather. Many of the ladies were clustered in small groups in or near Donaldson's. The noise of their chatter was quite deafening. Another keen look around reassured Giles that there was no sign of any danger to Anna in the shape of Sir Bilton Kelly, or his own brother, so he indicated to Ned that they should move on. They resumed their leisurely walk down towards the sea.

'Still looks pretty rough out there,' remarked Ned, gazing towards the horizon.

'Hmm. Not really a challenge though.' Giles stood very straight, hands clasped behind his back and frowned at the choppy sea. 'If I had thought to have the *Kestrel* sent round from Lyme, we could have enjoyed a few days riding the storm.'

Ned refused to be diverted. 'Why did you want me to talk to her?'

Giles shrugged. 'I wish to be certain that all is well with her.'

'Dash it, you can pass the time of day with 'em. It would not cause a scandal, especially when the old lady is there.'

Giles merely raised his brows. He was still uncomfortably aware that he had broken his own code of conduct towards his protégée. Was that the reason she had told him to keep away from her? He felt disgusted at himself and worried that he seemed to be developing a conscience. He had never hesitated to accept the favours of all those ladies who were more than ready to fall into his arms. He knew — who better — how to play the game of seduction. And he never, ever felt anything for any of them.

Yet the one girl he absolutely must respect and protect, had overcome his defences before he was even aware of it. It had taken just a hint of a tear in her clear blue eyes to melt his heart. He was deeply uneasy at this lapse, and at the uncomfortable feelings stirring in his breast. For both their sakes, Giles determined to keep his distance from Anna. Yet he would not allow any other young blood to take advantage of her, and if Sir Bilton Kelly, or the Regent himself, should offer her an insult, he would —

'You're mighty twitchy today,' came Ned's voice.

Giles found he had clenched both his fists and his jaw. He sighed. 'I have some — er — family matters on my mind.' Really, why did Ned have to keep such a keen eye on him? And would he be suspicious of Giles's brilliant idea when it was made public? The rhythmic crash of the waves drew his attention to the fact that the sea spray was splashing up onto their boots. The tide was in and the wind was blowing inshore.

The two men turned and crossed the road, ready to head back up the Steine again. They paused to chat with a group of friends, who had news of a cock fight to be held the next

190

evening. Parting from them, Giles found himself face to face with Lady Beveridge and her daughter. Belinda looked as cool and elegant as ever.

'Well, Longwood,' said Lady Beveridge, 'we have seen very little of you these last few days.'

'I trust you enjoy your customary good health, ma'am,' drawled Giles. He turned a sarcastic gaze on Belinda. She was smiling graciously at him. How different from her cold looks when she thought that Anna was compromising herself beyond repair. And this was the girl his father was ordering him to marry! It was enough to send him off on a month-long orgy.

'Will you be at the assembly this evening?' insisted Lady Beveridge. 'There are so few suitable partners for dear Belinda. Brighton has such a quantity of undesirable residents this year, do you not agree?' She tapped him on the sleeve with her lorgnette. 'We shall see you later then.'

Ned scowled at her back as she drifted majestically away. 'Do I rank as an undesirable? She completely ignored me.'

'Lucky you!' said Giles, clapping a hand on his shoulder. 'That's my evening ruined.' He paced on, surveying the crowd with disfavour. 'I wonder if my scheme will be a success,' he said in a low voice.

'What is this mysterious scheme?' Ned's eyes were alight with curiosity.

'Did I hear the word *scheme?*' Sophia's voice came from just behind them.

They were obliged to turn and bow to her. She was all smiles, dazzling in an eye-catching green spencer and yellow silk dress, with a ruched green bonnet sporting three ostrich plumes. It was without doubt the most ostentatious outfit in town. By her side was a really elegantly dressed lady. With a slight effort, Giles recalled it was the *contessa*. A pity she was so gaunt with her shadowed eyes and her pale cheeks. There was no sign of the obnoxious cousin, thank the Lord.

'Are you planning something splendid?' asked Sophia, pushing between Ned and Giles. She fluttered her eyelids and put her dainty gloved hand on his arm. 'Do tell.' She must have felt his muscles clench for she shot a sharp look up at him.

He looked down at her, unsmiling. 'Perhaps you misheard.'

'Oh, I am sure I did not.' She pouted prettily. 'But be disagreeable if you wish.' She kept her hand on his arm and smiled radiantly as she walked the short distance to Donaldson's at his side.

'This is such a charming place, is it not?'

she observed. 'See how everyone loves to gather here. And one is sure to meet all one's acquaintances. Ah, Lady Fording.' Her tone was just a little shrill, Giles noticed. No doubt she had seen Anna and was jealous of all that fresh, youthful beauty. Sophia never could stand competition.

Giles slid her hand off his arm and raised his hat. 'I trust the sea air continues to agree with you, ma'am?'

Lady Fording looked up at him with approval. 'Thank you, Lord Longwood. I am very well now — as I keep assuring my daughter.' She looked round. 'Have you finished your shopping already, Beatrice?'

Giles raised his quizzing glass and surveyed the tangle of ribbons in the box on her table. 'It seems you are doing some shopping also?' His eye caught Anna's for a second. She was looking wary. And rightly so, he thought, if she has got Sophia's measure. Yet again, it was not a good moment for any private conversation. He frowned, aware that five pairs of eyes were fixed on him. Then he found an unexpected ally.

'Anna, my dear, 'said the old lady, 'oblige me by taking this tray back into the shop. We will have the blue and . . . yes, the amber.' She waited for Anna to gather everything up and invited Giles to sit. 'It is very fortunate that you came by, my lord. I wish to consult with you.'

'At your service, ma'am,' Giles said promptly. Lady Fording was looking at the others. 'Do not let us keep you from your promenade.' She smiled in dismissal. Sophia glared at being thus outsmarted. She was obliged to walk off with the others. Giles gave a chuckle as he drew out a chair and sat down. His companion winked at him. 'You and I are past the age of needing chaperons, *non è vero?*' she said, her eyes twinkling.

Giles placed a hand theatrically against his heart. 'Let's give them something to wonder about, anyway.' He leaned close to her. 'In what way can I serve you, ma'am?'

She explained what she wanted.

'But that is so simple,' he exclaimed.

'Ah yes, but you have such impeccable taste, sir. I fear that if I ask anyone else, they would choose something too . . . ' — she waved one beringed hand as she sought the right term — 'too gaudy.'

They smiled at each other in great amity. 'And now,' said Giles, 'if I may make so bold, I have a favour to ask of you . . . '

20

Anna was out walking the dog. It was a pleasant morning, with enough blue in the sky to promise a dry, warm afternoon. That meant they would go for the usual promenade on the Steine or to look at the smart shops in St James Street, followed by tea in the Castle Tavern. Perhaps she would see Giles again. In the fleeting look they had exchanged yesterday, she had seen the roguish gleam in his green eyes. Although she wanted to talk with him, on this occasion she had made herself act with discretion. No more mistakes, she had sworn, just do not draw attention to yourself.

In addition, she had seen Mrs Chetwynd arriving with Giles and the others. Young as she was, Anna could tell a jealous woman when she saw one. So she had played the innocent and humble companion, while managing to observe the players in this drama. Her conclusion was that Giles was not pleased by Mrs Chetwynd's clinging attention but for some reason he could not ignore her.

Anna and Emily had enjoyed several very

satisfying discussions about Mrs Chetwynd, her scandalous reputation and her determined pursuit of Giles. Whenever they met, they reported to each other on her latest toilette, always so fine, as Emily said, that she could be on her way to court for tea with the Queen. In a seaside town, her elaborate robes and bonnets stood out as faintly ridiculous.

Anna crossed the road to look down at the beach below. The bathing machines were drawn up in a row near the water's edge. At this hour there was nobody in the sea. Anna had not ventured onto the beach since the day she went swimming. And she had not encountered Belinda since that evening at the Pavilion. Maybe Belinda knew she would get a sharp reminder of her lack of help, when they did meet again.

A fishing boat was approaching the shore. Gulls screamed and circled round its mast. It reminded her of her burning desire to travel to foreign lands. But was she ready yet? She was finding that there were many pitfalls to negotiating life as a single woman. She sighed and shook her head. I still have a lot to learn. But I do need a pistol, she decided. That would make me feel so much less vulnerable.

At her feet, the little dog barked at the gulls. 'Come, Beppi,' she urged him, 'let's try running.' She chased him along the road, laughing. Several carriages went past in the direction of the town centre. And behind her, she could hear a carriage approaching in a tearing hurry. It would pass her any minute now and she would see who was driving so recklessly. It drew abreast. Anna glanced up at a pair of gleaming black horses and a curricle she knew well.

She saw the dark face look towards her. Then he was checking the horses and the curricle stopped. Giles tossed the reins to Morgan and jumped down. He strode to meet her and grasped both her hands in his. 'What is wrong?' he asked urgently. 'What are you running away from?'

Anna gave a peal of laughter and saw his gravity disappear. 'Do you call it running? Poor Beppi can only scamper.' Her heart was beating hard but that was due to the exercise, she told herself. She could not help the smile that would stay on her face.

He smiled back now, a smile of pure enjoyment. His eyes were very green this morning. 'Egad, you are a refreshing change from all the other young ladies I see around. Running in the street!' He gave a low laugh and looked down at the pug. 'Yes, I imagine you do long for more energetic exercise.' He drew her arm through his. 'Come, but at a walking pace, mind!'

Anna's spirits soared. He was not offended with her. She was very conscious of his tall, elegant figure so close to hers. She could feel the strong muscles of his arm, see the length of his well-shaped legs as he strode by her side. The faint spicy aroma of his cologne reached her nostrils and she breathed it in eagerly. For a few moments she let these agreeable sensations wash over her. Her dear friend was here again and she felt safe.

'Well', he said at last, 'are you still not speaking to me?'

Oh! He *was* angry with her. When she had told him to leave her alone at that card party, she had been furious. But after all, she was just a young lady of no importance and he was a member of the aristocracy, on speaking terms with the Prince Regent himself.

'Miss Lawrence,' his cool, amused tones penetrated her embarrassment, 'are you trying to pull my arm off?'

'Oh, I do beg your pardon!' She released her death grip on his arm and stared in horror. 'Oh no! I have creased your sleeve, I — I ... ' She gave a huge huff of exasperation. 'It goes from bad to worse,' she muttered, trying to rub the crease away. She darted a look into his face. 'I saw how you smoothed your sleeve when Mrs Chetwynd had merely laid a hand lightly upon it.'

'Perhaps,' he murmured, his head bent close to hers, 'it depends on who does the creasing.'

She jerked back. A frown came into her eyes. 'Are you teasing me?'

There was a dull colour along his cheekbones. 'Alas, yes. However, you are too smart to fall for my rakish tricks. But let us turn to other matters. Is all well with you? Your appearance, may I say, is exactly as it should be.' His gaze travelled over her blue spencer, buttoned high to the throat over a yellow cambric gown.

Anna could detect nothing but critical appraisal. She bore the scrutiny with outward composure but her blue eyes kindled.

'Before you slay me with reproof for mentioning the matter,' he told her while she was still speechless, 'you must remember that I consider myself responsible for you. You are clever enough to have noticed how important appearances are.'

'Then I must be glad you find nothing amiss,' she snapped. It was impossible to decide if he was just teasing.

They walked along in silence, Anna fuming inwardly. He was still treating her like a schoolgirl. But then she recalled Sir Bilton Kelly ogling her almost naked bosom. Giles was right to urge a modest appearance. And he was always dressed with such elegance, that she must accept he knew what message clothes conveyed.

At last honesty made her admit, 'This is how I normally dress. It is only those wretched evening gowns that they insist I must wear . . . '

She felt him shake with silent laughter. 'Those gowns are stunning. But they are more in the Italian mode than what is considered suitable for a young miss to wear here. And you are well aware of the effect they have on the men.' He turned to give her a rueful grin, 'Witness my own sad behaviour in the Pavilion.'

She stared up at him silently, her cheeks paling. Then she bent her head down and said in a stifled voice, 'I must return now. Can you not hear poor Beppi wheezing?'

'Deuce take that animal,' he growled. 'Let me ask you, my infant, are you still determined to maintain this masquerade? If you have had second thoughts, I will convey you back to your home.'

Anna gasped. 'B-but you do not know where I come from . . . d-do you?' she added as doubt shook her. Surely there was no way he could have found out.

His eyes glinted at her. Then his expression relaxed into a lopsided grin. 'You minx. Does this mean you prefer your current situation?'

'Indeed I do.'

'What about that dandy of a cousin?' he growled. 'Does he annoy you?'

She shook her head. 'We scarcely see him. I find him very odd and I think even his relatives do not care for him. But I should not gossip about him.'

'Never mind that. You have no one else to look out for you. I need to know. In what way is he odd?'

She shrugged. 'He is very moody and easily enraged if his clothes are not just how he considers they should be. He is more concerned that his snuffbox matches his jacket than if his aunt is in good health.'

'So he is a peevish dandy.'

She nodded. 'He is also involved in some political society back in Italy. He gets many letters and pamphlets and these often put him in a rage. I was present when he told Lady Fording and her daughter how he dreams of a revolution. He appears to favour violent methods to achieve it. It makes them anxious.' She looked up. 'But he is such a dandy I cannot believe he would ever do anything that would — er — cause him to crease his jacket.'

Giles chuckled as she went on, 'I understand the Italian tongue, you see. Is it not a fortunate coincidence that I am with an Italian family? They are thinking of returning to Italy soon.'

'What? All of them?' He stopped in his tracks. 'And you would go with them?'

She tossed her head. 'It would be a wonderful opportunity to start my foreign travels. And I could never find a kinder employer than Lady Fording.'

He muttered something under his breath. Anna lifted her chin and gave him a mulish look. They walked a little further, she with her nose in the air and he frowning heavily.

'Suppose you did not like it there. What if you wished to return to your family?'

Anna clenched her jaw. He just did not understand! She tried again, speaking slowly and clearly. 'I confess, I am sorry if Mama is worried but there is no way I will *ever* go back.' She felt him heave a deep sigh and added, 'You see, I spent so many years away at school that I am not at all close to my family any more. And when the headmistress insisted that I come home, they were trying to marry me off as fast as possible. So . . . ' She swallowed hard and turned her head to gaze out over the sea.

He grasped her hand in both of his. 'My poor infant.'

Once again she wanted to bury her face in

his shoulder and sob out all the pain of that rejection. But they had reached the door of the villa. Beppi was tugging at his lead in his eagerness to get back inside. Giles just had time to add, 'So I must insist on continuing in my role as self-appointed guardian.' He squeezed her hand and let it go to rap on the door with the head of his walking stick.

Anna found that he was coming inside. She was so torn by conflicting emotions that she wanted to hide away for a while until she could calm her thoughts again. But that was impossible, so she forced a polite smile to her lips as she showed him up to the drawing room. If only he had not made that remark about her dress causing him to lose his self-control at the Pavilion. Now her memories of that kiss were spoiled.

She led the way into the drawing room, then stood aside as Giles bowed over Lady Fording's hand. Anna felt a little suspicious when Lady Fording showed no surprise. She had obviously been expecting him. When the greetings were over, Giles produced a long, slender package from an inside pocket and laid it down on the little table at Lady Fording's side.

'So prompt, Lord Longwood,' said the old lady, raising her eyebrows. 'I am sure it is exactly what I wanted.' Her dark eyes turned towards Anna, watching this little scene with eager curiosity, and she smiled. 'All in good time, young lady.' She indicated the refreshment tray.

Anna poured out wine and brought it to them both. Giles soon set his glass down and pulled out a gilt-edged card. He handed it to his hostess. 'I trust you will be kind enough to honour me by accepting this invitation.'

Lady Fording scanned it through her lorgnette. 'A picnic,' she exclaimed, smiling up at him. 'You may be sure we will.'

Anna's face lit up. 'That sounds delightful. But will it not be a lot of work to organize it?'

'Probably,' he answered indifferently. 'I have sent for my secretary, Mr. Dowling. He has a genius for all such matters.'

'And can he select a dry and sunny day?' she teased.

Giles looked down his nose. 'Of course. That is what I pay him for.'

The ladies laughed. The door opened and Signor di Cassagna appeared.

★ ★ ★

The laughter faded. Giles exchanged a bow with the *signor*, feeling more hostile than ever. And not just because Signor di Cassagna was dressed in a decidedly

Continental style, that Giles considered too florid. It was not even because of the man's extravagantly curled hair, or the strong aroma of Russian hair oil. What Giles instantly disliked was the blank stare and the pinched lips that expressed their owner's conviction that nobody else mattered, only himself.

That gentleman stalked over to the fireplace and planted himself there, hands clasped behind his back. Giles saw him glance towards Anna and look away impatiently.

So, he considers her to be a servant, who has to be tolerated, thought Giles. Aloud, he said, 'Ladies, it is time for me to take my leave. I shall have the pleasure of seeing you all at my picnic in five days from now.'

'Picnic?' echoed Signor di Cassagna, betraying a slight interest.

Giles inclined his head regally. 'The invitation includes you as well, sir.'

Morgan was walking the horses up and down the road. Giles jumped into the curricle and took over the reins. He resisted an urge to look up to the window of the drawing room he had just left, turning the horses neatly and setting off along the coast road to the east of town.

'That dandified gentleman was admiring the horses, my lord,' remarked Morgan.

Giles raised his brows. 'You astonish me.

He is, as you say, dandified to the point where I would not expect him ever to go near a horse.'

'Oh, no,' Morgan shook his head, 'very knowledgeable he is, indeed.'

Giles was not prepared to allow Signor di Cassagna any good points. In fact he spent the next few minutes savagely listing everything he had noticed about the fellow that marked him as a rogue. He had noted the extreme pallor that indicated either a fondness for long nights of drinking or perhaps a liberal use of laudanum. That might explain why he was moody, as Anna put it.

If they met again, Giles determined to sound the fellow out about his political ideas. If Anna should go to Italy with the family, he wanted to be sure she was not going to end up in the middle of an uprising. His lips twisted in a wry smile. She would probably like that, he thought, as part of the life of adventure that she craved. And if she did go, he would have to buy her a muff pistol as a parting gift.

21

By setting herself to collect up various magazines and books, Anna contrived to move around the drawing room and reach the bay window just as Giles was jumping into his curricle. He did not look up, however. She watched him turn his carriage in one neat manoeuvre and set off at a cracking pace towards the east. He must be going to Rottingdean. It was a lovely day for a drive. She longed to be free and able to do the same. It would be splendid to accompany him — or it would have been if she had not been so crushed by that remark about her evening dresses.

You are well aware of the effect they have on the men — and the one that hurt the most: *Witness my own sad behaviour in the Pavilion.* She had hoped that the kiss was a spontaneous expression of affection. It had certainly figured very largely in her mind ever since. But now she knew she must suppress all longing to have it repeated. He was her kind friend and that was all. In fact, he was a true knight of chivalry. Why that made her sigh, she just did not know.

It must have been a loud sigh because both Lady Fording and Signor di Cassagna broke off their conversation to turn their heads towards her. Anna bit her lip and flashed an apologetic smile in their direction. She moved on towards the next magazine and added it to her armful. The conversation was in Italian and it was more heated than usual. Anna could make out enough to understand that someone had written a very insulting letter to Signor di Cassagna. He was telling his aunt how he intended to prove his capabilities as a leader.

'I will show that arrogant dog how mistaken he is,' he raged, his eyes burning with fury. 'I will show them I am the natural leader of the Brotherhood. As soon as we return to Italy, I will be the one to lead them to victory in our struggle against the Austrian oppressors . . .'

Lady Fording made soothing noises. Alerted by his ranting, the *contessa* hurried in, to remind her cousin he must not alarm her mother. It all ended as it usually did. Signor di Cassagna made a few more grand statements about his own abilities and poured scorn on the ambitions of his co-conspirators in Florence. 'You will soon see,' he exclaimed, staring at each of them in turn, 'how ruthless I am. I will make the whole of Europe take note, I swear it!' When he had repeated all this with grand gestures and flashing eyes, he marched out of the room and shortly afterwards they heard the front door slam.

Mother and daughter looked at each other meaningfully. Anna overheard the *contessa* say, 'He grows worse, I fear.'

Lady Fording shook her head. She twitched her shoulders as if shrugging all the unpleasantness away. 'Anna,' she said, 'a glass of wine — for all three of us, I think.'

They saw no more of Signor di Cassagna for the next two days. The time passed in their usual occupations. Anna managed to maintain a calm outward appearance but she was conscious always of a heavy weight in her heart. What were you thinking? she scolded herself. How many times did he warn you he is a rake? A kiss is nothing to him. But he is still my friend and he keeps my secret.

And with that she must be content. She longed to confide something of her feelings to her three special friends, Elinor, Sally and Tess. As soon as she thought about them she realized how lonely she was. Dare she write to Elinor? No, it was too risky. Her mother and stepfather must have been to Elinor's home by now, looking for her. Anna did not doubt that her friend would pretend she knew nothing about the matter.

Meanwhile, here in Brighton, people were speculating about Giles's forthcoming picnic. Anna learnt that he was famous for throwing lavish parties and suddenly, from being spoken of as a disreputable rake, everyone was praising his generosity and anticipating a splendid occasion. The gossips were soon circulating snippets of information.

The Prince Regent had been invited. But would he risk spending time in the fresh air, when he was always afraid of catching cold? There was to be a large tent erected in case of cold weather. But would His Highness attend when he might take some illness from another guest? There was to be a second large tent just for the Prince and his attendants and those guests who were his personal friends.

The gossips also discovered that there was to be a cricket match. The Prince's own regiment would provide a guard of honour and the officers were to be among the guests. Excitement grew with each new item of information. The band of the Tenth Hussars would play during the event.

Anna listened to all the comments and speculation and felt her own excitement growing. She decided she would wear the blue dress she had worn for the visit to the Racecourse, together with her little yellow parasol and matching reticule. So she must change the ribbons on her bonnet. She was sitting in the drawing room measuring out lengths of yellow ribbon when Signor di Cassagna opened the door.

'Oh,' he said, when he realized she was there, 'where is my aunt?'

'She is resting at this time of day,' replied Anna. Perhaps you should do the same, she added silently. He looked grey, with dark circles under his eyes. At least he was not in one of his bad moods. In fact, he seemed almost pleased with life. She hoped he would leave but after standing just inside the doorway for a few minutes, he came across to look at what she was doing.

'Is this for the grand picnic?' he asked, picking up a piece of ribbon and examining it through his eyeglass.

Anna nodded. 'It will go well with my blue dress.'

He frowned in an effort of memory. 'Have I seen that one? I do not think so. I trust it is very stylish.' He leaned forward, one hand resting on the table and looked very intently into her eyes.

She blinked at him, suddenly uneasy. Why was he so interested in her appearance? Now he was staring at her as if examining an unusual specimen. Whatever could he be

211

planning? His mouth twisted, a warning his temper was about to explode, so she said in a calm tone, 'It is my smartest day dress. It was new when we came to Brighton.'

She hoped he would be satisfied with that. If he started shouting and upset the other ladies, the *contessa* would blame her for provoking him.

He continued to stare at her for a moment. 'Excellent,' he said at last, 'it is so important to be stylish. The Prince will be there.' His dark eyes gleamed.

Anna was struck by the tone of his voice. He sounded so pleased, yet when they met the Regent at the Pavilion, he had ignored Signor di Cassagna. But perhaps he was hoping for a more cordial reception this time. However, if he thought she was going to attract the Prince's attention by having most of her bosom on display, he was doomed to disappointment.

He straightened up and dropped the ribbon on the table. Anna went back to her sewing. He wandered over to the window and stood looking out. She heard him sigh and mutter something about grey skies. Then he whisked round and stalked out of the room. Anna listened intently and breathed a sigh of relief when she heard the front door closing. A discreet peep out of the window reassured her that he was walking up to the road where he had lodgings.

She soon forgot about him as she added a small spray of white silk roses at the right side of the bonnet and stitched the ribbons into place. She was considering the effect in the mirror when Lady Fording came into the room.

'Charming,' she said, after a moment's critical examination. 'And that puts me in mind of something.' She rummaged in the heap of pots, boxes and magazines beside her favourite chair. 'Here.' She held out a long, slim package. 'I am so glad I asked him to select a white one.'

Anna advanced slowly, her eyes fixed on the package. She swallowed. Giles had brought this on his morning visit. Her fingers trembled as she unwrapped the paper and revealed a fan. She gazed in delight at the carved ivory sticks and the white lace. 'This is beautiful,' she whispered. She blinked hard. 'But I cannot take it, dear ma'am. Lord Longwood brought it for you.'

Lady Fording chuckled. 'Wrong! I merely asked him to select a fan for me. You are a good girl and deserve a little gift. And after all my lessons teaching you the language of the fan, it is time for you to show your skills. At this picnic, there may be some opportunities to try it out, *non è vero?*'

'But . . . I cannot.' Anna frowned down at the fan. 'This is a most costly gift.' Reluctantly she made to give it back.

'Anna! Do not be silly. It was for you. And see how well it goes with your bonnet.'

Anna held the delicate fan as if it were a bird. 'Thank you, oh thank you,' she whispered. 'I shall treasure it.'

The next two days were spent anxiously watching the sky and discussing the prospect of a fine day for the picnic. Everywhere and at every event, people had only that one topic of conversation. Anna accompanied Lady Fording and her daughter on their usual daily outings. Sometimes they met up with Mrs Barton and Emily. Once or twice they encountered Mrs Chetwynd, usually if they went along St James Street to look at the shops.

There was no sign of Giles or his friend the poet. Anna hoped each day to see him, but she was disappointed. She did not even see his brother although the officers were often in the town, very visible in their blue uniforms. It was a tiny consolation, in Anna's opinion, that at least if Giles were not in town, Mrs Chetwynd could not pounce on him in her usual way, with that dazzling smile she managed to keep on her face for hours on end. She mentioned the incredible smile to Emily.

'She will soon be horribly wrinkled if she keeps smiling so widely,' Emily giggled. 'But have you remarked that when there is no gentleman to impress, her expression is most disagreeable. It quite spoils her beauty. Grandmama says she is desperate to find a rich husband.'

'Surely not,' responded Anna tartly. 'She cannot wish for a husband when she has far more freedom as a widow. And she cannot be poor — just look at her clothes. She is always wearing something new.'

They giggled again. 'She must spend a fortune on dresses,' said Emily. 'So of course she needs a rich husband. And Lord Longwood is very wealthy.'

'The poor man,' replied Anna. 'He is surrounded by ladies trying to catch him.'

'How can they help it? He is so striking and well made.' Emily clasped her hands at her rather ample bosom.

'What? Never say you are wanting to catch him as well? I thought you would at least wait until you had enjoyed a season or two before you would consider surrendering your freedom.'

'Of course,' said Emily with dignity, 'but I am entitled to admire a good-looking man when I see one.'

22

The tents were erected on a level stretch of land, just outside the town, close to the London road. There was a view of the sea from this area. The gossips passed along the information that cartloads of provisions were arriving, that a small army of servants were busy preparing the supplies and that a group of Hussars had measured out a cricket pitch. Chairs and tables were delivered, also by cart. Smaller tents and stalls with awnings were going up all over the ground. With each visible addition, promising a wide variety of entertainment, excitement grew among those people who had received invitations.

The day of the actual event dawned at last. Peeping out of her bedroom window as soon as it was light, Anna saw that the sky was clear. She breathed a sigh of relief. Even the *contessa* could not feel that her mother might get chilled on such a lovely day. But, after trying in vain to go back to sleep, Anna wondered how she would get through all the hours before the picnic began at one o'clock.

She was even more excited at the idea that she would see Giles again. Even a brief exchange of words with him would be precious to her. Anna resolved to keep her distance from any possible rakes or troublesome young bloods. But she was excited at the treats in store and hoped she could enjoy all the different entertainments of the afternoon.

The picnic ground was a mass of bright colours and intriguing little booths. There were various stalls set out in clusters here and there and small groups of blue uniformed soldiers stood near these. A number of small tents had been set up to one side of the wide field. In another corner, men in white aprons were busy around tables. Even from a distance it was clear that there were generous supplies of food and drink. Officers were trying out their bowling and batting skills on the cricket pitch.

The band was already playing when the first guests began to approach the largest tent. Anna and her party arrived early, due to Signor di Cassagna's insistence. As soon as she had helped Lady Fording down from the carriage, Anna looked eagerly towards the head of the line of visitors. Sure enough, there was the tall and elegant figure of Giles, greeting his guests. She saw Lord Charles Maltravers, resplendent as always in his blue and silver uniform, next to his brother.

When he saw Lady Fording, Giles came forward to greet her and take her by the arm.

'I have a table inside this tent for you, ma'am,' he told her. 'And if you need anything at all, Mr Dowling, my secretary, will procure it for you.' He indicated a tall, thin young man with an engaging grin, who bowed to the ladies.

'How kind,' smiled Lady Fording. She waved a hand towards Anna, who was carrying a basket. 'We have brought some of our special Italian cakes as a gift.'

Giles glanced at the basket, then he raised his eyes to give Anna a slightly quizzical look. She stared back, not sure now that this had been a good idea. But the *contessa* and her mother had been happy making their cakes. And in the family discussion a few days earlier, it was Signor di Cassagna who had suggested the matter. Anna saw Giles exchange a bow with Signor di Cassagna. He did not speak, however and returned his attention to the ladies, ushering them inside.

Lord Charles was blocking Anna's way. He looked at her with frank appreciation. 'Servant, Miss Lawrence,' he began. 'Allow me to tell you that you look most becoming in that colour. It almost matches my jacket, what?'

At once, his brother was there. 'Charles,'

— his voice was quiet but deadly — 'why not relieve Miss Lawrence of that basket?'

Charles raised his eyebrows but made no protest, simply doing as he was bid. Giles waited until his brother had followed the *contessa* into the tent. 'I trust you will have a pleasant afternoon,' he said, with a smile that made her heart seem to jump into her throat, as if his dear face and impeccable appearance had not already caused a flutter in her bosom. 'I shall do my best to keep an eye on you. Some of my guests are not very respectable.' He turned his head towards the other large tent close by and gave a tiny sigh.

'The Prince?' she exclaimed, with a gurgle of laughter.

Giles nodded sadly. 'Alas, yes — and especially his aides. You are warned.' He turned away then as more guests were approaching. Anna went inside, still smiling. She found Mrs Barton and Emily already seated with Lady Fording. Emily cast an eager glance at the basket. 'You have brought some of your delicious cakes, ma'am.'

'These are gifts for our host,' cut in Signor di Cassagna, 'as a mark of our esteem.'

He did not need to be quite so abrupt! Anna looked at poor Emily, red now with embarrassment. But Mr Dowling was murmuring in Mrs Barton's ear. A second or two later, waiters were pouring lemonade into glasses for the two girls and champagne for all the others. Long dishes of meat pies and savoury little patties were placed on the crisp white cloth, followed by bowls of fruit and cakes.

'I think we will not starve,' whispered Anna. 'And then, perhaps we can go and see the cricket match.'

Emily was already attacking a large slice of meat pie. 'It has been a long time since breakfast,' she whispered back. 'I am *famished*!'

It was noticeable that as they drank their champagne, the others became more relaxed and happy. Only Signor di Cassagna was rather silent, but at least he was not ranting about Italian politics. The ladies were happily settled, chatting and observing the other guests now filling the large tent. When Emily mentioned the cricket match, her grand-mother suggested she could go with Anna to watch for a while. The girls gladly jumped up and hurried out to enjoy the various activities and displays.

'I do not care very much for Signor di Cassagna,' said Emily. 'He made me feel like a thief.'

'Oh, do not let him trouble you.' Anna was casting an eager eye around as she spoke. 'He is very moody. It is best not to upset him, if possible.'

'Where are we going?' Emily had to scurry along to keep up with Anna, who was much taller and more athletic.

'Er . . . everywhere. We should see everything. Let's start over there.' She pointed to the musicians, seated under a canopy near the smaller tents. Many of the guests were seated round the small tables near the open air buffet. Waiters bustled to and fro, their trays laden. The conversations sounded louder and more cheerful now. Some people, like Anna and Emily, were strolling here and there.

The girls reached the cricket pitch and a couple of young officers bowed to them. 'Are you familiar with the game, ladies?' asked one of them. 'Only too happy to assist you in followin' it, y'know.'

With a smile, Anna led Emily away. 'There was no need to do that,' Emily said crossly, 'he was perfectly polite.'

'Yes, but your grandmother would not wish you to strike up a friendship until she has met the young man.'

'This is ridiculous,' grumbled Emily. 'If that same young officer asked me to dance at the Castle Tavern, Grandmama would say yes.'

'Of course, but that is another matter.'

There was no sign of Giles anywhere. Swallowing her disappointment, Anna was about to suggest that they return to their group when a sudden hum of activity caught her attention. Several carriages were arriving and now she saw Giles leave a group of guests and stride forward to bow as an immensely corpulent gentleman climbed down from the first coach.

'Oh,' breathed Emily, 'is that the Regent?'

'Yes, I recognize his figure. And he is as amiable as he is large.'

'It is a great honour for Lord Longwood, is it not? Grandmama says the Regent hardly ever goes outdoors because he is so susceptible to chills and putrid sore throats.'

Anna watched the Prince and his companions disappear into the tent. 'I do not think two minutes of fresh air can be harmful,' she said drily. 'If he took more exercise in the open air, he would be more healthy.'

The little stir of excitement was over. No doubt Giles would stay with his royal guest for some time. They had not met anyone they knew. If Belinda was here, she must be inside the main tent with her mother. Anyway, Anna knew she could not do or say anything that would create a stir. She must avoid attracting any notice whatsoever.

23

Anna hastened into the main tent and collided with Mr Dowling, who was rushing out. He stepped back with an apology. 'Miss Lawrence, I am mortified.'

She smiled at him. 'It is of no consequence. I am not made of china.'

He looked at her with a wry smile. 'Yet you have all the appearance of a delicate ornament.'

'That is an unusual compliment,' she said, 'that is, I *think* it was a compliment.' She felt herself to be blushing.

He hesitated, then grinned. 'Of course it was.' His gaze was certainly admiring. Anna noticed what a warm smile he had. She felt a slight stirring of interest. He might be someone worth talking to about many of her ideas. A figure materialized by them. Giles looked from one to the other, his eyes gleaming very green.

'Mr Dowling, I am so glad you have the time to entertain my guests.'

The young man gulped. His hand went up to tug at his neckcloth. 'I am on my way back, sir, but unfortunately I — er — accidentally collided with these young ladies.'

Giles simply nodded and watched as his secretary hurried out. He then transferred his gaze to Anna, his expression completely bland. Anna looked from him to Emily, who was grinning broadly. She raised her chin and waited.

'I trust you are tolerably well entertained?' enquired their host.

'Thank you, sir, it is a splendid picnic,' said Emily. 'Was that the Regent we saw arriving just now?'

'It was indeed,' Giles drawled. His eyes returned to Anna's face. She stared back, remembering his warning.

'I must return to Lady Fording,' she said, 'she might be waiting me.' Would he understand from that statement that she intended to stay in here, well out of harm's way?

'Lady Fording and her group have gone to listen to the band,' he told her, drawing out his snuffbox and taking a tiny pinch between finger and thumb. Languidly he raised it to his nostrils, all the time keeping his emerald gaze on Anna. Why was he cross with her? She was doing her best to be discreet.

'We have already been to watch the band,' said Emily, 'and I am thirsty. Perhaps we could have some lemonade while we are here.'

'Or some milk,' murmured Giles.

'I beg your pardon?' Emily was bewildered. Anna simply glared into those mocking green eyes.

'Ah, my lord, you are still here.' Mr Dowling was back, his eyes fixed earnestly on Giles. 'The Prince has another request, sir . . . '

'Mr Dowling,' said Giles, in a tone of reproof, 'that is twice you have upset these ladies.' His shoulders shook slightly as they both reassured him it was no such thing. 'I regret we must leave you,' he interrupted them, 'but you are quite safe in here.' With a polite smile, he took his secretary by the arm and stepped aside with him.

They returned to their table, where Emily pounced on the lemonade jug and filled two glasses. 'Did he really offer us milk?' she asked. 'What a strange idea. Ugh!'

'There is a stone in my sandal,' said Anna. 'Let us sit down for a few minutes. No one will see what I am doing behind this long tablecloth.' She proceeded to unknot her shoe ribbons to slide the sandal off and remove the sharp stone. There were very few people left in the tent now. The footmen were clearing away the used dishes and refilling the fruitbowls. Leaning down to retie her sandal, Anna breathed in the smell of crushed grass and the rather steamy warmth of the enclosed space. She straightened up to see Emily popping something into her mouth.

'Shall we go and watch the cricket match?' she was saying, when her friend's face dropped. 'Oh no,' murmured Emily.

The reason for this quickly became apparent. Signor di Cassagna rushed up to them, his expression impatient. 'The Prince Regent is just setting off to watch the cricket match,' he announced. 'Quickly, take our little gift to him.'

Anna stared at him, wondering if she had heard aright. 'To the Prince? Surely not at this moment! And it is for the *contessa* to offer them. She went to so much trouble to make them.'

He waved his hand urgently. 'No, no and no! She is not here. It must be now. The Prince will accept them if you hurry. Come . . . if you please,' he growled. His eyes bored into her.

Anna darted a glance at Emily. The girl was shaken by nervous giggles. At the same time, she was looking guilty. Anna frowned. 'But sir, it is not proper for me to approach His Highness. It will look most indelicate. And maybe his aides will not allow me close to him,' she added hopefully.

He muttered something under his breath.

His face was thunderous. 'How dare you deny my express order. You are simply a paid companion and must do as you are bid!'

At that she stiffened and went pale. He ground his teeth. 'I will not tell you again,' he spat out. He grabbed her arm and pulled her to her feet. 'Do it. Now!'

Very reluctantly Anna took the basket he thrust into her hands. Surely the gift was not worth so much fuss. It was just a few little sweetmeats. Moreover, it would seem as if she was flaunting herself in front of the Prince. She turned back towards him. 'Really, sir . . .'

'*Maladetta!*' With one stride he reached her and thrust her towards the tent doorway. 'And remove this,' he snarled, pulling her wrap off her shoulders. She gave a gasp of outrage. He was indeed using her as a bait. But he was in such a dangerous mood she decided to appear to follow his wishes. Once outside she would seek help.

Slowly, head erect, she walked out of the tent. And then, there was Emily by her side. 'That was terrible,' whispered the younger girl, 'do you think he is mad? I will come with you.'

'Oh, Emily, how very kind. But your grandmama would never permit it — or forgive me if I let you do so . . . Emily . . . ?'

Emily was holding a hand to her stomach. Her face was greenish-grey. She lurched towards Anna. 'I f-feel so unwell,' she whispered, 'my stomach burns . . . ' She staggered a couple of steps away and bent over. She began to retch violently.

Anna put the basket down and started towards her. In a flash, Signor di Cassagna seized her arm. 'No!' he thundered. 'Leave her to me. Take this gift to the Prince now. Hurry.' He pushed the basket at her.

Anna wrenched her arm free. 'How can you be so cruel? Emily needs help.'

'Yes,' he hissed, 'I will help her. Do as I say, now!'

Her eyes narrowed as she watched his face working. 'Why is it so urgent? Just what is in those cakes?'

He clutched his hair and swore loudly in Italian. Anna rushed over to Emily. The girl was on her knees, trembling and sobbing. She appeared to have brought up the whole contents of her stomach. *Just as well*, thought Anna. She put a hand to Emily's forehead. It was clammy and her skin was pasty.

They had begun to attract attention. A woman came forward to help and Anna requested some water and a cloth. They wiped Emily's face and made her rinse her mouth out before she sank to the ground and curled up, moaning with pain. Desperately, Anna looked around. She realized Mr Dowling was hovering nearby. Leaving the other lady to stay by Emily, Anna hastened to him.

'My friend is very unwell,' she told him, 'we need to take her home.'

'I will have a carriage brought up at once,' he said.

'Thank you. Her grandmother should be fetched.'

He shook his head. 'It would be best to avoid creating a stir. First let us tend to the invalid.'

He hurried away and she turned back towards where Emily was lying on the grass. As she looked at the pathetic little form, so limp and lifeless, Anna felt a stab of fear. Emily must have eaten one of the cakes from the basket. It was true that she had found them delicious when she came for tea. But this time it seemed that someone had put some kind of poison in them.

There was no time to think about the matter now. She hurried back to Emily's side. The other woman looked up. 'I cannot rouse her,' she whispered. 'Whatever has happened to her?'

'I think she ate or drank something that disagreed with her,' said Anna. She drew in a shaky breath. 'I think — ' She bit the words off. She must not give voice to her suspicion that Emily had been poisoned. 'I think she will be better if we can get her home,' she finished lamely.

She looked round for the basket. If anyone else ate one of those cakes and suffered the same fate as Emily, the scandal would be too awful to contemplate. It would probably give poor Lady Fording another heart seizure. But there was no sign of the basket, or of Signor di Cassagna. And then there was too much to do for Anna to think of him for quite some time.

Mr Dowling returned together with Giles. Emily was completely limp and her breathing was shallow. Anna saw Giles exchange a grave look with his secretary. He bent and slid his arms under Emily's shoulders and knees and lifted her easily. He took a pace towards the carriage which had been brought up.

'Miss Lawrence,' he said over his shoulder, 'will you accompany us, if you please.'

She hastened to his side and at his request climbed into the carriage first to support Emily's head as he lifted her in. Giles climbed in as well and they set off back towards the road.

'What is going on?' he asked in an undertone.

Anna hesitated. Her suspicions now seemed too fantastic to be true. She looked at Emily's pale face and then lifted her head to see Giles looking very grave.

'Well?' His voice was cold. 'Just what were you doing with that basket of sweetmeats? You were on your way to the Regent's tent, were you not?' His eyes swept over her, lingering on her bare shoulders and the creamy flesh of her bosom. 'Why have you removed your wrap? I would consider your appearance to be . . . shall we say, inviting, especially to that bunch of roués.'

By now, Anna was nearly as pale as Emily. He suspected her of being a willing partner in that plot. She stared into his cold, haughty face and felt a strange, icy sensation in her head. How could he even think such a thing? She clenched her teeth together and sat stiffly upright. Her throat ached so much she could not say a word.

'I suppose this young lady sampled one of those cakes,' his cold voice went on. 'I do trust nobody else did so or there will be the devil to pay. Do you know what the punishment is for such a crime, Miss Lawrence? And are you aware of how much more serious it is to attempt to kill a member of the Royal Family?'

Anna could hardly breathe. This was a

worse nightmare than anything she could have dreamed of. She felt a grey mist rise about her and was afraid she might faint. She fought it down by concentrating on Emily. But the nightmare could still get worse.

'The basket?' she croaked.

'Ah, the evidence.' She heard him draw in a deep breath. 'I trust Mr Dowling has found it.'

The coach slowed and stopped. They had reached the Bartons' house. With some difficulty they got Emily out of the carriage and Giles carried her into the house and up to her room. Anna followed, still icy cold with shock and despair. How could Giles assume she would want to harm anyone? And what was going to happen to poor Emily? She gave a sob as she thought of all the people who were going to be alarmed and distressed by this.

The housekeeper rushed off to find a hot brick to put at Emily's feet. Her maid was called to undress her. Giles took Anna by the arm and led her downstairs to the sitting room. Anna realized she was trembling. His hand on her arm felt warm and solid. But he was so angry with her! He thought she was a murderess.

He shut the door and led her over to an upright chair. 'Now then,' he said, 'you must tell me the whole story. It was only a short while since I left you. How could your friend poison herself in that time?'

'Do you truly believe I was trying to poison the Prince?' she asked, staring at him painfully.

He gripped the back of a chair. He kept a frowning gaze on her. 'I am not assuming anything. I am dealing in facts. And looking at you, it is obvious you are — yet again — dressed to attract attention.'

She glanced down briefly. 'Signor di Cassagna took my wrap,' she muttered.

Giles stepped forward and inspected her arm. 'Did you know you have bruises on your arm?'

She rubbed it. 'Are there? It certainly feels painful.' She looked up at him warily. 'What are you going to do with me?'

He sighed and straightened up, moving across to the fireplace. He set one hand on the mantelpiece and scowled down at it. 'I have yet to decide.'

There was a knock at the door. A maid came in, carrying a cup and saucer, which she set down by Anna. Astonished, Anna saw it was hot milk.

'How did she know . . . ?'

'I told her,' Giles snapped. 'I remembered your taste for such a comfort. You had better drink it,' he added when she sat there, frozen. 'You are almost as pale as your friend.'

There was another interruption. A doctor had arrived, sent by the efficient Mr Dowling. Giles went out to speak to him. During the long pause that followed, Anna fretted about Emily and wondered whether the contessa had had any part in the plot to poison the cakes. She decided that it could not be possible. Even if her cousin ranted endlessly and showed his displeasure with everything they did, the contessa did not appear to be afraid of him, or even very well disposed towards him. He had accompanied her from Italy at his father's orders. He had no hold over her.

At last, Giles came back into the room. 'The doctor has examined Miss Barton and says she should make a good recovery,' he announced.

Her face shining with relief, Anna jumped up. 'May I see her?'

He shook his head. 'Not at present.'

She clutched at her throat. At the same moment her temper flared. 'You *cannot* believe I-I . . . ' She choked on the words. From long experience she knew that it was no use to protest when people did not want to listen. Her own mother was always deaf when Anna tried to tell her about Sir Benjamin's drunken attempts to corner her. The anger drained away. Her hands dropped to her sides in a defeated gesture.

She realized that Giles was right in front of her and forced herself to lift her chin so she could meet his eyes. He was examining her face very keenly. He held out a long scarf. 'Put this on,' he said. 'The housekeeper has provided it. Now I will return you to the picnic.' He opened the door and waited for her.

Without a word she settled the wrap about her shoulders and preceded him out of the room, back into the road and into the carriage. She found that he was climbing in beside her, but she turned her head to stare blindly out of the window. If he truly thought she was guilty, why was he not taking her to the prison?

24

They completed the short drive without a word being spoken. Anna found the tension unbearable. She was devastated by his lack of trust in her. How could Giles consider her to be guilty of such a criminal act? She kept her head turned to the window but in truth, the scene outside was a blur.

The coach rounded a corner and lurched, throwing Giles against her. He murmured a word of apology and grasped the strap-handle. Anna folded her arms tightly round her ribs and lifted her chin, still keeping her head towards the window. She breathed in that enticing scent of cologne and wondered desperately how she could clear up this misunderstanding.

When they stopped moving and the coachman opened the door, she stirred at last and focused on her surroundings. She saw the tents, the bright colours of the stalls and the flags. To her surprise there were people strolling around and the sound of cheers and shouts coming from the cricket match. Anna felt she had been away for many hours but everything was continuing just as it had been before Emily ate the cake.

Why had he brought her back here? She was too numb to reason it out. Giles had already jumped down. He offered his hand to Anna. She looked at it as if it were a snake about to bite her.

'If you please,' he said in a soft, cold voice, 'you will get down and smile and laugh with me. We are going to show everyone that Miss Barton's indisposition is nothing serious.' He looked at her pinched face. 'Come, my infant, we cannot have any scandal.'

Grasping the good sense of his words, she nodded and took his hand. It held hers firmly and somehow communicated a sense of comfort. Unbidden, a memory came into her mind of how he had helped her that day in Alton. She gripped his hand rather tighter than manners allowed, but he made no comment, merely smiling at her as if she had made a witty remark.

'Speak and smile, dammit!' he whispered, a pleasant smile on his own face.

'Ah — er . . . yes,' she stuttered, coaxing her unwilling lips into an upward curve. She shook herself mentally. If Mrs Chetwynd could smile endlessly, then so could she. By thinking that Emily was recovering, she brightened and gave Giles her usual beaming smile. Just in time, as the woman who had helped Emily was coming up to them to enquire how the invalid was doing.

'Such a brave young lady,' said Giles, 'to have ventured out with a bad migraine, but her maid assured us that after a period of rest, she will soon recover.'

'She did so want to see the cricket match,' put in Anna and had the satisfaction of seeing Giles give her an approving nod. They repeated this story a number of times as they slowly made their way over to the cricket match. There were many cheers and shouts of encouragement coming from that part of the field. It seemed that not everyone had noticed Emily's indisposition and sudden departure.

'A migraine was an inspired idea,' whispered Anna, under cover of another burst of cheering, 'but why go to all this trouble?'

He gave her one of his enigmatic green looks. 'Do you think I will allow my party to be spoiled by a cowardly and murderous plot? Especially when the target was my chief guest, the Prince Regent himself.'

Her hand clutched hard on his arm and he bent his head to look closely at her face. 'Did you know just what you were doing, Miss Lawrence?'

She drew in a shuddering breath. 'I was only going out of the tent because he was becoming violent. I had no intention of taking those cakes to anyone.'

'Ah, Longwood!' Lady Beveridge pounced on Giles. 'Splendid event, splendid. Dear Belinda is enjoying it all. But it is an age since we saw you. Pray stay a while and tell me how your dear father is doing?'

'I fear, ma'am, that it is a long time since I had any communication with His Grace.' drawled Giles, at his most languid. He was ready to move on, but Belinda was blocking his way. She stared coldly at Anna's hand, still on Giles's arm.

'Oh, dear me, poor Belinda,' said Anna very clearly, 'I fear you are not enjoying this delightful picnic as you ought.' She smiled sweetly and had the satisfaction of seeing Belinda's eyes flash.

'Come, Miss Lawrence, we have a commission to execute. Ladies, pray excuse us.' He gave an irresistible smile and led her away.

'I see how useful it is to be a rake,' Anna hissed through her smiling lips. 'Your charm reduces them all to a jelly. Even Lady Beveridge ceases her hostilities.'

'It is just as well I can charm them,' he retorted, 'when you seem determined to ruin my picnic. I am in constant apprehension of what you might do next.'

'Well, I did not do anything to provoke that horrid woman,' she retorted. Giles seemed amused by this but he would not explain. And in another moment they were again talking to more people. Anna spotted Lady Fording and Mrs Barton seated on one of the benches and apparently enjoying the cricket, the company and the fine weather. 'It seems a shame to spoil their pleasure,' she murmured to Giles.

'We must do it, however. Miss Barton's grandmother should return home at once. She will have to know what happened as soon as she reaches the house. For now, let us stick to the story of the migraine.'

Mrs Barton went off, escorted by Giles, while Anna sat down next to Lady Fording. She did her best to answer that lady's questions but all the while the realization was growing of how close they had come to a catastrophe. Had she made herself into an accessory to murder? Giles appeared to consider that her actions constituted guilt. However, he had not had her arrested — yet! A chill swept over her, making gooseflesh rise on her arms.

She began to feel so wretched that it was a struggle to sit calmly on the bench and clap with everyone else when the batsmen hit a boundary or made a good run. And when she thought of Emily, lying on the grass, curled up into a limp little ball, her face grey, she wanted to be sick herself.

'Anna, will you fetch me a glass of lemonade, if you please. I find all this cheering has made me thirsty.'

'Do you wish to return to the tent, dear ma'am?'

Lady Fording shook her head. 'I am enjoying the sunshine.'

Anna was glad to have a few minutes to be alone. She crossed to the tent and went in. It was deserted now. The smell of grass and hot humanity made her wrinkle her nose. Suddenly she remembered her wrap and looked around for it. She was searching among the tables and chairs when a hand clamped on her upper arm and squeezed cruelly.

'You *puttana*, you spoiled everything!' hissed Signor di Cassagna.

'Let me go!' Anna tugged in vain. 'You are hurting me.'

He bared his teeth. 'You think I care for that? If you did as I told you, I would now be celebrating a great success. I would be famous throughout Europe as the man who killed the Prince Regent.'

'By using your own cousin — and me.' Anna stuck her chin out. 'You coward.'

For answer, he brought his free hand across her face in a stinging slap. It drew the attention of a group of men just coming into the huge tent. Anna gasped with shock. The pain made her eyes water and her head ring. Then he began to shake her violently. She was so dizzy she scarcely realized when someone prised his grip off her and gentle hands pushed her down onto a chair. Her head was firmly pressed down onto her knees.

When at last the whirling sensation faded and she could look up she found a number of men close by. Lord Charles Maltravers and Mr Dowling were standing one each side of Signor di Cassagna. Between herself and the *signore* was Giles. There was a heated exchange going on but she simply could not take any of it in. She felt decidedly unwell.

'Lemonade,' she muttered to no one in particular, 'Lady Fording wants lemonade.' And with that she slipped to the ground. She revived before any of them could reach her. 'How could I do that?' she mumbled angrily. 'Not the thing at all.'

Someone was offering her a glass of water. It was Ned. She managed to hold it although her hands were trembling. There were so many things to cope with. 'I must find my white wrap,' she told him.

He looked at her in concern. 'In a moment. Is your face very sore?'

She put up a hand and winced at her own

touch. 'Have you found the ba — ' She broke off, remembering it was a secret.

'Don't worry,' he replied, 'we have the basket safe.'

She gaped at him. He gave her a gentle smile. 'Giles left us to do that while he took the young lady home. All's well — er — that is to say, except for you.'

'How can I get home without being seen?' she asked, then thought of her errand, 'and who will take Lady Fording her drink?'

Ned went over to a table and filled a glass with lemonade. He disappeared, to return shortly afterwards. 'That is done,' he assured her. 'Now, excuse me, business to deal with.' He rejoined the others, who were marching a protesting Signor di Cassagna outside. Anna's head was clearer now. She heard him say, 'I demand swords . . . ' Her eyes grew wide. They were going to fight a duel.

'No!' she called out, jumping up too hastily and spilling the water onto her skirt.

Giles looked round. He sighed and came back. 'Don't you think that is enough for one day? What a pickle you are. I will have a carriage brought for you in a few minutes.'

'But I cannot leave . . . ' she protested. 'must stay until L-Lady — '

'You are in no state to remain here,' he said coolly, taking her arm and urging her back onto her chair. 'Your left eye is swelling fast. Your appearance will cause a scandal.' He smiled faintly. 'And we are determined to avoid that.'

'What will you do with *him*?'

He straightened up. 'It is all decided. He will not bother you again.'

She wanted to ask him a dozen questions, but she was too exhausted to think any more. In addition she could hardly see out of her left eye. It felt very puffy when she put up her hand to touch — and even that was painful.

When Mr Dowling came a short while later to escort her to the carriage, Anna meekly took his proffered arm and found she needed his support to walk such a long way.

★　★　★

Giles watched the carriage set off. Beside him, Charles stood, frowning angrily.

'Brother, a simple picnic would have sufficed. We did not need all this intrigue as well. Life is quite exciting enough, being pursued by Lady Beveridge and the beauteous Belinda.'

Giles ignored his brother's grumbles. 'I look to you to find a pair of swords immediately.'

Charles snorted. 'Why me? Where am I

going to find swords? Barbaric, that's what it is! Why can't he go for pistols like normal men?'

Giles grinned. 'Because he's Italian . . . and he's seeking to establish his reputation as a great leader.'

Charles gazed in stupefaction. 'Reputation? Never heard such a load of rubbish. The man's a villain. Should be in gaol. And to strike Miss Lawrence in the face like that on top of the rest! Poor girl, I should think everyone here heard it.' He put a hand on his hip and shook his head severely, 'Fellow don't deserve you should call him out.'

'Now where have I seen that particular look before?' Giles considered. 'Ah yes. Our esteemed father — you have caught the mannerism exactly.'

'You don't fool me,' retorted Charles, 'just trying to put me off the scent. It's because of the female, ain't it? I tell you, Giles, this time you're caught.' He gave a satisfied chuckle.

'Swords! Now!' Giles punched his brother's arm and Charles shrugged, grinned and swaggered off, whistling. With a sigh, Giles made his way to the Prince Regent's tent for a polite visit. His royal guest would never know what schemes had been set in motion and how close he had come to an untimely end.

25

Anna frowned at her reflection in the mirror. Three days since the picnic and she still had rainbow colours round her eye. She stuck out her lower lip. She was desperate for some fresh air and exercise but the *contessa* kept insisting that she must not be seen in public. In Anna's mind, it was Lady Fording who was most likely to cause comment. She had become grey and shrunken with shame over her nephew's crazed plan and how close he had come to carrying it out. It was no use for Anna to assure her that she would never have gone near the Prince Regent with the basket of cakes.

'But he poisoned little Emily, my dearest friend's flesh and blood,' was Lady Fording's reply. Then she would press her handkerchief to her eyes and shake her head. Today, however, Anna found a more cheerful atmosphere when she entered the drawing room. Lady Fording was actually smiling. 'Henrietta has just this minute sent a note to say that Emily is quite recovered,' she announced.

'I am truly thankful to hear that,' beamed

Anna. 'It is such a relief. Dear ma'am, do you think we might venture out in your carriage this afternoon? You truly would benefit from a change of scene.'

A little to her surprise, Lady Fording nodded assent and even the *contessa* agreed with her. But then, she was always anxious to see her mother get well again. 'If I give you some rice powder,' she said, looking closely at Anna's eye, 'it will mask the bruise from a distance. How clever you were to tell the servants that you slipped and banged your head on a table . . . but I still dread any scandal.' She shuddered.

It seemed almost like an adventure to leave the house and breathe in the fresh sea air. Once they were in the barouche and driving along the road out of town Lady Fording seemed to revive.

'By now Enrico must have left the country,' she said. 'Dear Lord Longwood informed me that he would personally see him embark. But oh, my poor brother, what anguish he will feel when he learns what his youngest son has done this time.'

'But surely your nephew will not leave without trying again to carry out his plan,' objected Anna.

'He has no choice,' put in the *contessa*, 'he was wounded in the duel.' She stopped at

Anna's gasp of horror. 'But *of course* there was a duel. And Enrico is too weak to attempt anything else.'

'And . . . Lord Longwood . . . ?' faltered Anna. She imagined Giles with a wound that would slowly kill him. Previously she had thought having a duel fought over her would be romantic and exciting but in reality it seemed a brutal way of settling a problem.

The *contessa* shrugged. 'I believe my cousin had the worst of it,' she said. With that, Anna had to be satisfied.

They reached the house again and were preparing to descend when two horsemen approached. Anna shrank back and pulled her hair over her left eye. Then she heard a well-known voice and dared to glance up. Giles was raising his hat.

'How fortunate that we met you,' he drawled. 'Mr Caldecott and I are just on our way back from Newhaven.' Lady Fording gave him a sharp look and he smiled at her. 'Yes, ma'am, he has sailed on the packet. All is now well.'

She took a deep breath and reached up to clasp his hand. 'Thank you for that.'

Watching this exchange, it seemed to Anna that Giles looked more weary than she had ever seen him. *Oh! He must be wounded!* She sat in silence, wishing she dared ask about it. Nobody spoke to her. But at the last second, as Giles was touching his whip to his hat, he gave her a wink.

★ ★ ★

'Miss Lawrence is a good sport,' remarked Ned, when they had trotted out of earshot of the ladies. 'She doesn't make any fuss over a black eye. But that fellow di Cassagna, is a rank coward. Fancy using a girl to carry out his attempt at murder. And then to assault her like that!'

'He is obviously deranged,' responded Giles. 'Whatever one thinks of the Regent's political views, there is no way he should meet his end in a sordid poisoning.' His jaw tightened. 'And at my party of all places.'

He had exacted revenge for that. Signor di Cassagna had chosen swords and he had drawn the first blood, wounding Giles in the shoulder. But Giles had always enjoyed fencing and he was a master with the rapier — as Signor di Cassagna then realized when Giles dealt him two wounds in quick succession and forced him to yield. Even then the villain would not admit that he had poisoned the cakes. But Giles considered it was proof enough that when they set the basket of cakes in front of him and ordered him to eat them, he had refused to touch them.

'Well,' Ned said, breaking in on his thoughts, 'life has certainly taken some unexpected turns this summer.'

Giles gave his oldest friend a suspicious look. 'What is that supposed to mean?'

Ned blew out a long breath. 'Been watching you, ever since that night you came to my room and drank a bottle of brandy. Knew then something fundamental had changed.' He grinned at his friend's outraged face.

'How many times do I have to say that it is a completely different situation?' protested Giles. 'She is a young lady who needs protection.'

Ned guffawed.

'Not that kind of protection, you dolt!' He simmered in silence, but Ned had not finished.

'You've given Sophia the brush-off in no uncertain way.'

'I told you she wearied me when we were still in London.' Giles shrugged and caught his breath at the sudden sharp pain in his shoulder. The long ride had not helped. 'And there are plenty of other willing females.'

'Ah, but these days you're not showing interest in any females bar one.'

'You know, Ned, you can be tedious. Just keep your observations to yourself,' snapped Giles.

'Just acting as a good friend should.' Ned was still grinning, damn him. 'But I would not wager on Sophia giving up gracefully. And if she thinks she's been slighted, she's one who will take revenge.'

That night, as he lay in bed and eased his throbbing shoulder into a more comfortable position against the pillows, Giles recalled that comment. Ned was an astute observer of people. He had spotted the changes that Giles did not yet fully accept. And he was quite right about Sophia. He frowned up at the canopy as he wondered what form her revenge would take.

★   ★   ★

Now that a dusting of rice powder was enough to disguise Anna's fading bruises, the *contessa* let it be known that her mother was well enough to receive visitors. As Anna had guessed, the first visitor was Sophia. She entered the drawing room in yet another striking ensemble and with her usual dazzling smile. The greetings were scarcely over when she plunged into the latest gossip.

It was plain even to the *contessa* that

251

nobody had any idea about the poisoning plot or the duel that had followed. If anybody had the faintest suspicion, it would be Sophia — and she would have enjoyed rubbing salt in the wounds with spiteful comments and teasing questions. Listening to her tittle-tattle about some of the more indiscreet holiday-makers, Anna breathed a silent sigh of relief. She acknowledged just how skilled Giles had been in concealing the whole episode from so many people.

Sophia now came to her main item of news. 'I myself am being very ardently pursued.' Sophia smiled around generally. She contrived to keep her eyes on Anna as she spoke. 'He is so impatient for my answer, but I told him I need time to consider.' She batted her eyelashes and looked down modestly.

'But this is so exciting,' cried the *contessa*, setting her cup down and clasping her hands at her bosom. 'Is it someone we know, dear Sophia?'

Sophia tittered, one hand over her mouth. 'Oh, everyone knows him. Such a rake . . . can he ever reform? That is why I need time before I decide.'

The *contessa* leaned forward eagerly. 'The only rake I know is Lord Longwood.'

Again Sophia simpered and folded her

252

hands in her lap. Watching her discreetly, Anna was *almost* certain it was all an act. But her heart seemed to have dropped into her boots. She set her own plate down, the slice of cake quite untouched. There seemed to be a big lump in her throat. Nothing, she thought, could end her friendship with Giles more effectively than his marriage to Sophia.

By the time she was able to attend to the conversation again, Sophia was urging the ladies to visit the shops, where, she said, there were some very stylish new gowns on display. The *contessa* was so tempted by her friend's description of these new garments that she felt able to face the world again.

When Sophia had left, Lady Fording rubbed her hands together and announced, 'If that woman can persuade you to get back to a normal life, I am almost in charity with her.'

'Whatever can you mean, Mama? Sophia is always gracious — and she has such an eye for fashion . . . '

Lady Fording looked at Anna and raised her brows. Anna gave a half smile in return. It was comforting that Lady Fording also mistrusted Sophia. But Anna still felt downcast by the story of the ardent suitor and an offer of marriage. After the weeks in Brighton, she had seen enough of society to know that the strict rules of behaviour taught at her school in Bath might be essential for young debutantes but in reality life was more complex. So many married ladies seemed to have a great deal of freedom. And young, widowed ladies could get away with perfectly scandalous behaviour, so long as they had enough money to maintain their independence.

As she walked Beppi the next morning, Anna saw some riders returning from their morning outing on the Downs. How she longed to gallop freely over the countryside. She still had over thirteen months to wait before reaching the age of twenty-one. Then she would have an allowance and buy a superb horse for herself. Meanwhile, she pondered on the many problems confronting her. It was by no means certain that she would be asked to go to Italy with Lady Fording. And if Sophia managed to draw Giles back into her net, Anna knew she would be unable to look to him for any more help.

She was still wondering what the future held for her when she returned to the house. Opening the drawing-room door to let Beppi in, she saw a gentleman bowing over Lady Fording's hand. He straightened up and turned. 'Ah, Miss Lawrence, I am delighted to see you are well enough to go out once more.' Giles was regarding her, his mocking green gaze travelling from her head to her toes and back again.

Her heart was thudding at such a rate she could not speak. She feasted her eyes on his arrogant face and dark curly hair. That lock that tumbled over his brow . . . how many times had her fingers itched to smooth it back. As always he was dressed with immaculate style, his russet jacket fitting him exactly. She was aware how tall he was and what long legs he had. All this in the time it took to curtsy and sit down.

Giles turned back to his hostess. 'And I trust you will join me for tea at the Castle Tavern this afternoon,' he said, resuming the conversation that Anna had interrupted. 'It is time you all took up your usual activities before people remark on your long absence from the social scene.'

'You are right,' nodded Lady Fording. 'Beatrice has been very upset, but thanks to her friend, she is now willing to venture out again.'

At the mention of the 'friend' Giles frowned for a moment. Anna saw it. Her spirits rose a little. But then he said, 'Oh, Sophia has no doubt discovered some new fashions to inspect.' And her heart sank again. He must be close to her to call her *Sophia*!

Anna brooded on how unsuitable Sophia was for Giles. Behind the dazzling smile she was sharp and spiteful, her clothes were flashy and she was much too selfish to make him happy.

'Miss Lawrence?'

'Anna!'

What had she missed? Bewildered, she stared from one to the other.

'Anna,' repeated Lady Fording, mild reproof in her tone, 'were you not attending? Lord Longwood wishes to invite Mrs Barton and Emily as well. It is a good opportunity for you to call on them. A drive in an open carriage is quite unexceptionable.'

They were both watching her. She did not want to be alone with him, but at the same time she craved his company. She pressed her hands on the arms of her chair and slowly pushed herself upright. Surprisingly, her legs held her up. Giles rose to his feet at the same time, obviously impatient to be off. He was holding the door open even as Lady Fording was still giving Anna messages for Mrs Barton.

'Will you remember even the half of all that?' he asked, as he opened the front door for her.

'Oh — yes! It is always the same message. And in any event, they will meet this afternoon. It will be good for Lady Fording to go out and forget her woes.' She heaved a sigh. Her own woes were just beginning. But she was going to have one more ride in his curricle. She settled herself beside Giles. Morgan smiled and touched his hat to her. He swung up behind as Giles set off. How different things were now from that first journey from Alton to Rosevale Park. That seemed like a whole lifetime ago. She stared at her clasped hands, brooding on the events of the past two months.

'It is easy to see you are overjoyed to be in my company again,' Giles remarked in a chatty tone. She gave him a quick sideways look and raised her chin. Keeping her face rigidly towards the front, she said, 'I am sure it is always a pleasure to see your lordship.'

His face darkened. 'That was unworthy of you. I have gone to all this trouble, merely so I could get a few minutes alone with you to ask if all is well — '

'Well?' she exclaimed in a shrill voice. 'How can things be *well* — after what happened at the picnic.' She gave a shudder as the horror of that day swept over her again. She felt his hand grip her arm just above the elbow but she shook it off.

There was a muttered oath and the curricle stopped. Giles jumped down and lifted Anna down as well. 'We will walk the rest of the way,' he told Morgan, 'walk them.' He took her arm firmly and led her to the side of the road. There were plenty of people about now as well as carriages taking visitors in and out of the town. 'We only have a short time,' he said patiently, 'and I wish to know how you are. But we will not mention the events of the picnic in front of anyone, not even Morgan.' He looked at her face keenly. 'I am glad those bruises have faded. And now you must put the whole episode out of your mind. It is over.'

Unconsciously, she drew herself up. 'It has been a hard time.' The words tumbled out. 'So many shocks and a sense of shame at being caught up in a madman's plot — and the fear that Emily might not recover. I will never forget her lying there.' She gulped and turned to him, gripping his arms impulsively. 'You were simply marvellous. I cannot conceive how you managed it, but you have brought us all through the whole business without anyone else knowing anything about it.'

He gave an embarrassed shrug and then winced. Anna looked more closely at him. 'What is it? Oh, heavens above! That duel . . . you *were* injured.'

'It's nothing.' He smiled at her. 'Just a

scratch. See, we have arrived.' He gestured towards Mrs Barton's house on the other side of the road. Anna looked round and saw a cabriolet driving past. Its two occupants were both staring at her. She sighed. Lady Beveridge and her daughter were like a pair of avenging angels, always resentful and always appearing when least wanted. She forgot about them, however, in her relief at seeing a smiling Emily waiting to greet her in the entrance hall.

26

Giles's invitation was accepted with many smiles and exclamations of pleasure. Promising Emily that they would have a good talk that afternoon, and staying just long enough to be introduced to Emily's newly arrived brother, Jack, Anna allowed Giles to hurry her back out to his carriage for the short ride home. Giles took the reins and set off at a trot.

'I see you are wondering why Morgan is not accompanying us,' he began, glancing at her with a half smile.

Anna clasped her hands together tightly. 'I am glad of it because I wished for a moment alone with you.' She shook her head vigorously as he leaned forward to give her a roguish look. She gulped. 'Because I . . . to apologize for sometimes being troublesome.'

Giles raised his brows. 'Miss Lawrence, now I am alarmed. You are not yourself. I thought you spent every waking moment in devising adventures to lead yourself into danger and to keep me in constant anxiety.'

But Anna was too overwrought to appreciate his teasing. She was attempting to say a private goodbye to him before they all went their separate ways. Then she realized that the curricle had stopped moving. Giles was holding out a neatly wrapped package. 'Pray accept this,' he said, 'with my apologies for taking so long to find it.' His eyes were gleaming. 'Do open it,' he urged, 'I must see your face when you do.'

'For me?' Anna hesitated. He nodded and pressed the package into her hands. She pulled off the brown paper covering and stared wide-eyed at the slim, leather-bound copy of *The Corsair*. 'Oh!' She clutched it to her bosom as she raised her face to his. 'Oh, sir . . . '

He smiled again. 'My infant, it is not often you are so lost for words.' His face softened. 'But your expression speaks for you.'

Anna looked from the treasure in her hands to her dearest friend, so soon to be only her former friend. 'Th-thank you,' she whispered, and burst into tears.

At once he pulled out a snowy handkerchief. 'I was prepared for that,' he remarked to no one in particular and mopped her eyes. The whiff of his spicy cologne made her weep even more.

'Come now, that's enough,' he told her. 'I do not wish you to appear with red eyes at the tea party.'

She sniffed. 'It was so unexpected — and you do not like Lord Byron.'

'But you do.' He looked closely at her. 'Are you all right now?'

'I am sorry. Perhaps I am not quite myself yet.' She glanced at the precious book. Was it proper for her to accept it? But how could she refuse? He was her dearest friend and this was a fitting token to remember him by.

'Well,' he said, as he set the blacks trotting again, 'I hope I did the right thing in giving it to you today. Now I worry that you will begin reading it at once and we shall wait in vain for you this afternoon.'

'Of course not,' she protested, 'but tonight I shall read for as long as my candle lasts.'

Punctually at four o'clock the guests assembled at the Castle Tavern. Giles was waiting for them in the main reception room. Under the interested gaze of everyone there, he bowed and offered his arm to Lady Fording. 'As you have only just recovered from your indisposition, ma'am, I decided we should take a private room today,' he stated with a rakish smile at the old lady. She agreed without a blush that indeed, she must avoid too much excitement.

'Just so,' he nodded, 'although I trust you can cope with the addition of my brother and Mr Caldecott to our party?' Both these smartly dressed gentlemen bowed and Lady Fording nodded at them graciously. Giles led them all through into a cosy parlour, where a table was set invitingly with a crisp white cloth and dainty porcelain plates. There were enough dishes piled with fruit, patties and cakes to make Emily's eyes sparkle with anticipation and her brother to exclaim, 'Now this is something like!'

Giles seated Lady Fording in the hostess's place. 'I am sure Miss Lawrence will assist you, ma'am,' he purred, 'so that you need not overtax yourself.' He drew out the seat next to her and Anna sat down demurely. She was in her role as companion and helper, so was determined not to argue with him, or draw attention to herself.

In effect, it was Anna who poured and served the tea, handing cups to people as Lady Fording directed. She did her best to enjoy the occasion, even though it was painful to watch Giles. He was the perfect host and Anna was acutely aware of his charm. She recalled some verses by Lord Byron about dark torments of the soul and this time she understood the meaning of the word *anguish*. While Giles watched over her he had given her a sense of security that she had been missing for so long.

'Miss Lawrence, I fear you do not care for

those lobster patties. You have not touched the one on your plate.' Giles's voice roused her. She was obliged to smile and protest and force a mouthful past her unwilling lips. As soon as he turned his attention elsewhere, Anna carried a fresh cup of tea to Ned. She gave him a warm smile. 'I have been wanting to thank you for the glorious bouquet of roses you sent me. I never saw such beautiful flowers.'

'It was a trifle,' he protested, 'I did not know how to express my sympathy. Never saw such a shocking thing as when that villain attacked you!' He brooded for a while, his large dark eyes smouldering. Anna wondered whether she should rescue his teacup, which seemed in imminent danger of spilling its contents over his natty buff breeches. At the last second, just as she was reaching out her hand, he recalled himself and set the tea down.

At last the party divided into smaller groups. Anna and Emily were able to discuss the picnic and Emily's illness, but they were soon interrupted. Jack Barton sat down next to Anna.

'My sister tells me you are a famous rider, Miss Lawrence,' he said enthusiastically. 'What do you say to a gallop across the Downs on the next fine day?'

Anna shook her head. 'I am here to assist Lady Fording, sir, I am not free to go on pleasure outings.'

He slapped his hand hard on the table. 'That is not right. You should be able to have some leisure . . . Did not you say,' he went on, leaning forwards to address Emily, 'that you were both dancing at the assembly?' When his sister nodded, he turned eagerly back to Anna. 'At least I shall have the pleasure of standing up with you then, at the next ball. Is it agreed?'

Anna could do nothing other than smile and accept. He chatted on, monopolizing her attention until Emily at last told him they had something urgent to discuss. He moved away reluctantly and Emily confided in a whisper, 'He is very attracted to you. Can you not see?' She spoiled this, however, by giggling and adding, 'Jack is very susceptible to a pretty face. He is forever fancying himself in love.'

★ ★ ★

Giles moved from one guest to another, spending a few minutes with each. And all the time he was aware of Anna. She looked pale and heavy-eyed. Perhaps that was due to her injuries. He noticed how she talked to Ned for a short time. Then that puppy, young Barton, accosted her and settled in for a long conversation. It was obvious the young man admired her.

That was no surprise, but, as he watched discreetly, Giles could not tell how Anna was receiving the young man's advances. Of course, the three young people were all much of an age. He had shielded her from rakes such as his brother and Sir Bilton Kelly but now Giles felt he must not interfere. Perhaps this youngster was the right age to appeal to her. As he thought this, he became aware of something that should have been obvious: he was too old for her.

A hand squeezed his shoulder. Giles looked up to see Ned regarding him thoughtfully. 'Not the time to look so melancholy, old man. Your guests will notice.'

Giles took a deep breath. He assumed a bland expression. 'Ned, old fellow, you are too observant. But thank you.' He rose and strolled over to talk to the *contessa*. When he heard that she planned to take her mother to Italy before the end of September, he became seriously alarmed. This masquerade had gone on long enough. He must talk to Anna again and persuade her to return to her home.

27

'What a shame there is no dancing this evening, Miss Lawrence. We shall have to wait until tomorrow to stand up together.' Jack Barton was hovering eagerly as Emily and Anna found themselves seats within sight of Lady Fording and Mrs Barton. The two older ladies were settling down to an evening of cards and gossip with some of their acquaintances. The rooms were not so crowded tonight. There were definitely fewer people in the town these last few days.

However, Anna noticed that Belinda was present and she was taking a turn around the room with Charles. They were talking earnestly and for once, Belinda seemed animated. Giles had explained that the Beveridges were old family friends. No doubt that was why Belinda seemed to be confiding something to him. Anna saw him pat her hand and say something that made her smile — actually smile.

While she was marvelling over the difference that smile made to Belinda's face — making her ten times prettier than she was already, she heard an exclamation from Jack

Barton and then he asked his sister, 'Who is that beautiful creature over there, by the pillar?'

Emily turned in her chair. 'Goodness! Can you mean the dark-haired girl talking to Lord Charles Maltravers.'

'I do. Why is he so friendly with her?'

'Oh, Jack,' she sighed, 'never say you find her attractive. That is Belinda Beveridge and we are not on good terms with her.'

'Well, that is about to change,' he growled. 'Never saw anyone more taking in my life.' He continued to stare at Belinda, while Emily exchanged a speaking look with Anna, who was trying not to laugh. She found that Jack made her think of a puppy, full of good humour and eager to play with whatever caught his eye.

He was an amiable-looking young man, fairly tall and willowy and his clothes were very fashionable, although Anna considered his pantaloons were rather too yellow to be truly stylish. His brown hair was carefully arranged in the windswept style, which meant he was forever going across to a mirror to check that the upswept locks were still in place.

'Do sit down, Jack,' said Emily, 'we are getting a crick in our necks from looking up at you.'

He did sit down but was constantly twisting round to take another look at the latest object of his admiration. Meanwhile, Anna went to ask whether Lady Fording required any refreshment. She smiled fondly at the old lady, who was apparently winning at the card game. Satisfied that all was well, Anna returned to the group of young people. To her surprise, Charles and Belinda had joined the group and Jack was now happily chatting to Belinda. Even more surprising, Belinda was talking to him. She had abandoned her usual cool manners and seemed pleased with life.

Perhaps that was the effect Jack had on everyone, constantly rattling on with his cheerful nonsense. They were all laughing and talking animatedly, Anna included, when she became aware of a pair of green eyes in a very dark face. Giles was watching her, tight-lipped. Her brow creased as she wondered why he was so angry. Then he gave her a curt nod and walked on.

Emily laid a hand on her arm. 'I fear Lord Longwood is displeased,' she whispered.

Anna nodded dumbly. He had not even wanted to speak to her. She clasped her hands tightly against her stomach, trying to stop the sick feeling inside. Idly, she stroked the sticks of her fan while she went through the events of the day to see what had provoked such fury.

Then a voice spoke in her ear. 'Miss Lawrence, pray spare me a moment. I need to speak to you privately.' It was Sophia. She was wearing another shimmering gown, daringly low-cut and sewn with quantities of seed pearls. Her lips were smiling but her eyes were cold. Anna rose obediently and accompanied her across the passage into the other room. Sophia led her to one of the window recesses, where a draped curtain gave some privacy.

It was growing dusk outside, so this part of the room was in shadow. Wondering what Sophia was going to say, Anna stepped into the recess and found Sir Bilton Kelly standing there. She immediately turned round to walk away but her path was blocked by Sophia.

'Oh no, Miss Lawrence,' said that lady, her face stony now, 'I am sure you will be very interested in what dear Bilton has to say.'

Anna shot her a look of intense dislike. *Dear Bilton*, indeed! This was the woman's revenge because she suspected something between Anna and Giles.

Sir Bilton Kelly bent forward confidentially. He cleared his throat. 'Miss Lawrence, I have to tell you that His Highness has expressed a desire to see you again. I do assure you that he would be delighted to have you join him this evening. There will be music and you are partial to that, are you not? Eh, what do you say now?' He came a step closer.

The pair of them thought they had her neatly trapped but she was no wilting little miss to obey their orders! She took a step sideways, putting a space between herself and this obnoxious man with his dissipated face. As she moved she felt her fan knock against her hip. She opened it and fanned her hot face.

'I believe I told you before,' she said through gritted teeth, 'that you mistake me for some other kind of female. Please do not do so again.'

'Oh dear me,' drawled Sophia, 'I do believe the little milkmaid is vexed, Bilton.' She gave a shrill laugh.

'What do you mean — *milkmaid*? And I am not little!' Anna stared fiercely at Sophia, who was a head shorter than herself. Sophia's sneer changed to a look of alarm but she was not going to give up yet. Anna sensed the woman's determination, but to her relief, at that moment she spotted Giles across the room. He was with a group of his friends but he was looking her way. Then she realized that everyone was looking her way, some more discreetly than others. There was a slight hush, as if they were waiting for the outcome of this encounter. Anna knew then that Sophia was determined to compromise her. Well, even if Giles was angry, he would not refuse a direct appeal. She snapped her fan shut and placed the tip of her finger against it. She saw his suddenly intent look as he read the message. At once he was coming towards her. Relief shone in her face.

Sophia gave her a puzzled look and then glanced over her shoulder. Giles was close behind her. Sophia assumed a smile and placed herself directly in his path. 'Darling!' she purred, 'What a lovely surprise! I thought you had left town.' She reached out a hand to him but he ignored her.

'Is anything amiss?' His eyes bored into Anna.

She beamed at him. 'Not now.'

'Longwood, you interrupt us.' Sir Bilton Kelly puffed his chest out. 'We are having a delightful chat with Miss Lawrence, is that not so?' His face dared her to contradict him. At his most arrogant, Giles raised his quizzing glass and coldly examined the man through it. Anna found it surprisingly menacing. And sure enough it was not long before Sir Bilton Kelly's eyes fell and he began to fidget with his cravat.

'Darling!' Sophia protested, her voice sharp, 'do go away and let us finish our conversation.'

'I will speak to you shortly,' Giles told her. To Anna he said, 'Your friends are looking for you,' and offered his arm. She allowed him to lead her back through the large room and into the wide entrance hall.

'You have rescued me again,' she said, fanning herself.

He swung round and looked at her, his face dark and hard. His jaw seemed to be sticking out.

'Are you angry with me?' she blurted.

He shook his head in denial. Then he seized her arm and drew her towards the main door. 'Let us take a turn in the fresh air while I recover my temper,' he growled. 'It is quite the done thing,' he assured her when she looked a little doubtful. 'We can stroll outside for five minutes. It gives us more privacy to talk.'

But she waited in vain for him to speak as they paced along the footpath in the direction of the Pavilion and then turned back to walk down the road towards the sea. The evening air was mild and soothing. At last Giles remarked, 'How glad I am you carried my fan this evening.'

'How glad I am that Lady Fording taught

me how to convey messages with it — and that you can read them.'

'Well for you that I was there. But I fear Kelly is very persistent, like his master,' he added in an undertone.

'Why did Mrs Chetwynd call me a milkmaid?'

Giles breathed hard. 'You are flaxen-haired and blue-eyed. Exactly the style the Prince Regent favours.'

Anna raised both hands in exasperation. 'Surely his aide understands by now that I am never going to accept an invitation to the Pavilion.' She gave a faint smile. 'Yet when I arrived in Brighton, it was the summit of my ambition to attend a reception there.' They paced on a little way before she added, 'I have grown up a great deal, I think. But I do thank you with all my heart for your care of me.'

'Do not thank me. I am ashamed of the way you have been treated. But as for growing up — ' A short laugh broke from him. 'That leads me to another point — '

'I will not go home,' she interrupted, raising her chin. 'I can see by your face that you plan to suggest it once more.'

He sighed. 'Very well, I will refrain. But I am seriously concerned for your safety. And I can no longer protect you. Tomorrow I will be returning to London.'

The words echoed in her head. Her heart plunged down, down, into a deep, dark place. This was the last time she would see him, hear his voice, watch him smile! How could she bear it?

'So this is goodbye?' In spite of her efforts, her voice shook.

They walked to the bottom of the road and turned back up again before he said, 'Yes, Anna, this is goodbye. Promise me you will be very careful.'

She raised her face to his. 'If this is goodbye, may I ask you something?'

'Anything, my infant.'

'I want you to kiss me — properly.'

He gave a gasp of laughter. 'But that would be very improper.'

She grasped his jacket. 'Please . . . '

Giles darted a quick look around. The road was empty of people. He pulled her a few steps further along to a doorway. There he stood and looked at her intently. She gazed hopefully up into his green eyes. Then his mouth curved in a very slight smile and he slid his arms round her shoulders. She tensed, her hands by her sides, her heart hammering. But she wanted him to kiss her. Not like the time in the Pavilion when he had not meant to do it. This would be a proper kiss, to remember him by. She swallowed nervously.

'Properly, then,' he murmured and bent his head towards her face. He brushed his lips along her cheekbone, and down to her jaw. Anna shivered in anticipation. Her hands came up to grasp his upper arms. Giles tightened his hold, the hand at her shoulders pressing her closer to him, his other arm circling her slender waist. Then he kissed the hollow at the base of her neck and she tilted her head back. Her soft mouth opened on a long sigh and suddenly she was moulded against him. Her arms were round his neck.

He pulled her closer still and at last met her lips with his own. It was a totally unexpected shock of pleasure that swept away all power of thought. Her body seemed to be dancing on the inside with the excitement and pleasure of what he was doing to her. She loved the way she was squashed against his hard chest. She tightened her hold on him, breathing in the subtle fragrance of his cologne. Mindlessly she plunged one hand into his thick glossy hair. Giles increased the pressure of his kiss and Anna responded as best she could, aching for him to continue creating these magical sensations and never let her go.

All too soon he broke the kiss. His hands slipped up to her shoulders and grasped them firmly, prising her away from him. He lifted his head and looked at her out of glittering eyes. Anna's lip trembled. Reluctantly she let go of his hair and trailed her hands down his arms. Her legs felt decidedly unsteady at that moment. Her eyes never left his face.

He gave her a lopsided grin. 'Properly,' he said in a husky voice. 'Come, Miss Lawrence. We have been outside long enough.'

Anna continued to clutch at his arms. She shook her head, a puzzled frown on her face. 'I do not understand,' she said slowly, 'I thought a kiss would be complete in itself but somehow I feel — here' — she pressed one hand against her stomach — 'that something is missing?' She looked at Giles for an explanation.

He began to laugh. 'I am not about to answer that. Come along, my pickle, it is time to return.'

She was still preoccupied with trying to sort out the strange mixture of sensations and allowed him to propel her towards the entrance with a hand at her back. She felt as if she was floating, rather than walking as they went inside.

In the entrance hall, Giles ran a critical eye over her. 'You are quite tidy,' he murmured, a smile lighting his eyes, 'and now you really should rejoin your young friends. Farewell to you.' Suddenly his face went bleak and he turned away.

Anna wanted to call him back and beg him not to leave her. But she reminded herself sternly that she was just a little schoolgirl he had been kind to. She could never show that she loved him. She gulped. Dignity! Rather blindly, she went into the card room, stopping first by Lady Fording and then going back to sit down next to Emily. The young people were all still talking and joking together. When there was a pause in the conversation, Emily turned to look at Anna.

'Whatever did Mrs Chetwynd have to say that took so long?' she whispered. 'But I can see it was something nice. Your eyes are shining like stars.'

28

The *contessa* was upset, the following day, to receive a scented billet from Sophia, stating that that lady would not be able to attend the play as agreed that evening. 'Here is a disappointment,' she exclaimed, looking up. She flourished the letter and read aloud, '*By the time you receive this, I will no longer be in Brighton.*' The *contessa* looked at her mother. 'She says it was arranged very late last night so that she could not inform me at the card assembly. She folded up the letter and sighed. 'Mama, shall we leave Brighton as well?'

Lady Fording put down the magazine she was reading. 'Why should we do that, Beatrice? I shall not miss that one, with her artificial smiles. But while dear Henrietta remains in Brighton, I am happy to stay a little longer. I enjoy the animation here. *Non è vero*, Anna?' she added, turning to smile at her.

But Anna was not listening. *Sophia had gone to London!* Had she gone together with Giles? Had he known about that when he was walking outside with her? Her sewing had slipped to the ground. Realizing that Lady Fording was speaking to her, she gave a start. 'I — I beg your pardon, dear ma'am. I was not attending.'

'So I see.' Lady Fording looked as if she could see too much. Anna forced herself to concentrate on the conversation.

'We have no man to escort us,' lamented the *contessa*.

'*Davvero*, Beatrice, I will not abandon Henrietta. And besides, Enrico rarely went anywhere with us. We managed very well on our own.' Lady Fording sighed.

The *contessa* looked significantly at Anna. 'I think after all, we will join the promenade this afternoon. Mama will benefit from a change of scene.' And so they went to town in the afternoon and later that evening, they went to the theatre. The *contessa* was somewhat cheered when, during the interval, they received visits from Charles and Ned and shortly afterwards Jack Barton brought Emily into their box.

'Grandmama sends her fondest greetings,' she told Lady Fording, 'and she begs that you will come to take tea with us tomorrow.' When this invitation had been accepted, Emily moved over to talk to Anna. She opened her eyes very wide. 'Do you have the headache? You look very pale.'

Anna clasped her fan tightly. 'No, it is nothing. I am just a little fatigued today.' Before Emily could probe any further, she murmured, 'Is your brother still in love with Belinda?'

Emily screwed up her nose. 'He is *besotted*! At the promenade this afternoon he managed to find her outside Donaldson's and actually sat there with her and her mother for a full half-hour.'

'Oh, then it is really serious!' Anna could smile about that. 'It seems she is also taken with him. But what about Lady Beveridge? Does she scowl as much as ever?'

Emily did not think Lady Beveridge had been too ferocious. 'Maybe she knows that Jack will inherit a large fortune,' she said, 'but of course, he cannot compare with the son of a duke. We shall see if she allows Jack to dance with Belinda at the ball tomorrow evening.'

★   ★   ★

Anna entered the Castle Tavern with some trepidation. With no Giles, there was no pleasure to be expected from the evening. And now she realized that one kiss was simply not enough. She longed for him to repeat the magic he had wrought on her.

How could a kiss have such an effect on her whole body — as well as on her mind? But she must learn to live without him. It was another dark secret to bear in her soul. Perhaps going abroad would help her endure this loneliness.

She stuck closely to Lady Fording for a while. However, it was not long before that sprightly old lady met with Mrs Barton and another elderly lady who often played cards with them both, so she was no longer required. Emily, who had come with her grandmother, was hovering nearby. She beckoned Anna to come with her into the ballroom. A country dance was underway. There were plenty of blue and silver uniforms among the men, while the ladies were mostly in white gowns.

The two girls walked towards the end of the room and found seats on a long padded bench. Anna opened her fan and studied it, recalling how it had saved her only two days ago.

'You have trimmed your gown,' observed Emily. 'It is very pretty, but not so dashing as it was.'

Anna had spent the morning sewing the lace and ribbon to the bodice of her silk and net evening gown. She hoped she now looked demure enough not to attract any attention.

'Oh look over there.' Emily put a hand up to her mouth to hide a smile. 'Belinda has just arrived — what a charming gown she is wearing. And Jack is already making his way over to them.'

The girls watched as Jack bowed and chatted to Lady Beveridge and her smiling daughter. He found them seats and he remained by them. Anna saw Charles drift over to join them. They were still watching to see which young gentleman would lead out Belinda in the next dance when Anna became aware of someone by her side. She looked up and found, to her relief, that it was Ned. His long face was serious and his gaze a little abstracted.

'Glad to see you here,' he said. 'I trust you are completely recovered now . . . the two of you, that is.'

They both assured him they were in excellent health. 'You have decided to stay on in Brighton for the present, Mr Caldecott?' Emily asked him.

Ned drew up a chair and sat down. 'I am in the middle of composing an epic poem,' he explained. 'I prefer to stay where I am while I work on it.'

Both girls gazed at him with interest.

'Is it very difficult to write poetry?' asked Emily.

He shrugged. 'Sometimes,' he said, 'but mostly I am able to keep it flowing.'

'What theme have you chosen?' asked Anna. She thought of *The Corsair*, her most precious possession. She had already read it through twice and was beginning to memorize some of the more dramatic verses. However good a poet he was, Mr Caldecott could not equal Lord Byron.

'I am writing about elemental nature,' he said at last, 'and using a gothic style. But I am not sure it is the right way to achieve what I wish. I need more time.'

'One of my schoolfriends writes poetry,' Anna told him. 'The teachers consider her to be very gifted.'

He looked interested. 'What kind of verse does she favour?'

Anna began to tell him about her friend Tess, but then Emily broke into their conversation.

'Look, look,' she exclaimed, 'he has done it!'

'By Gad, is that Miss Beveridge dancing with your brother?' Ned's eyes were almost bulging. He shook his head in amazement. 'She looks so different.'

'I do hope your brother is truly taken with her,' said Anna. 'It is a pleasure to see her looking so happy.'

By the end of the evening Anna had decided on two important issues. Firstly, after dancing with Emily's brother, she knew he was far too juvenile in his attitude to please her. She was very glad he had turned his attention to Belinda. And whether they became seriously attached to each other or not, it was definitely good for Belinda to be so pleased with life. Could it be that she had never had an admirer before? Or perhaps her mother had bullied her into thinking she must marry Giles and that she had no other choice.

The second — and more important — issue was that Ned had obviously been told to keep an eye on her. She was touched that Giles cared so much about her. Ned was a dear, kind man and she was very fond of him. Indeed, she often felt she should be keeping an eye on him, especially when he wandered around with that vague look on his face and inkstains on his fingers.

But still she was faced with the dilemma. Was she going to be invited to go to Italy with Lady Fording? And if not, whatever was she to do? But each time she considered her future, she ended up putting off the decision for a little longer.

29

That disagreeable job was done! Giles's eyes were still green slits in a dark face as the hackney turned into Cavendish Square. Sophia had finally accepted that their liaison was over. The diamond necklace he had produced had helped to calm the worst of her rage but it had been an unpleasant half-hour. Giles did not care for shouting at a woman. Neither did he care for the noise of crashing china ornaments. At least she had spared him any weeping. But her attempts to ruin Anna had swept away the last shreds of any kindness he still felt towards her.

He paid off the hackney driver and dashed up the steps of the town house. He vaguely noted that the butler was not in the hall to greet him. Flinging his hat onto a side table, he strode into the library — and checked at the sight of his father, seated at the great desk and calmly writing a letter. What the devil . . . ? His father rarely stirred from his estates in the north west. His grace made no sign he had noticed Giles's arrival and continued to write. Giles's mouth tightened. He trod over to the fireplace and planted his clenched fist on the mantelpiece. That was a mistake! He winced at the sudden twinge from his healing sword wound. His father raised bushy eyebrows but kept on with his task.

At last Lord Hawkesborough put his pen down and placed the letter to one side. He folded his hands on the desk and surveyed his heir. 'Well, Longwood! You have taken your time in responding to my — er — letter.'

Giles compressed his lips still further. Anger blazed in his eyes as he looked steadily into his father's equally green eyes. But the older man remained cool and slightly disdainful. After a long pause, he said, 'Well, well, I did not expect my arrival in Town to strike you dumb.'

Giles pulled himself together. It was time and more for him to confront his father on the issue of his marriage. He came forward and bowed slightly. 'My apologies, sir. It is indeed an unexpected pleasure to see you here.'

'Ha!' This was accompanied by an ironic look. 'And what have you done to your shoulder? Another duel? That must make three this year alone.'

'You are well informed about my movements, sir.' Giles's tone was arctic. He still stood before the desk, rigid with anger and

287

tension. His father was up to something. 'Who has been sending information about me?'

Lord Hawkesborough drew out his snuff-box and flicked it open. 'I have my methods. You are my heir, after all.'

Giles swung away and went to stand in front of the window, looking out. Not that he saw anything other than a red haze. Why did his father treat him like a schoolboy? His temper still had not cooled from dealing with Sophia and now he was going to engage in one of the heated arguments that seemed to be the only conversations he ever had with his father. No wonder Bilden had avoided him in the entrance hall.

Giles closed his eyes and counted to twenty. He turned round, clasped his hands behind his back and took a few steps towards the desk. 'Do you make a long stay in London, sir?'

Lord Hawkesborough met his gaze. 'That depends on how quickly I can deal with the current . . . ah, problem.'

'Problem, sir?' Giles's voice dripped menace.

His father picked up a quill and turned it idly between his long fingers. The great old-fashioned emerald ring he wore caught the light and flashed. 'Let us not beat about the bush, Longwood. I told you in my last letter that this year you must set aside your ruinous lifestyle and settle down. It is well past time for you to marry and produce an heir.' He raised his bushy eyebrows. 'If you continue fighting duels at this rate, there may be one that will prove fatal.'

Giles let out a scornful 'Hah!'

'So you say,' his father continued calmly, 'but you have sustained an injury.' He rose and strolled across to the bell pull. Bilden appeared promptly and was ordered to bring wine. Giles resigned himself to the fact that his father was determined to have the matter discussed fully.

They sat in deep leather armchairs facing each other. Bilden brought their wine. He cast an impassive glance at Giles as he set the glass down by his elbow.

He knows, thought Giles. My father's arrival has been enough to tell the whole household. And servants gossip! Soon all London will know that I am to be married . . . but so far, nobody knows who the bride will be.

He took a mouthful of wine and considered. A quick look showed him that his father was seated comfortably and sipping his drink. He was watching Giles from under hooded lids, his face its usual disdainful mask.

'Very well, sir,' said Giles, 'it is more than time for us to reach some understanding. Let us suppose that I am ready to alter my way of living,' he added, and saw a flicker of some emotion cross his father's face.

His Grace set his glass down. He breathed hard. 'That is something I would be mighty glad to consider.' He steepled his fingers. 'Pray go on. What . . . ah reforms do you plan to make?'

Giles dashed a hand through his hair. 'It is not so very difficult, in fact. I find I am no longer drawn to the lifestyle that has given me such a bad reputation.' He shook his head, a half smile on his lips. 'The time I spent at Longwood Hall gave me a taste for living on the land. It was . . . more worthwhile than the pursuit of pleasure in Town.'

Lord Hawkesburgh remained perfectly still. His expression was unreadable, but his eyes grew brighter as he digested this revolution in his son's attitude. Giles picked up his glass again and stared into it. Without looking up, he said, 'In addition, I have found the girl I wish to marry.' He set the glass down sharply and looked at his father. 'That does not mean I *will* marry her.'

His father blinked and leaned forward. 'Somehow I feel certain you are not talking of Belinda.'

'Of course not. We would never suit. And I will not tolerate being pursued, especially when it is by the mother. Belinda is currently enjoying the admiration of some cub who will deal with her far better than ever I would.' He lapsed into silence again. He was not ready to speak about Anna. Dearest Anna. Her freshness and clear-cut views on life enchanted him even when they exasperated him. With Anna there was no time to be bored.

He was conscious of a terrible weight somewhere inside. Ned would probably say his heart was pining for her. But he must overcome this. She had demanded a goodbye kiss, but otherwise she never gave any hint of wanting his attentions. She seemed to view him as a favourite uncle, which meant she thought he was too old for her. Since when had he, Giles Maltravers, become so sensitive to any woman's feelings? But he would not clip the wings of his brave protégée. She had made a desperate bid for freedom and he would respect that. But he would never know such sunshine and laughter again, or breathe in her fragrance of roses and sweet youth — or even battle his way through another argument. She would no doubt seize the opportunity to travel to Italy. His lips twisted in a wry smile. She would maintain that it was her choice, not his, to decide her fate. He eventually raised his head to find his father waiting patiently. Was that a look of understanding in his eyes? 'Won't she have you?' he asked in a mild tone.

Giles looked at him, not knowing how much anguish showed on his face. 'It's not that, sir. She is so young, so full of ideals and plans of her own. I can't trap her into the kind of routine that goes with my rank. Once I do marry, I am aware of all the social implications — the balls, receptions, dinners . . . committees, charity work, a life endlessly busy yet so dull it would squeeze all the freshness and joy out of her.'

Lord Hawkesborough's face was very thoughtful now. 'You are all consideration for this young lady. I take it she *is* a lady?'

'Of course!' Giles glared. 'But not a member of the *ton*. Her name is Annabelle Lawrence.'

'Lawrence,' repeated his Grace. He rubbed his chin and stared unseeing towards the window, his eyes narrowed. 'Lawrence — from Hampshire?' When Giles nodded, he went on, 'Hah! It must be the daughter of Four-Horse Jim Lawrence.'

Giles sat up sharply. 'You knew him?'

'I certainly did. He was a famous whip and a great sportsman. But he finished himself in polite society when he eloped with Swinton's eldest daughter. She was one of the beauties of that season, I recall. Had all the men at her feet. Her father accepted an offer for her hand from a man twice her age, Viscount Henry, but she ran off with Jim Lawrence and the pair of them have never been seen since. Swinton disowned her — you know what high sticklers they are in that family.'

Giles digested this in silence. It fitted the meagre facts he knew from what Anna had told him. She had once said that her mother was a beauty. And she herself was lovely, especially when dressed fashionably. His face darkened again as he remembered those evening gowns that displayed so much of her snowy bosom. She really needed him to care for her!

'So how did you meet the daughter?' Lord Hawkesborough interrupted Giles's attempts to piece the facts together. Giles shook his head. It was not his tale to tell. And all at once he was filled with such a longing for her that he knew he must try once more. Deep inside, a tiny spark of hope sprang into life. His mood lifted. He fixed an eager look on his father. 'Do you know where Mr Lawrence lived in Hampshire?'

30

'Grandmama says we are to leave Brighton after the weekend,' announced Emily. She was walking along Marine Parade with Anna and Beppi, while Lady Fording paid a visit to Mrs Barton.

'That means we shall probably leave at the same time,' said Anna. She sighed. Brighton was dear to her because every corner held some memory of Giles. But it was no good to cling to the past, as she knew all too well. Her great consolation was her copy of *The Corsair*, which she more or less knew by heart. It was her most precious possession, along with her fan, of course. She made a determined effort to concentrate on Emily's chatter. It would never do to reveal her heartache. And the memory of that kiss was a torment. Why had she thought one kiss would be enough?

She missed the feel of Giles, the scent of him, the way his voice vibrated along her spine and thrilled her. Most of all, she mourned the loss of his presence, her friend and her guardian whenever she had needed him.

'I beg your pardon,' she said, aware that Emily was apparently expecting an answer to something. 'I — er — suddenly began to think of travelling to Italy and my mind wandered.'

'Your mind does seem to wander a lot these days,' remarked Emily with a secret little grin. 'No doubt the idea of going to Italy is rather daunting. Oh, heavens above!' She gripped Anna's sleeve. 'Suppose you meet Signor di Cassagna when you are there.'

Anna shrugged. 'I do not think so. He lives in Florence and that is very far from the *contessa*'s home. Stop it!' This was to Beppi. The little dog was barking at the donkeys on the beach below them. A group of women were riding along with great shrieks and squeals. The two girls watched for a moment and then moved on.

'Are you looking forward to your come-out?' Anna asked, 'you will soon be so busy visiting the modistes and so on . . . '

'I would look forward to it all far more if you were there to accompany me,' sighed Emily. 'You have so much confidence.'

'I spent several years at school,' replied Anna. 'One soon grows accustomed to being part of a group — and of taking the lead when necessary. You will find some agreeable friends in no time, I feel sure.'

Emily looked doubtful. 'If only Jack will give me some support. But he can think of nothing but Belinda. He is totally smitten by her.'

'And she with him, if we judge by appearances,' agreed Anna, following Emily into the Bartons' house. 'At least now we are all friends.'

Lady Fording and her daughter were reading a letter while Mrs Barton and her son looked on. As the girls entered the room, Mr Barton exclaimed, 'Ah, here they are. And I warrant we shall see Miss Lawrence cheer up wonderfully at the news.' He gave Anna a mischievous grin.

'News, Papa? Has something marvellous happened?' Emily danced forwards. Anna cast a furtive glance towards the mirror. Surely she was looking cheerful already. But her reflection did look rather pale, with shadows under her eyes. She swallowed nervously and made herself smile. Mr Barton was joking with his daughter and for a fleeting second, Anna felt jealous. If only her own father had lived. She pulled herself together and took the seat Mrs Barton was indicating to her.

'Now then! Here we are,' said Mr Barton, taking the letter back from Lady Fording. He wagged a finger at Emily. 'Mind you, I have not yet decided whether I shall accept.'

'Is it an invitation to the Pavilion?' Emily enquired, polishing her father's reading glasses and setting them on his nose.

'I think it is more interesting than that.' Mr Barton looked at the older ladies, who nodded in agreement. Satisfied that he had drawn the moment out to the full, he said in a provocative tone, 'But indeed, I wonder if Emily should go.'

'If Jack is to be there,' put in Mrs Barton, 'and Miss Beveridge as well, it would be perfectly acceptable for Emily to attend. And Miss Lawrence is always so very sensible . . . '

By now Emily was quivering with impatience. It was no good to hasten her grandmother so she merely rolled her eyes at Anna, who looked back in bewilderment. She felt too tired to take much interest in yet another of these family discussions in what was or was not suitable for Emily. They wrapped the poor girl in cottonwool.

Soon Lady Fording would take her leave and they could return to their own home. Anna would slip up to her room at the first opportunity and read her favourite cantos from *The Corsair* to kindle some enthusiasm for her future adventures. A squeal from Emily made her start and look up.

'That will be the perfect way to end our stay in Brighton,' the girl was saying, 'and I may go, may I not, Grandmama? Of course I will not be seasick. How often have I been out in the boat on the lake with Jack when he went fishing?'

Anna looked from Emily to Lady Fording. The old lady was watching her with a decided twinkle in her eye. 'So we are agreed,' she said, rising to her feet, 'Emily is right, my dear Henrietta. It is a perfect event to mark the end of our time here. And while the young folk enjoy their outing, we more sober creatures will have one last tea party at the Castle Tavern.'

They took their leave. When they were in the carriage going home, Lady Fording said, 'Well, Anna, you have been moping for some days now and you do not take any interest in events. But I am sure this excursion will cheer you up.'

Anna gave her employer an apologetic glance. 'I am very sorry, dear ma'am . . . ' she began, but Lady Fording waved a hand to silence her. She exchanged a look with her daughter. 'Did you ever see such a lack of enthusiasm? When first we came here, Anna was excited even by an outing to the shops. Well, if you do not wish to join the other young people, you may stay and take tea with us. But the letter was from Mr Dowling, Lord Longwood's secretary. It is an invitation to take a trip round the bay on Lord Longwood's yacht.' She watched with satisfaction as Anna's face brightened. 'I thought that would please you.'

'I have been wanting to try a sea journey,' protested Anna, 'to see if my stomach is strong enough to endure it.' She frowned. 'Lord Longwood is very kind to lend us his yacht when he himself has left Brighton.'

* * *

Mr Dowling escorted Anna and Emily down to the long pier where the *Kestrel* was moored. The graceful boat swayed slightly as the waves rocked it. Emily gave a gasp of alarm. Anna also felt her stomach flip uncomfortably when she saw that tall, elegant figure waiting on the deck. Giles had come back! She trembled with anticipation. But she must be prudent and keep very calm.

They were the last to arrive. Giles came forward to assist them onto the boat. Emily clung nervously to his hand and he led her slowly over to the stern, to a seat next to Belinda. Anna followed them across the deck. A sudden lurch nearly threw her off-balance. She sat down abruptly next to Lord Charles.

'Bravo, Miss Lawrence,' he grinned. 'Not easy is it, to measure your steps when everything is bobbing about? Give me a horse any day.'

'I want to test myself on a ship,' she replied, grabbing at her bonnet as the wind tugged it. 'Oh, we are already moving.' She watched the sailors pulling on the ropes and saw the sails unfurl. At once they billowed out. She sat, fascinated, as the yacht swept away from the shore. Gulls cried and wheeled above the mast. She soon noticed that the air was much fresher so close to the water.

Mr Dowling and Giles were offering refreshments to their guests. Anna wondered if she dare venture to the front rail to look down into the sea as they moved through it. She rose and suggested it to Emily. But Emily shook her head vigorously and indicated that she would stay where she was.

Belinda stood up. 'Miss Lawrence,' she said in a low voice, 'we have met several times recently, but so far I have been too cowardly to do what I must. Let me put matters right and apologize now for not coming to your aid that evening at the Pavilion. There were reasons why — ' she bit her lip. 'Mama . . . well, I can only assure you I have felt very bad about it ever since.'

Anna took her hand. 'Pray do not say any more. It is over now and we are friends.'

Belinda blinked rapidly. 'Thank you.'

The *Kestrel* swung into the wind and Emily shrieked as her bonnet almost flew away. The girls all giggled as they settled their hats securely and pulled their wraps closer about them. The young men had all abandoned their hats and the wind ruffled their hair into tufts and curls.

'Now you have a truly windswept hairstyle,' Emily told her brother. He shrugged and glanced half shyly at Belinda. From the smile she gave him, it was obvious to everyone that his tousled hair did not matter.

Giles came up to Anna. 'Well, Miss Lawrence, does this satisfy your craving for adventure? I am sure Lord Byron would approve.'

'So far so good,' she answered, 'but it is a calm day. We need a storm before I can judge.'

There was a chorus of laughing protest from the others.

'Come to the prow,' Giles invited her, 'you will feel the swell more there.'

Anna's eyes gleamed and she jumped to her feet. The boat tilted and she hastily grabbed the hand he held out to her. Both Giles and his brother laughed. After an indignant moment, Anna joined in. 'That was unexpected,' she said, moving cautiously forward, 'but I will soon learn.' A couple of steps further on, the boat rose suddenly to a large wave and Anna found herself thrown against Giles's side. 'Oh dear, is it always so difficult to move around?' she exclaimed, righting herself with difficulty.

He laughed. 'I am not complaining. But you will notice that I do not stagger when the boat rocks. That is your first lesson — how to balance. Watch Sam over there.' He indicated one of the sailors, who grinned and touched his forelock to Anna as he ran along the deck.

'I see,' she exclaimed, 'he keeps his knees bent.'

They reached the prow and stood side by side as the *Kestrel* began to dip and rise in a deeper, more regular motion. Anna clung to the rail, watching the shore grow distant until they were well out in the bay. Her bonnet brim fluttered and strands of hair blew across her face. She pushed the hair back impatiently. She gazed into the swirling water as the bow cut into the waves.

''*O'er the glad waters of the dark blue sea,*
Our thoughts as boundless, and our souls as free,'' she murmured.

Beside her, Giles chuckled. 'So we're back to Lord Byron, are we?'

'What else? I already know most of *The Corsair* by heart.'

'Dear me,' he said faintly.

A larger wave tossed against the bows, sprinkling her with foam. 'It seems like a journey into a magical world,' she exclaimed, entranced. She smiled sunnily at Giles as he gave a low laugh. They grinned at each other in perfect amity. Then, suddenly, their smiles faded. Anna's eyes fell to his mouth, that firm, full mouth that had stolen the soul out of her body. Her heart hammered crazily in her throat. With a huge effort, she made herself look away. 'I wish we could sail off on an adventure,' she said.

He put his hand over hers. It was large and warm and very comforting. But the sensations it awoke in her were far from comfortable. 'We can if you wish,' he said. His eyes were glowing and his expression was surely much softer than she had ever seen it. Suddenly she was desperate for him to kiss her again.

Behind them a voice called out, making her jump. It was fortunate, though, reminding her of the need to quell this longing for him. Seeing him again this afternoon had severely shaken her carefully built defences. She stared blankly at the horizon and swallowed down the anger and frustration. How long they stood at the prow she never knew. At length she realized that they were approaching the pier and their voyage was nearly over.

She put up a hand to brush her hair aside.

Mr Dowling was speaking to Giles in a low voice. When Anna turned to look, she found the other guests still sitting in the stern. They were decidedly windswept, even Belinda. The boat came alongside the pier and there was a bustle as the sailors made all secure. Emily rose to her feet, evidently glad to be going ashore. She looked towards Anna and wrinkled her nose.

'First and last time, eh, Miss Barton?' Charles stood up with a laugh. He offered her his arm and she eagerly stepped towards the gangplank put in place by the crew. The others were rising and getting ready to follow her.

Anna turned away while she dragged a comb through her tangled hair and twisted it up again. She tied her bonnet strings and turned back.

'Oh . . . ' She stared in disbelief. She was all alone. There was not even a sailor in sight. How could they do this to her? Even if Emily did feel unwell, surely Belinda or even Mr Dowling, would see that all the guests disembarked safely! Feeling very angry, she made her way to the gangplank. Giles appeared, striding up it and back onboard.

'At last,' he said, taking her hand. 'It has been such hard work to get you alone.'

Anna blinked at him. 'Whatever do you mean? We were alone for most of the journey — and I suspect the others are cross with me because of that.' She waved her free hand towards the shore. 'See, they all left without a word.'

Giles captured her free hand and held it warmly. His face was taut. 'They all left because I asked them to go. There are not many places where we can be private — and I absolutely must be private with you, Anna.' He gave her an unusually serious look. Yet at the same time she sensed that he was uneasy. Now what could be wrong.

Giles gripped her hands tightly. 'Dear Anna, this is a difficult question, I know. You have made such plans for your life of Byronic adventure. But I want to know if — if . . . instead of wandering the world, you would be willing to consider becoming my wife?'

She stared blankly. *His wife?* Had she heard correctly? *Not Sophia, then . . . but he didn't know . . .*

'I know I am asking a lot of you, young as you are,' went on Giles, gripping her hands even harder, 'but you are energetic and brave . . . '

Anna felt numb with shock at this sudden proposal. He had not said one word about loving her. And although she loved him with all her heart, she had never dreamed of being his wife. He was a haughty aristocrat from a world where she could never have a place because her parents had been banished from polite society when they eloped together. How often had her mother told her not to dream of a London come-out because she would be shunned by the great families of the *ton*?

★   ★   ★

Giles's heart sank. He had made a complete mess of it. For once in his life he had wanted to do everything according to the rules. He had stated the facts. Marrying him came with a huge burden of responsibilities in tow and he must allow her to choose with a level head. He waited, still holding her hands. They had gone icy cold. And her face was white.

She licked her dry lips. 'I never thought of marriage,' she whispered, 'no, it is not possible. I can not marry you, do not ask me why.'

He gazed into her troubled eyes and saw the honesty there and the distress. To her he was no more than her guardian and friend. The only woman in the world for him, and she was the one woman who would not have him. There was something blocking his throat. He swallowed several times. He dropped her hands and took a step back.

'Anna . . . ' he began again, but she shook her head.

'You will be glad I said no,' she said, in a strange, high little voice. 'You do not know all my secrets.' She was very pale, even her lips had lost their colour.

He moved to catch her hand again but she backed away. 'I thank you for the honour you have done me but truly, believe me, I cannot . . . '

'Stop,' he said in a harsh tone, 'you need not say any more.'

'I do not mean to argue with you,' she faltered, 'but you must believe . . . '

'Enough of this.' Giles crushed down the pain. 'We must rejoin the others. Can you cope?' He looked at her closely.

Anna straightened up. 'Of course.' But her face was stricken.

31

In response to Lady Fording's express command, Anna made her way down to the drawing room.

'*Santa Madre di Dio!* Did anyone ever see such a picture of woe?' tut-tutted Lady Fording, peering closely at Anna's pale face and the shadows under her eyes. 'Why did you refuse him if it makes you so miserable?'

Anna blinked at her. 'H-how do you know . . . ?'

The *contessa* tittered. Her mother raised both hands and shook them, her expression incredulous. 'Is there anyone who cannot see how things are between you two?'

Anna's shoulders slumped. 'He d-didn't say anything about love. And even if he did, I am not able to show my face in his world.'

'Why ever not?' Both ladies were looking at her keenly. 'It is obvious you received an excellent education,' said the *contessa*, 'you can take your place at any level in society.'

'And you are young, pretty and in good health,' put in Lady Fording.

Anna hesitated. 'You have been very kind to me and have never asked me about my origins,' she began.

'Ah, but I recognized the name Lawrence.' Lady Fording nodded, as Anna stared, whiter than ever, if that was possible. 'Your father's family owned Wickleigh Hall. My dear husband knew of the sport crazy Jim Lawrence. So I was sure you had a connection with that family. Of course,' — she gave her little shrug — 'you gave us to understand you were an orphan . . . '

Anna hung her head. 'I would have told the truth if I dared . . . but . . . '

Lady Fording spread her hands, palm upwards. 'I saw at once that you were an intelligent and kind young lady, and there are many reasons for running away from home, *non è vero?*' There was a wealth of understanding in her voice, making Anna feel even more wretched.

'Yes, dear ma'am,' she whispered, raising her head to look the old lady in the eye.

'Now you must be honest. It is plain for all to see that you love Lord Longwood. So why did you refuse him?'

Anna wrung her hands. 'My parents eloped and were cast out of society. Mama's family disowned her . . . we have always lived retired . . . so you see — '

'I see nothing!' snapped Lady Fording. 'A rake like Lord Longwood is not going to care for a twenty-year-old scandal. Goodness, child, he is the one who has been trailing scandals everywhere for the last dozen years. He has given the newspapers plenty to fill their columns. Even I followed his exploits.'

There was a tap at the door. The housekeeper came in with her arms full of flowers. 'From Lord Longwood, ma'am,' Beaming, she handed a charming bouquet to each of the ladies. Anna buried her face in the sweet smelling roses and swallowed a sob. How cruel of him to woo her when she must resist at all costs. The other two were reading a note and looking very pleased. They nodded at each other.

'Anna,' said Lady Fording briskly, 'you must do exactly as I say.'

Wearily, Anna submitted. An hour later, bathed, dressed in her yellow muslin gown and with her hair styled by the *contessa*'s maid, Anna stood for Lady Fording to inspect her. The old lady nodded approval.

'So far, so good. It is time for you to take some exercise. You have not been out for two days. Off you go then.'

Anna looked round. 'Where is Beppi, ma'am?'

'No, no, no, and no! Just go.'

When she opened the front door, Anna discovered the black horses and the curricle drawn up by the step. Morgan was standing by the horses' heads. He smiled and touched his hat. She nodded to him and even in her confused state, noticed how the blacks gleamed like satin. They were facing in the direction of Rottingdean.

Slowly she forced herself to look towards the other figure standing silently by the door. A very grave Giles raised his hat, then indicated that he was waiting to hand her up. With great difficulty, Anna raised her eyes to his face. A shock trembled through her. He looked haggard, deep shadows under his eyes and his features completely rigid. Yet he was as impeccable as always. Numbly she took the hand he held out and climbed up into the curricle.

Giles swung himself up and took the reins. Morgan stepped back. The blacks needed no urging but set off at a smart trot. They drove along as far as Rottingdean without a word being spoken. There were a few other coaches on the road and a small crowd strolling in the main street. Giles kept on through the village at a trot. Once they were out in the country again, he slowed his horses to a walk. All this time, Anna sat rigid beside him.

Were they going to have another argument? She felt too weary for that, yet she was determined to stick to her decision. But when he finally broke his silence, Giles surprised her.

'Are we still friends, Miss Lawrence?'

Anna gripped her hands together in her lap. She nodded, still looking straight ahead.

'Are you sure?' His tone was dry.

She swung towards him. 'Always,' she asserted, 'wherever I go I will never forget that you were my true friend.'

Giles's face thawed a degree or two. He inclined his head. 'And when do you go to Italy?'

She fidgeted with her shawl. 'Before the end of September.'

'I suppose I shall have to give you a pistol as a parting gift. I am not easy about you going where I cannot keep an eye on you.'

The concern in his voice threatened to shatter her resolution. It was so hard to pretend she wanted to go away. But, she told herself sternly, kindness was not love. She loved him and it was impossible to stay unless he truly loved her. She heaved a great, shuddering sigh. Immediately Giles slipped an arm round her shoulders and pulled her close.

'Enough,' he murmured against her hair. 'I will not upset you any more.' The carriage came to a halt. Giles slipped his other arm round her and pulled her against his shoulder. 'There, there,' he soothed as she stifled a sob against his jacket front. Suddenly, the rigidity left her. She clutched at his jacket and leaned gratefully against his hard, warm frame. She could smell his cologne. She heaved another sob.

'Stop that,' came his deep voice. 'My little love, look at me . . . '

'Mmm?' she mumbled. 'W-*what* did you s-say?'

'I said 'My love', my love.' She felt his hand underneath her chin, gently urging her face up. In the next instant he had swooped and was kissing her. This was quite different from both their previous kisses. It was very thorough, very insistent and so sweet Anna felt her heart would burst for the beauty of it. Her hands twined round his neck, pulling him even closer.

'You little witch,' he breathed, rubbing his cheek against hers. The light was back in his eyes. He kissed her again, with an extra dose of passion. Anna's head was swimming, and she felt the same longing he had aroused in her before. It was making her lose the will to say no to him. Even as the thought formed vaguely through the haze of pleasure, she struggled.

At once he slackened his hold. She looked at a new Giles; his eyes were heavy lidded, his face hawklike. His hair was ruffled and his cravat untied. Anna smiled in spite of herself. Giles swooped again.

'No,' she protested when she was able, 'stop this . . . you *must* listen. It is not that I do not like you — '

He raised his brows, 'I should hope not after such a display!'

'But it would ruin you to m-marry me . . . ' She stopped in bewilderment as he gave a shout of laughter.

'Oh my sweet infant, are you referring to your parents' elopement?'

She gaped. 'You know about that? Your father will never accept me.'

'My father,' Giles told her, pulling her closer to kiss her again, 'remembers yours as a great sportsman. There, I knew that would make you smile. It was my father who told me where Wickleigh Hall is situated. Even so, it took Morgan and me two days to find it. You certainly were living in a remote place. And having seen your father's estate, and then Foxley Manor, I understand why your stepfather resents you.' He stroked her cheek and tucked a stray curl behind her ear. 'I have your mother's permission to pay my addresses to you.' He smiled at her round-eyed astonishment. 'All it needs is for you to tell me whether you can bear the idea of marrying such an old man as I am.'

'Old?' She blinked at him. 'Whatever makes you say that?'

He sat back, watching her keenly. 'Your friends are so very much younger than I. And I recall that you spoke of the *old* suitor your family had found for you.'

Anna gave a peal of laughter. 'He was old in his ways. I do not much care for very young men. My friend Elinor's brothers are so childish. As for Emily's brother . . . ' She rolled her eyes. She put a hand against his firm chest and smiled shyly up at him. 'I think I have loved you from the first moment I saw you — ' She was interrupted as Giles gathered her into a rib-cracking hug.

'I love you so very much,' she went on, when she could draw breath, 'but I was not at all sure if you . . . O-ooh . . . ' This shriek was provoked by Giles scooping her off the bench and onto his knee.

Eventually he raised his head and looked at her flushed face. 'I trust you are convinced now that I love you.' He set Anna back on her seat and pulled out a comb. 'I may be a rake,' he told her, as he ruthlessly tugged the comb through her hair, 'but I love only you and I always will love you.'

She blinked hard and touched her fingers to his lips. He caught her hand and pressed a kiss into her palm. 'Time to return,' he said. 'I do not trust myself any further. And the ladies are waiting anxiously to see how things have turned out.'

'You have been in league with Lady Fording,' Anna said. 'Why should I be surprised? You have charmed her as well.'

'Of course,' he murmured, turning the horses to set off on their return journey. 'But the price is that she wishes us to celebrate our engagement at Rosevale Court before she leaves for Italy.'

Epilogue

No thought had man or maid of rest or home,
While many a languid eye and thrilling hand
Exchanged the look few bosoms may withstand,
Or gently pressed, returned the pressure still:
Oh Love! young Love! bound in thy rosy band,

Anna closed her battered copy of *Childe Harold's Pilgrimage* and clutched it to her bosom. She shut her eyes and smiled happily.

There was a tap at the door and in came Elinor. 'Are you drawing strength from Byron's verse?' she said in her musical voice, taking the book away and running a critical eye over her friend's appearance. 'You look radiant — and no wonder. Wait until I describe Lord Longwood to Tess and Sally. They will be so jealous. Your adventure was short, but it led you to the ending we all swore we would achieve. So you are the first of our group to find the love of your life.'

Anna looked at her seriously. 'I would not have given up my plans for anything less. Oh, Elinor.' She moved forward impulsively to squeeze her friend's hands. 'I only hope you and the others can find such happiness also.'

Elinor gave a wry smile and glanced at her reflection, 'It will not be for my looks,' she murmured.

'You are the brightest star of us all,' Anna told her.

'Everyone is here now,' said Elinor, 'I have come to fetch you.'

Anna took a last look in the mirror. Her white gown was sufficiently modest to satisfy Giles, she hoped. It was a simple puff-sleeved robe of silk, trimmed with pale pink ribbon. Maria, the *contessa*'s maid, had dressed her hair into a topknot with little ringlets over her ears.

They set off down the two flights of stairs to the large drawing room where Anna had first met the *contessa* on the day that Giles had driven her here. 'I am so grateful you came to support me on this special occasion,' she told Elinor. 'Furthermore, you accompanied Mama on the journey, which was certainly no easy task.'

There was no need to elaborate. Both were well used to Lady Fox's butterfly mind. She could never have made the journey alone and Giles was adamant that Anna's stepfather was not to be present, either at her engagement or her wedding.

Anna's heart beat fast as the footmen threw open the double doors. She had yet to meet

Giles's father and it was possible he might decide he did not approve of his son's choice of bride. But, almost as soon as she walked into the room, she was surrounded by the ladies, admiring and commenting on her radiant looks. Anna kissed Lady Fording's rouged cheek, smiling fondly at the kind old lady.

'I have been waiting for this since first I saw you dance with our dear Lord Longwood in Brighton,' she whispered to Anna. 'Even then, I saw how he cut his brother out.' She chuckled and gestured for Anna to turn round.

Giles was close by, as elegant as always, but it was the glow in his eyes that made Anna catch her breath. The rest of the people in the room faded away as she returned his smile and stretched out her hand to him. With a start, she realized that he was leading her up to someone. She gave a gasp; this was an older version of Giles, his hair greying at the temples but the green eyes just as striking and the lopsided grin just as endearing.

'Miss Lawrence,' the duke bowed gracefully over her hand, 'I cannot begin to tell you how delighted I am to meet you at last.'

Anna's mother fluttered forward. 'Oh my dear, you look so ravishing in white. Indeed, you remind me of myself at your age.' Lady

Fox blinked her long lashes and patted her blonde curls. She offered her cheek for Anna to kiss her, then fussed round exclaiming over her daughter's hair and clothes until Elinor drew her away towards the bay window to admire the garden.

Next Charles came forward to greet Anna. 'It takes an event such as this to get all we Maltravers together,' he said with a laugh, 'and since I am here and you are going to be my sister-in-law, I claim the right to greet you with a kiss.'

Charles kissed Anna's cheek while Giles watched like a hawk. Then he drew her hand through his arm and led her over to Lady Fording.

'Dear ma'am, you have been my secret ally and it is thanks to you that we have reached this point at all. May I ask you to fulfil the next vital part of this ceremony?'

Lady Fording beamed and pulled out a scarlet leather box. Opening it, she offered it to Giles. There was a sparkle of fine stones as he drew out a ring and, taking Anna's left hand, slid it onto her finger. It fitted perfectly. Anna gazed open-mouthed at the three glittering diamonds surrounded by a myriad of winking chips. She was shy all at once, and it was with difficulty that she raised her eyes to his. Then she had to smile. Devil! He was enjoying her surprise.

'This is only the second time I have ever known you to be speechless,' he said with his wicked grin. Swiftly he bent his head and kissed her. There were cheers and laughter.

All their friends were toasting them in champagne, but Anna heard only Giles as he whispered, 'My sweet, I warn you our wedding day will take place very soon.'

'Yes, oh yes,' she murmured, 'and can we spend our honeymoon cruising on your yacht?'

Everyone turned in surprise at Giles's sudden shout of laughter. 'Life,' he informed them all as he pulled Anna to his side, 'is never going to be boring, ever again.'

We do hope that you have enjoyed reading this large print book.

Did you know that all of our titles are available for purchase?

We publish a wide range of high quality large print books including:
Romances, Mysteries, Classics
General Fiction
Non Fiction and Westerns

Special interest titles available in large print are:
The Little Oxford Dictionary
Music Book
Song Book
Hymn Book
Service Book

Also available from us courtesy of Oxford University Press:
Young Readers' Dictionary
(large print edition)
Young Readers' Thesaurus
(large print edition)

For further information or a free brochure, please contact us at:
Ulverscroft Large Print Books Ltd.,
The Green, Bradgate Road, Anstey,
Leicester, LE7 7FU, England.
Tel: (00 44) 0116 236 4325
Fax: (00 44) 0116 234 0205

Other titles published by
The House of Ulverscroft:

APRIL AND MAY

Beth Elliott

Rose Charteris arrives in Constantinople, little expecting to confront Tom Hawkesleigh, the man who broke her heart four years previously — but she does. And Rose must work with Tom on a top-secret document for the Sultan. Spied on by all sides, she must affect a polite indifference and complete the job, despite her inner turmoil. When Rose finally returns to London danger follows her, and, although Tom is desperate to help, she remains fiercely independent. Rose is still in love with the man who abandoned her — is it too late to swallow her pride and let him in again?

HENRY TILNEY'S DIARY

Amanda Grange

Growing up in an abbey with an irascible father, a long-suffering mother, a rakish brother and a pretty sister, Henry Tilney's life bears more than a passing resemblance to the Gothic novels he loves to read. And Henry is undoubtedly cut out to be a hero. Yet he cannot find his heroine — until, that is, he meets Catherine Morland. With her refreshing innocence and love of reading, Catherine is the perfect match. But will the scheming of Henry's father and the scandalous behaviour of his brother destroy their happy ending?

THEODORA IN LOVE

Ann Barker

After her father's death Theodora Buck-leigh's new adopted family want to give her a London season. But though she is a pretty girl, Theodora has limped from birth, and dreads exposure to the social round. She takes evasive action, accepting an invitation from Dorothy Wordsworth to stay with her and her poet brother, William, in Dorset. Here she will find love, danger and intrigue. Might Coleridge and the others be engaged in treason? Can Theodora's chaperone, Alex Kydd, rescue her from this dangerous company; and even if he does, could there ever be any more between them than friendship?

THE KYDD INHERITANCE

Jan Jones

In Regency England, Nell Kydd is at her wits' end and it's easy to see why. Her father is dead, her brother, Kit, is missing and her loathsome uncle, with his mismanagement, is wrecking the family estate. She must contend with a perturbing lack of funds, an unwelcome proposal of marriage and a mother who lives in a reality of her own. Cue the arrival of the unsettling Captain Hugo Derringer: an old schoolfriend of Kit's who blows hot then cold, and is discovered at odd times — in odd places — asking very odd questions. How far can Nell trust him?

LORD WARE'S WIDOW

Emily Harland

Lady Georgiana Ware is delighted to be the object of the Earl of Thornbury's admiration, so when her hopes of being his wife are dashed, she flees south to the seaside resort of Sidmouth to recover her dignity. She is dismayed when his lordship follows her, determined to correct her opinion of him. Georgiana may find him handsome and charming, but she doesn't trust him one bit. However, can Georgiana conceal her growing feelings for this seductive man? More importantly, can Lord Thornbury penetrate Georgiana's defences and help her to realise that things are not always what they seem?

GRETNA LEGACY

Marina Oliver

Abigail Barton was brought up in Bath by Lady Jordan; her own parents died when she was a baby. Now her trustee, Mr Wood, insists that she goes to London for the Season, but Abby has no desire to marry. Abigail's sponsor, Lady Padmore, is bringing out her own daughter, Caroline, this Season, determined to marry her to cousin Julian. Meanwhile, Julian, intrigued by Abigail's unconventionality, lends his house for the ball. Then Abby's childhood friend, Hartley, arrives in London, Caroline's brother Dudley sells out from the army, and among the offers of marriage, she must accept someone — but whom?